"Her Unexpected Star"

Bulbs, Blossoms and Bouquets #6
By Laura Ann

This is a work of fiction. Similarities to real people, places, or events are entirely coincidental.

HER UNEXPECTED STAR

First edition. February 8, 2022.

Copyright © 2022 Laura Ann.

Written by Laura Ann.

DEDICATION

To my grandmother.
Your kindness and sweet heart
will forever be in my memories.
Thank you for everything.

ACKNOWLEDGEMENTS

No author works alone. Thank you, Tami.
You make it Christmas every time
I get a new cover. And thank you to my Beta Team.
Truly, your help with my stories is immeasurable.

NEWSLETTER

You can get a FREE book by joining my Reading Family!
Every week we share stories, sales and good old fun.
To get in on the action, just visit lauraannbooks.com

CHAPTER 1

Brooklyn's phone felt like lead in her pant pocket as she sorted a rack of shirts back into order. She was desperate for a chance to take a break and read all the news on her lifelong celebrity crush. She'd been glued to her screen for the past couple of weeks, ever since her friend's wedding, where she'd learned about the stunt accident.

Brooklyn had been in love with Grayson Cordova since she was a young tween in braces. He'd been the star of a weekly TV show and the ultimate teenage heartthrob. Now he, and she, were all grown up and Grayson had continued to build his career, this time as an A-list actor for action movies.

Through it all, Brook's attention had never wavered. She was realistic enough to know she'd never meet him, so it wasn't like she'd never had a boyfriend. But somehow, always sitting in the back of her head was the thought that her date could never live up to Grayson's reputation. A long sigh slipped through her lips before she could stop herself, and Brook's store manager looked her way.

"What's wrong, boss?"

Brook forced a smile and shook her head. "Nothing. Sorry. My thoughts were wandering."

Ainsley Taylor was quite a bit older than Brooklyn's twenty-seven years, and had been around since the boutique had opened. She was a solid worker, rarely complained, and did a wonderful job of keeping Brooklyn grounded in reality.

Ainsley stopped folding shirts and put her hands on her hips. "You've been sighing like that for the past two weeks. Are you sure you don't want to talk about it?" She tilted her head to the side, trying to catch Brooklyn's gaze, but Brook refused to look.

Her emotions were bubbling too close to the surface at the moment, and any sign of compassion was going to be enough to push her over the edge. "Thanks, but I'm fine," she assured her friend and employee. Patting the top of the rack, Brook backed up. "I'm gonna go get some paperwork taken care of. You all right out here?"

Ainsley was frowning, but she nodded. "Sure. It's slow right now, so go ahead."

Feeling Ainsley's eyes boring into her back, Brook disappeared down the hall and into her office. It took less than half a second for her to be on her phone, scrolling for any new information she could find on Grayson. After a moment, Brook blinked, coming back to herself for a moment. "What is wrong with me?" she muttered, dropping her phone on the desk. Another heartfelt sigh escaped and she buried her face in her hands. "When am I going to get past this? I'm too old to still be in love with a movie star." *And too lonely.*

The past couple of years had been filled with drama and fairy tales in Brook's world. A good chunk of her friends had met and eventually fallen in love with their perfect spouse. Brook was happy for them...she was! But being happy for her friends didn't help alleviate the loneliness that their absence was leaving in her life.

Add to that the fact that she compared every date with a man who was more fantasy than reality and it made for a difficult life, emotionally speaking.

She had always been the type to believe in fairy tales and happy ever afters, but with each passing year, Brook was afraid she'd somehow missed her chance. Not a single man that she spent time with ever kept her attention for more than a few minutes. None of them were as handsome as Grayson. None of them were as manly as Grayson. None of them were as much of a gentleman as Grayson...

She groaned and scrubbed at her cheeks. "I can't keep doing this. Something has to give."

Her phone buzzed, making Brook jump. Tentatively, she turned over the device and made a face at the text.

I'm open next Friday. Want to grab a bite?

Brendon Perkins had been asking Brook out for several weeks and each time, she'd found an excuse. He was...okay...technically speaking, there wasn't anything really *wrong* with him. He was attractive enough with his light brown hair and trendy glasses. *Which isn't the same as black hair and blue eyes.* He taught high school science and was unfailingly polite. *A little too polite.* He wasn't in bad shape physically speaking. *Just a bit on the thin side.* All in all... *He just isn't Grayson.*

"When did I become such a jerk?" she whispered to herself. "Brendon is fine. Why can't I work up some kind of enthusiasm about him?" Her forehead thunked against her desk. "Ow."

Turning her face sideways, she lay there for a minute. In her mind she called herself all kinds of names, but none of them were enough to spur her into action. Nice as he was, and lonely as she was, Brook just wasn't feeling the kind of pull she wanted when it came to a relationship.

Her stomach was free of butterflies and her heart didn't skip a beat. She didn't wonder what it would be like to kiss him and didn't crave his touch. In fact, she felt numb. None of those things appealed to her at all...at least in regards to Brendon.

Growling, Brook raised her head. "This is so stupid." She grabbed her phone and took a deep breath. "You need to get your head out of the clouds and back on the ground where it belongs." Before she could talk herself out of it, her thumbs began to fly.

That would be nice. Thank you.

Brendon didn't answer right away and Brook could just see him standing in shock at her answer. She'd been holding him off for a long time, so she could only imagine how he was taking her agreement.

Perfect. I'll pick you up at seven.

Brook swallowed the bile that wanted to rise in her throat. "He's nice," she reminded herself as she sent back a thumbs up. "He's cute." She set down her phone and took in a deep breath through her nose. "And best of all... he's available."

She kept herself busy the rest of the day with paperwork and catching up on her notes for the boutique, adamantly keeping thoughts of Grayson and Brendon on the back burner.

When she finally turned the sign to "Closed" for the day, Brook was wrung out. Surprisingly, it took a lot of energy to keep from thinking about something. After driving the couple of miles home, she collapsed on her couch and laid her head on the back cushion. Her stomach let out a vicious growl, letting her know her afternoon cheese stick was long gone.

Her legs protested adamantly, but Brook forced herself to her feet and into the kitchen of her apartment. If her steps were slow and slightly shuffled, no one could blame her. Brook was just proud of herself for actually getting up and moving when all she wanted to do was sit down, check on news of Grayson, and then fall asleep with pictures of his oh-so-kissable lips in her dreams.

"You're an adult..." she told herself. "Act like one."

Her phone sat on the table, face down, as she worked to scramble a couple of eggs and butter some toast. It was a simple dinner, but it would do its job, and during none of it had she been looking for updates on injuries and celebrities or analyzing grainy pictures that might or might not show Grayson walking around like normal.

Grayson isn't real. He's just a face on a screen. She salted her eggs. *Brendon is here. He's real and he's here and best of all, he actually knows who you are.*

It wasn't a truth she wanted to hear, but they were necessary and Brook knew it. Her obsession with Grayson had gone too far. She'd been walking around like a zombie, checking the media every five minutes and dying inside from loneliness. It was time she tried something different. And right now, that meant going on a date, no matter how unwanted, with Brendon Perkins.

"AT THIS POINT, ONLY time will tell if you'll ever walk normally again."

The words entered Grayson's ears, but he struggled to mentally comprehend them.

Carson, his younger brother, scoffed. "You can't be serious! You guys can keep people from dying of cancer, but you can't fix my brother's leg?"

The arguing in the room seemed to buzz in his ears, becoming incomprehensible as Grayson sunk into the shocking revelation. *Might never walk normally again. Might never walk normally again. Might never walk...*

"Come on, Gray."

Grayson blinked a few times, coming back to the present to see his brother grabbing the handle of his walker.

"Let's get you home and we can discuss your options."

Carson's words were tight, letting Grayson know his brother was angry, but for the life of him, he couldn't figure out why. It wasn't like Grayson's injury affected Carson. It was Grayson's career on the line, not his. Even if he had a bum leg, Carson would be able to continue his career as a lawyer.

But Grayson? If his leg didn't heal correctly, his career was over. Completely. He'd spent so much of his life in front of a camera that he had no idea what he would do if that was taken away from him. Acting was all he'd ever done, from the time he was a young teenage boy, still trying to grow into his wide shoulders. Now he was a household name and hadn't planned to stop any time soon.

"Up we go." Carson put his hands on Grayson's back to help him transfer from the seat to the passenger side of the car.

Grabbing the top of the car, Grayson used his upper body strength to make the transition easier. It only took moments for him to be settled into a reclining position, and then Carson took the walker to the back of the vehicle and folded it up.

Carson grunted as he got settled in his own seat. "Ready?"

Grayson nodded. Currently they were both ignoring the elephant in the car and that was fine. He wasn't sure what there was to say. Carson had said they could discuss options, but it didn't feel like there were any options. Either Grayson got better...or he was finished.

He rubbed his thigh absentmindedly. The meds he was on couldn't quite take away the ache that seemed to plague him all day long. The sharp pain from the original injury had since died down, but it had never completely gone away, often choosing to flare up at the most inopportune time.

"Are you due for another pill?" Carson broke into Grayson's thought and it took a second to respond.

"No. Not for another hour."

Carson's dark gray eyes darted to Grayson's leg and back to the road. "Okay. Well, if it gets out of control, let me know, okay?"

Grayson nodded. Words just weren't coming to him at the moment. He let his gaze relax as the scenery blurred while they whipped down the freeway.

"Amelia's going to meet us at the house," Carson said as he looked over his shoulder to change lanes.

"What for?"

"We need to talk about what's going to happen going forward."

Grayson pinched his lips together. His hands clenched and unclenched multiple times. He didn't like the fact that his whole family was having to come together to discuss his future. Grayson had been providing for himself for a long time. Now, suddenly, *he* was something that needed to be dealt with, and he didn't like it.

"Hey."

He looked over to see Carson glancing rapidly between him and the road.

"We're your family," Carson said sternly. "Don't sit there and think you're some kind of martyr." He smirked. "I see them all the time in the courtroom and I'll sweep the floor with you just like I do them."

Grayson grunted and gave a half-smile. "Thanks," he muttered before going back to the scenery.

"We're going to get through this," Carson continued. "Maybe now it's our turn to take care of you for a while, huh?"

The last question had been said quietly, but that didn't make it pierce Grayson's chest any less. He knew his brother meant well, but the words were like a slap in the face.

At the age of fifteen, Grayson hadn't auditioned for that TV show because he had a burning passion to be an actor, but because his parents were convinced they were going to strike it rich by putting their "unusually handsome" son in front of the camera.

To their delight...it had worked.

Unfortunately, it also brought on some challenges. As the middle child, suddenly everything in their family revolved around him, something Grayson wasn't used to. His father quit his minimum wage job and went into managing Grayson full time, taking every bit of income he made and raising their family from the ghettos to a Beverly Hills mansion.

The changes had been sudden and had ultimately torn the family apart. His parents divorced only a few years later, and it wasn't until Grayson was a legal adult that he was finally able to kick his father, and his father's greed, out of his life forever. Having no other marketable skills, it had seemed wrong to look a gift horse in the mouth, so Grayson had continued in the profession his father had begun for him. Since his career was already established and plenty profitable, it simply made sense for Grayson to stay in Hollywood and continue doing what he was doing.

For their part, Carson and Amelia had never blamed Grayson for his stardom, which had wreaked such havoc on their family. Grayson was more than grateful for their understanding and allowed them to still be friends as adults, which was the best and worst part of Grayson's life.

His siblings were his biggest cheerleaders, but they were also the only thing that kept him tethered to the ground and in touch with reality.

"Home sweet home," Carson said as he pulled into his garage. The hard set of his jaw was a sign to Grayson that his brother was still upset, but just like in the courtroom, Carson kept his emotions to himself.

"About time you two got here."

Grayson's head snapped up at the sound of his sister's voice.

She stood in the door of the garage with a tired smile on her face.

Grabbing the handle on the door, Grayson, with Carson's help, got himself back on the walker. Then he looked up with a small smile. "Hey, Am. You look amazing."

She struck a pose. "You would too if you'd given birth only a month ago." She winked as she came forward. "You should try it sometimes. It does wonders for the complexion."

Grayson snorted and pretended to be patient as they shuffled him into the house. "And just where is my little niece?" he asked as they entered the family room. "Surely she's too young to be left at home?"

Amelia gave him a wry look. "I'm a mother, not an idiot."

"I've heard mom brain is a real thing," Carson said, heading to the attached kitchen. "They did a scientific study on it. I'll bet it would hold up in court."

Their sister rolled her eyes. "Matt is taking care of her, thank you very much. I fed her before I came and now I should have a couple of hours before I'm needed again."

Grayson grabbed her hand and gave it a squeeze. "Thanks for coming," he said softly.

Amelia's eyes were misty as she smiled. "I wouldn't have missed this for the world." She played with a piece of hair that often fell into his eyes. "You've done everything for us. I'm grateful we can help repay that just a little."

Again, Grayson felt as if he had been slapped, though he knew his family was sincere. It just felt wrong, though, to let someone else take care of him. He'd been independent for too long to take all this lying down. He sighed and slouched in the chair. *Only time will tell...*

It was true. Only time would tell. Now if only Grayson was patient enough to see what it would say.

CHAPTER 2

"Don't you like the shrimp?"

Brook jerked slightly as her thoughts came back to the present. "What? Oh!" She plastered a smile on her face. "Sorry. Daydreaming." Stuffing another bite in her mouth, she chewed with a smile. "It's good. How's yours?"

Brendon smiled and looked down at his nearly empty plate.

Heat infused Brook's cheeks as she realized she had been daydreaming long enough for him to eat his entire meal. She swallowed hard. "Sorry."

Brendon shrugged and set his fork down. "It's fine. Whatever's on your mind must be big though."

Yeah...so big it's national news. "Uh...just stuff at work." She poked at her plate, not really hungry anymore. "Sometimes running your own business can be stressful, ya know?"

He nodded knowingly. "Yeah. I get that." His fingers tapped the table. "You own the little clothes shop, right?"

Brook pinched her lips together and managed to keep herself from saying something rude. She worked hard to have a good store and his wording just irked her. *But he isn't trying to,* she reminded herself. *Give him the benefit of the doubt.* "Yes," she said in a tightly polite tone. "I own Blushing Pink Boutique. We specialize in women's clothing."

Brendon nodded. "Right. I think I've seen it a few times."

Her jaw remained tight as she chewed another bite of overcooked shrimp.

"I'll bet your business fluctuates a lot, huh?" He gave her a half-grin that might have been charming if he wasn't degrading her work.

"Why do you say that?" she asked, picking up her glass for a sip of water. She wasn't normally much of an alcohol drinker, but right now Brook was wishing for something stronger to get her through the evening.

"Well, I'm guessing it fluctuates with the tourism trade. Do you actually make enough during the summer to survive all winter?" His eyes were open and honest and that made it difficult to get frustrated, but why did men always assume that women didn't do as well as a man-run business?

"Actually, it might interest you to know that women buy clothing all year round," she replied with a sweet smile.

Brendon blinked, then laughed softly. "I suppose they do. Sorry. That all came out wrong." His neck grew red and Brook realized he was nervous.

It made her pause. She had come into this date semi-unwilling, and here he was nervous about spending time with her. It made her ire melt a little and she determined once again that she would try a little harder to push past her celebrity obsession. "It's all right," she said softly. "I get it."

Brendon cleared his throat. "So...maybe I'll try something safer. Like why did you decide to go into fashion? Was that always your dream?"

Brook pursed her lips and ticked her head back and forth. "Sort of. I loved playing dress up as a child." She grinned. "I'm an only child, so I spent a lot of time playing imaginary games, and how better to do that then with pretty clothes?"

Brendon returned her smile, but didn't speak, obviously giving her the floor.

"My mom was big into fashion and Hollywood, so we spent a lot of time together pouring over magazines and dissecting all the outfits of the A-listers." A sarcastic laugh broke free as she thought about how that was currently affecting her love life...or lack thereof. "So, a store with all the clothing I'd spent so many years admiring seemed like a good fit."

"Did you jump into it right out of high school? Or..."

"I have a bachelors in business," she offered. "During college, I paid my way through by doing online selling." She shrugged. "I sold small things, like scarves or jewelry. When I was done, I knew I didn't want to continue with dropshipping. I enjoy being around people and helping women find that one special outfit that makes them feel like a million bucks." Her smile grew wider and more genuine the longer she talked. It didn't matter who her audience was. Once Brook got going, she had a hard time stopping when talking about her dream life. "So, a storefront was the perfect answer to that. Those looking for help can get it, while others who simply want to browse only have to say so."

Brendon nodded. "Sounds like you're pretty happy with what you're doing."

"I love it." She took another bite and chewed. "What about you? What made you become a teacher?"

He grinned and sat back. "It wasn't my first choice of jobs, but it ended up being a good career."

"What was your first choice?" Brendon might not be the most interesting person she'd ever met, but the conversation was getting a little easier between them.

"I wanted to be a veterinarian."

Her eyebrows shot up. She hadn't expected that. "Wow. What stopped you?"

His neck turned red again. "An unfortunate incident with a cat, and a good grade in chemistry."

She gave him a look. "I think you might need to explain."

His eyes dropped to his plate and his voice dropped to a whisper. "It's pretty cliche, actually." He glanced up under his eyelashes. "We adopted a cat from the shelter and I spent the next three years fearing for my life."

Brook frowned. "What?"

"I swear that cat was out to kill me," he said in earnest. "It used to follow me with its eyes, glaring and plotting my death. All while that stupid tail would swish back and forth in perfect rhythm. After that, I knew there was no way I could deal with animals all day every day."

"Wow...that's kind of crazy." She turned to head to the side slightly while she watched him. "How old were you?"

"Fifteen."

Brook tried to hold it in, she really did, but the laughter refused to be controlled. Her vision blurred with tears as she laughed, covering the sound with her napkin to keep from drawing any more attention than she was already drawing.

Brendon huffed, but gave her a small smile, letting her know he wasn't offended. He leaned back with a resigned sigh and folded his arms over his chest. "Why is this the reaction I always get?"

"I'm sorry." She gasped, wiping at her eyes. "I just...you were so serious."

"Have you ever had a cat?" he asked. "They're like evil incarnate."

Another burst of giggles slipped through her lips. "I'll remember that for future reference," she responded, pulling herself back under control.

He nodded.

"And the chemistry thing?"

Brendon took a drink. "Once I realized animals weren't my thing, my mom noticed that I sailed through all my science classes in high school like a pro. After heading to college, I tested out a few courses, gave some tutoring sessions, and realized that I enjoyed teaching the concepts to others." He shrugged. "The rest, as they say, is history."

"Well, I couldn't do what you do, so kudos to you," Brook said, setting her napkin across her plate.

"Done?" he asked.

She nodded. "Yep."

"Ready to go home? Or would you like to walk down Main for a bit? Maybe get a little dessert?" His eyes were hopeful and Brook found herself torn.

She still wasn't finding herself drawn to Brendon in any kind of romantic way, but it was nice that he was entertaining. Her eyes hadn't drifted to his muscles and she didn't find herself wanting to sit closer to him, but he'd made her laugh and she wasn't hating their time together. Taking a deep breath, she forced herself to take the plunge. "You know what? A walk would be nice. Thanks."

"I CAN'T STAY HERE!" Grayson cried, leaning back against the wall. His leg was burning today, putting him in an even worse mood than usual. Nothing seemed to be able to touch the fiery sensation from the compressed nerve, and yet he wasn't supposed to sit down. It was either all down or all up. As each day went by and the weakness in his leg didn't improve, Grayson found his outlook becoming more and more bleak. "The media is hounding at the gate. We've already had three of them arrested for climbing the fence." He sneered. "Everyone wants to get a glimpse of the invalid."

"You're not an invalid," Carson snapped. He sighed and pushed a hand through his hair before turning to Richard Silverman, Grayson's agent.

Rich shrugged and splayed his hands out to the side. "I don't know, Gray. What do you want me to do? We've got the best security company on it, but they're only human."

Grayson snorted and shifted his hips to try and alleviate the pain in his leg. It didn't work.

"What do you *want* to do?" Carson asked, walking over to put a hand on Grayson's shoulder. "I know everything happening right now is stressing you out and Dr. Timson said you'll heal better if you're not stressed, so what would be the perfect scenario for you?"

Grayson hung his head. Truth was, he didn't know. All he knew was that he was angry, he hurt in a way that defied description, and he had no way of knowing if it would get any better. He hated that he couldn't walk correctly. Some days he could manage on a cane, but other days he needed a walker because he could barely lift his leg. He had always been active and on the go and this was killing him, mentally as well as physically.

But what could he do? He couldn't force his body to recover. Time had been the answer reiterated to him over and over again. He needed to give the injury time, and keep up other exercises to help his body stay strong. But how could he do that when he was constantly looking over his shoulder for the next flashing light or trespassing paparazzi trying to make a buck. They drove him crazy in the best of times, and these were not the best of times.

"I don't know," he grumbled. "I need... I need to be somewhere else."

"Do you want to go to one of your other houses?" Rich asked as he fiddled with his phone. "We can book you a private jet and find a new doctor closer."

Grayson shook his head. "The media will just follow."

Carson sighed. "He's right. If he goes to any of his normal places, those vultures will just tag along. It won't take it long to be just as bad there as it is here."

"I don't know what you want, then." Rich threw up his hands. "It's not like one of the biggest movie stars alive can just drop off the edge of the earth."

Grayson stilled. "That...doesn't sound so bad."

"Hey, now, wait a minute," Rich hurried to say, storming across the room to confront Grayson. "I said you *can't* just drop off the face of the earth. Where the heck would you go that the people wouldn't know who you are? And where you can still get the care you need?"

"Somewhere people don't expect you to go," Carson offered.

Grayson nodded slowly and turned to look at his brother. He grimaced slightly and shifted his weight again. "Where is the last place on earth that the paparazzi would expect me to be?"

Carson pursed his lips and squished them to the side. "Probably some podunk tiny town that doesn't show on a map."

"Wait, wait, wait," Rich argued. "I need you in top notch condition if we're gonna have a comeback from this." He pointed a finger in Grayson's face. "And we *will* have a comeback." Dropping his hand, he sighed. "But the point is, you need to be where you're close to the medical help you need."

"We could hire a personal physical therapist to go with you. I'll bet Jude would do it," Carson said, speaking of a family friend.

Rich glared at Carson. "You're not helping."

"Actually, he's the one who is helping," Grayson stated firmly. He put a hand on Rich's shoulder. "I know you want me to jump back from this, but Rich...I can't even walk. It's gonna be a while, and I can't function in this environment."

Rich scoffed and shook off Grayson's hold, walking away before turning back to face the men. "I can see you're really suffering," he said wryly. "A mansion with a private pool and personal security." Rolling his eyes, Rich shook his head. "You have everything you need here and the best doctors in the country at your disposal. Why would you want to throw that away to go sit in some shack being catered to by a quack?"

Grayson wasn't impressed with his agent's tantrum, although he understood the sentiment. Rich's career relied on Grayson's career. If Grayson wasn't able to work, Rich lost money. A lot of money. "At the risk of sounding like a spoiled brat," Grayson said tightly, "I need to get away. None of my properties will work since the media will be watching them." He straightened, holding back a groan when the fires of purgatory continued climbing his leg. "I have no doubt that if we look around, we can find a place where I can hide and will still be close enough to a city with the medical help I need." He turned to look at Carson. "And I think taking Jude with me would be a good idea. That's something I'll need almost every day, so it'd be better to have him close."

"You guys are insane." Rich huffed, slumping onto a couch.

"Lie down," Carson said softly to Grayson. "You're getting pale and I can tell you're hurting."

Grayson clenched his jaw, but couldn't argue. He could feel sweat beginning to trickle down the back of his neck. If he didn't take the pressure off soon, he was afraid he would faint, and that would be far worse than just lying down to begin with. With a curt nod, he hobbled over to a sectional and Carson helped him lie flat on his back. "Now what?" he muttered.

Carson sat on the coffee table and pulled up his phone. "Now we start looking at maps."

Grayson held out his hand and Carson handed him the device. Pulling up a map of the Western Coast, he began zooming in and out, trying to find something small but not too small.

"What about something in Washington?" Carson murmured, his eyes glued to his screen.

"The coast side is full of bigwigs and the eastern side is all farms." Grayson huffed. "I don't think cows are what I'm looking for and there'll be paparazzi on the coast."

"Oregon?" Carson said, not deterred in the least. "It's not exactly a glamorous state, but it has Portland, which should have the doctors you need."

Grayson pursed his lips. "That might work."

"Cannon Beach, Rockaway Beach, Tillamook." Carson began reading cities.

"Those are really touristy places," Rich drawled. "You'll still have troubles there."

Grayson pressed his lips together to keep from snapping at his unhelpful agent. Seriously, if the guy wasn't so good at getting him the roles he wanted, Grayson would rid himself of the whiner.

"Found it!" Carson said excitedly. He leaned in and showed his phone to Grayson. "The place is small, but close to some of the bigger cities. It would only take a couple hours to get to Portland for your big appointments, but because of its size, there shouldn't be any paparazzi there at all."

"Where is it?" Grayson asked, looking at the idyllic pictures of the beach and wooden boardwalk.

"Seaside Bay."

CHAPTER 3

Brook's eyes were on her phone as she walked. Brendon had been pressing her for another date, but she was working hard to hold him off without hurting his feelings. It wasn't that there was anything really wrong with him. He just didn't stir her at all. *Surely I want to at least be attracted to a guy if I'm going to date him.*

I'm sorry, I'm not available. Have a good time!

Chatting with him the other night had been fun and had helped stem some of her loneliness, but that didn't mean she wanted to spend an hour in the car with him to go see a movie in the theatre to the south of Seaside Bay.

It's running for the next while. When is a good time for you?

"Geez, this guy won't give up," she muttered. Scrunching up her nose, she stopped walking. *How do I do this without making an enemy?*

She pinched her lips together, contemplating the situation. Why was dating so hard? *And why do nice guys who are right down the street not ring my bell like a make-believe guy who lives hundreds of miles away?*

Sighing and stuffing her phone back in her pocket without answering, Brook started to walk again. Her eyes roamed over the swarm of tourists to her left who were moving all over the beach like a bunch of little crabs. Kids chased the waves, adults sat under umbrellas, seagulls dive-bombed leftover lunches. It was a picture-perfect day on the white sand of Seaside Bay. Having taken the afternoon off, Brook was tempted to go home, grab her gear, and come back to sunbathe for a while, but the idea of doing it by herself just sounded pathetic.

She was already fighting off one unwanted suitor. She wasn't about to put herself on display and open herself up to being hit on by tourists. Nothing said "I'm available" like laying on a towel by yourself in nothing but a bathing suit.

"I can at least sit on the benches," she muttered. Glancing up and down the beach, she found a long one with only one other person on it. *Plenty of space.* She pumped her arms a little, walking with a purpose until she got to the long, wooden seat. She glanced at the man sitting on the far end. A bushy beard, sunglasses, and hat hid his face and apparently his peripheral vision, because no matter how Brook moved her head, she couldn't seem to get his attention. "Excuse me," she said, putting a gentle smile on her face. She waved when he looked her way. "Hi. I just wanted to make sure it was okay if I sat down here."

Something about his body seemed to tighten at her words and Brook wondered if she said something wrong. Finally, after an awkward moment of silence, he grunted. "It's a free country."

Brook's eyebrows shot up her forehead. *Wow. Mr. Nice Guy, huh?* "Thanks," she said with forced politeness before sitting down. She made sure she was as far away from him as she could get. No point in seeing if rudeness was contagious.

She settled into the hard seat and took in a deep breath filled with the salty tang of the sea. *Ahhh...* This was her happy place. She loved the beach, and especially loved that it wasn't nearly as busy as her home in California had been. Hollywood was fun to read about, but Brook wanted nothing to do with living there anymore.

Ha! That might make things difficult if miracles really happened and you met Grayson Cordova.

Without conscious thought, her eyes drifted to the side. The man on the bench was shifting around and the soft sounds he was making made him seem in pain. She studied him as he moved. Thick muscles rippled through his arms and the thin fabric of his T-shirt.

His dark skin looked smooth and was just as mouth-watering as his body.

Realizing she was practically drooling, Brook snapped her head forward and pinched her lips together. *Are you kidding me? Why the heck are my hormones kicking into gear now? Why not the other night with Brendon?*

She looked through her periphery again and suddenly it felt as if her thin, long-sleeved shirt was too much. Had the sun shot the temperature up a few degrees that quickly? Her eyes went to his beard, which seemed completely at odds with the rest of him. He obviously took care of his body, but then why couldn't he be just as conscientious with his face?

With a low groan that caught Brook's full attention, he pulled a cane from his side and started trying to get to his feet. The sand, however, wasn't very cooperative and his cane kept shifting.

"Oh my gosh," Brook said breathlessly, jumping to her feet. "Let me help you." She grabbed his arm and her heart stuttered. Shaking off the odd sensation, she wrapped one arm around his back. "Do you have someone close by you want me to call?"

The man shook her off with a growl and stumbled to the side. Even through his glasses and hat, Brook could see the grimace of pain on his face. "I don't need help," he snapped. He seemed to realize just how rude his comment was because he followed it up with a gruff, "Thanks anyway."

Brook huffed and folded her arms over her chest. "Good save," she said.

He glared at her from under his glasses. "Look...I'm not looking for a handout. I made it here, I can make it back." He started to turn himself, his right leg dragging in the sand.

Despite his behavior, Brook found her heart going out to him. "You didn't answer my question," she said loudly enough for him to hear.

He stopped and glanced over his shoulder. "What was that?"

"You obviously don't want *my* help, but is there someone close by you do want?" Heat traveled into her cheeks as she realized how awkward that question sounded.

He must have realized it too, because his beard quirked and Brook was positive that if he was clean-shaven, she would find a smirk on that strong jaw of his. "I'm here alone," he finally said, his amusement audible. "Is that what you wanted to hear? Planning to fleece the cripple?"

"What?" Brook made a face. "Are you this skeptical of everyone?"

He shrugged and her eyes immediately went to his large shoulders. Shoulders that were big enough to be...

She mentally smacked herself. *Stop thinking about GRAYSON!*

"Everyone wants something," he said, the humor gone from his voice. "I have yet to find otherwise."

"Wow." Brook stepped back and blinked a couple of times. "So, you're a pessimist."

"Realist."

She huffed a sarcastic laugh. "Tomato, tomahto."

He shrugged again and began to turn away. "Now, if you'll excuse me, I need to get back."

Brook watched him go, torn between helping and being indignant at his rude treatment. *It's not like I can force him to accept my help. If he doesn't want it, he doesn't want it.* She looked around carefully, hoping to find someone who was heading their way to help him get back on the boardwalk and take him home, but no one was paying any attention to them.

Her heart lurched when he stumbled to get onto the sidewalk and she lunged forward, only to pull herself back. "He doesn't want help," she scolded herself. "Leave him to his pride." Knowing there was nothing else she could do, she plopped back down on the bench and stared at the water.

Eventually it would help calm her racing heart and overly flushed skin. Which, of course, were only because she'd just dealt with a jerk. They had nothing to do with the pull of his physical attractiveness. Nothing whatsoever. She just needed to take a few deep breaths and everything would calm down. And forget about Mr. Rude Pants and his horrible manners. She had no room or desire for someone like him in her life...

Not at all.

GRAYSON'S PANIC BEGAN to subside the longer he went without the woman chasing him down. He'd been terrified at her persistence that she would recognize him, even with his itchy beard and hat. Really, the beard was getting out of control, but he didn't dare cut it. It was a good thing he'd already been letting it go after his surgery. It made being ready to come to Seaside Bay easier.

Several sets of eyes darted his way as he shuffled down the sidewalk. He probably looked like a circus act as he slowly made his way to his rental home. The place was comfortable, well kept, and most of all...quiet.

He'd avoided the flashiest of the rental houses, not wanting to appear ostentatious to the locals, but still wanted enough room to do his exercises at the house, and he definitely wanted to be right on the water. Once a beach bum, always a beach bum.

A flash of dark brown hair went through his mind's eyes and he scowled. The woman had been pretty. Very pretty. But in his line of work, Grayson worked with and even sometimes kissed, the most beautiful women in the world. Why the heck was a small-town beach bunny taking up residence in his head?

An unwanted smile tugged on his lips as he thought of her growing embarrassed about asking who he wanted. He had known exactly what she meant, but the wording had come out wrong and they'd both realized it. A delicious blush had flooded her cheeks, making them very tempting.

"Not tempting," he growled as he punched in the code to his rental. Cool air hit him in the face and he relaxed slightly. The walk to the beach had been great...on the way there. But then he sat too long on the bench and now his entire right side was in flames.

He hobbled to the couch and almost fell in his haste to lie down. His doctor had warned him about sitting. It wasn't going to be good for him for a while. But how was he supposed to go through his day-to-day life without ever sitting? Standing was uncomfortable for long periods of time, not to mention awkward. And lying down only seemed appropriate in the bedroom or while watching a movie.

Sighing, he grabbed the bill of his hat and threw it across the room, along with his glasses. Perhaps he'd pushed things a little too far today. Maybe walking by himself to the beach was just too much too soon.

"You're back," Jude Lisbon, Grayson's friend and physical therapist, said cheerily. "How was the beach?"

Grayson threw an arm over his face. He liked Jude. The guy had been a buddy for a lot of years, since he worked with other actors, but he was also annoyingly chipper most of the time and Grayson didn't feel like being chipper. "Fine." He grunted.

"That good, huh?"

Grayson glared from under his arm. "I can still whip you," he threatened.

Jude laughed and flexed his arms. "I've been putting on a bit of weight, Gray. Or can't you tell?"

The move made Grayson crack a smile. Jude couldn't seem to put on weight if his life depended on it. He wasn't scrawny, but he was definitely thinner than Grayson and no matter how much Jude worked out, he stayed athletically thin.

"Ah...the sun does exist," Jude teased.

The smile immediately left Grayson's face. "Maybe I'm just trying to live up to my name."

Jude rolled his eyes and sat down in a seat near the couch. "I'm guessing from the sweat plastered to your head that you weren't quite ready for that walk." He tsked his tongue. "When are you gonna listen to reason, man?"

Grayson tucked his eyes under his arm again. "I don't know if I can do this," he admitted softly. "I've never been helpless before."

A sympathetic sound came from Jude's direction. "You're not helpless, Gray. Just...hurt. It'll pass."

"Will it?" Grayson asked harshly. "No one seems to be very sure of that." He dropped his arm and looked at his friend. "What if my back never recovers? What if I have to walk with a cane for the rest of my life? How can I live like that?" He was breathing heavily after his little rant and he squeezed his eyes shut, forcing himself to calm down. "I'm sorry, Jude. I didn't mean it."

"Between the two of us, we both know that's the lie," Jude said easily. "But don't feel bad about it. I think it would be good for you to get that all off your chest."

Grayson gave a harsh chuckle. "What? Are you a therapist for my mind as well as my body now?"

"Not a chance," Jude said. "But I deal with a lot of people when they've been hurt in some way, and I know well how much better they feel when they're able to get past the emotions of the accident."

There was some truth in what Jude was saying. Grayson felt bottled up. Like no one understood what he was going through, no matter how nice they were to him. None of them had ever gone from hero to zero in two seconds flat. None of them had ever had their entire future ripped from them. Try as they might, they just didn't get it. *Maybe I should talk to someone...*

Long dark hair and a plush mouth swam through his mind again and Grayson groaned.

"What's wrong?"

He shook his head. "Nothing. Just remembering this nosy woman at the beach."

"Nosy, huh?" Jude inquired. "How nosy? Do we need to look at getting a different place?"

Grayson shook his head. "No. I don't think she came close to recognizing me, but she certainly thought I was some kind of charity case." He snorted. "She's pretty tiny and yet she tried to help me get off the bench."

"You were sitting down?"

Grayson huffed. "Yes. What else are you supposed to do at the beach?"

"Follow your doctor's orders," Jude shot back. "Dude, you're never gonna get better if you keep pushing your limits."

Grayson didn't respond. Jude was right, but Grayson was tired of arguing.

"You're sure she didn't know who you were?"

"Considering she was younger than me and didn't squeal or throw her arms around me in delight, I'm gonna say no."

Jude snickered. "Must be tough to be you."

Normally Grayson would have laughed as well and rolled his eyes, but not today. Jude's joke was just another reminder that his life wasn't what it used to be. What it *should* be. After a too-long silence, Grayson changed the subject. "What're our plans for the rest of the day?"

"Hmm..." Jude slapped the arms of his chair and rose up. "I was gonna have us do some light exercises this afternoon, but you already pushed yourself too hard. How about I get lost and you take a nap? Sleep can be just as curative as work."

Grayson didn't answer. He was tired, but it just made him feel even more helpless.

"Mrs. Flores said she'll have dinner ready at six, so you take it easy until then." Jude's voice changed as he began to walk out of the room. "Want me to take you to your bed?"

Grayson shook his head. "Nah. This is fine. If I sleep too much, I'll never sleep tonight."

"'Kay. See ya in a while." Footsteps echoed down the tiled hallway and once more, Grayson found himself left alone.

The feeling magnified the loneliness he was already struggling with, but there was nothing for it. Once again, a shift in his life had led to something that separated him from everything else, cutting Grayson off from his family and friends. Only this time...he wasn't sure it would have the same happy ending as before.

CHAPTER 4

A restless energy seemed to keep Brook company for the next couple of days. There was just something about that rude guy at the beach that she couldn't get out of her head. She knew some of it was sympathy. He was obviously hurting, which is probably why he was so rude. Plus, the man had appeared to be alone. *Which was no wonder with his attitude.* It pricked her heart to think of someone going through all that pain by themselves.

But along with that feeling, Brook found herself slightly intrigued. For the first time in ages, she had felt a stirring of attraction. It was a feeling she only ever had when she saw pictures of Grayson Cordova. Those butterflies and heartbeat skips had been wholly prominent when she'd studied the man at the beach. She hadn't felt a draw to his personality, but she'd definitely been attracted to him physically.

In direct contrast...Brendon was very nice, but he didn't stir any of those pesky feelings in her stomach and heart. Two men and two completely different reactions. It would be smart to go with the nice guy, right? Someone who at least knew how to say hello and not bite your head off when you ask a question?

I must be an idiot. Despite Brendon being the logical choice, Brook couldn't find it within herself to ignore the feelings the beach guy had stirred.

She wanted to see him again. She wanted to see if he'd gotten home all right. She wanted to ask about his injury and hear his story. If she was being honest with herself, she also wanted another chance to see his muscles and study his face. Even with the bushy beard, she could tell he was handsome. What she wouldn't have given to see his eye color. With his dark coloring, could he be lucky enough to have light-colored eyes? The kind that stood out in a crowd and arrested attention without even trying?

Ones like Grayson Cordova?

"Oh my gosh, stop," Brook muttered to herself. She really did need to let this all go. Grayson Cordova was a star who didn't even know she existed, and the guy at the beach didn't sound like he was looking for a friend.

"What is it with me and men who are unavailable?" she grumbled as she continued to punch numbers into her computer screen. "Maybe I'm just a glutton for punishment."

The afternoon wore on, but no matter how hard she tried, Brook just couldn't get the man...or Grayson...out of her head. She hated thinking of him being alone and wounded. It caused a physical ache in her chest and made her want to cry. She knew what it was to be lonely, even as she was surrounded by friends. But he didn't even have anyone around him. He was completely alone. Or, at least, it had looked that way.

"Give it up, Brook," she muttered. "He could be married for all you know." She huffed. "Plus, he's obviously a tourist. There's no way he lives here, because you've never seen him before."

With a groan, she put a hand to her heart. The thought of him being a tourist hurt even more. He was on vacation...on the beach...and was by himself. There were so many things wrong with that picture and Brook wanted to fix every one of them.

What if he doesn't want you to?

She stilled. The thought was a good one. Despite the fact that she was fiercely loyal to friends and her crazy celebrity crush, she was not, in fact, one to push herself on others if they didn't want her around.

The reminder had her slumping in her seat. Her pen began to bounce against the desk. "Well, the only way to know for sure how he feels about making a friend is to actually meet him properly," she mused.

She glanced at her clock. If she left now, the crowds would still be at the beach, which meant she'd have a chance of running into him again. Her eyes went over her work. She still had some inventory stuff to take care of, but she was having trouble focusing with thoughts of the stranger on her mind.

"Just go see him," she told herself. "You'll get the work done tomorrow, or you can do it at home." A grimace spread across her face at the thought. Just another clear indicator that she had too much time on her hands and that her evenings were spent by herself.

"Whatever." She closed down her computer, stuffed the binder on the shelf, and grabbed her purse, keys and phone. What good was being the boss if she couldn't take a little time off once in a while, right?

After saying goodbye to her employees, she pushed open the door and headed out into the sunshine. Today was a beautiful day. The salty tang of ocean permeated her sinuses and the heat of the sun beat down on the top of her head. The bright blue sky was a rarity and suddenly Brook was grateful she'd come outside. Pushing her sunglasses onto her nose, she began sauntering toward the beach.

Even on a weekday, the tourists were swarming. Seaside Bay might not get as many visitors as Florence or Cannon Beach, but they saw their fair share during the summer. Many of them weren't staying in the city. They drove in from other bigger cities in order to take advantage of less crowded beaches. *But that only makes them more crowded,* Brook thought with a snicker.

The sand lay ahead of her and her eyes automatically began scanning benches. With his leg, she knew he wouldn't be walking along closer to the water. He could barely walk on the sand at all. But she hoped he was sitting around somewhere, taking in the sights and enjoying the sunshine.

Once on the boardwalk, she looked left and right. Which way should she choose? There were benches in both directions and he could be on any one of them. Squishing her lips to one side, she turned her feet to the right. The bench he'd been on earlier in the week was that way. Hopefully going back to the same place would give her a better shot of seeing him.

As she walked and dodged running children, Brook let her mind roam free. Right now it was easy to imagine that she had no cares in the world. The beach was her happy place. Her solace. And it was working its magic as she strolled. The sounds of seagulls, children squealing in delight, and the rush of mighty waves could warm even the hardest heart, and Brook was definitely *not* hard-hearted.

In fact, she sometimes thought she was too soft-hearted. She hated seeing people in pain. She loved to see others happy. Maybe that's what she loved so much about Hollywood. Pictures of glamorous people with perfect smiles... It made it seem as if fairy tales did come true.

Her phone buzzed with a notification and she pulled it out of her purse. A news blog she followed had a new article and it was about Grayson Cordova. Brook's thumb hovered over the notice. She wanted to know what was going on, but she also wanted to learn how to let go of a dream that was doing more harm than good.

Swallowing hard, she forced herself to erase it. Her hands shook as she put the phone back in her purse. Why did it feel like she was tucking her heart onto a shelf, never to be seen again?

Shaking her head hard, Brook put her feet back into motion. Grayson was a dream. But her life wasn't. It might not be awesome. She was alone, only being pursued by someone she wasn't interested in and wasting her afternoon looking for a man who might hate her, but it was hers.

And it's real. That's the most important part. This is reality. And I need to remember that.

GRAYSON FROWNED. A single line of sweat worked its way down his back as he stood leaning against a building across from the boardwalk. The woman he'd met the other day was walking as if she didn't have a care in the world. He couldn't see her eyes because of her sunglasses, but it seemed like she was scanning the beach.

Is she looking for someone?

A small part of his brain hoped she was looking for him, but Grayson quickly pushed the thought away. He didn't want her looking for him. He wasn't trying to get close to anybody at the moment because he was in hiding. All it would take was one person to recognize him and it would be all over. He couldn't risk that. He needed peace and quiet. The ocean and beach could bring that to him, but not if it was mixed with fans who wouldn't leave him alone.

Growling softly under his breath, he turned away from the woman. He didn't need her kindness. It would only lead to trouble. He'd only gone a few steps before he paused then stepped back to lean against the building. He was breathing heavily as his leg began to burn like a poker was stuck straight down the middle of it. He gasped, trying to breathe through the pain, and felt his knee wobble.

Not now... Please, not now...

His grip on his cane tightened as he tried to keep himself upright. He closed his eyes and turned so his upper back was against the building. Grayson forced his breathing to slow down as he tried to wait out the pain. Several minutes later, however, it was no better. He needed to lie down. But where? Maybe he could get to one of the benches on the beach?

"Crap," he muttered. If he went out there, that woman would see him. He couldn't afford that. No matter how kind she'd been or how beautiful she was. Her image floated through his mind as he tried to grit his way through the pain. Her dark hair and soft, lightly tanned skin was hard to ignore.

His knee shook even harder and Grayson couldn't stop himself from sliding to the ground. Bending at the waist, however, only made things worse and he let his body fall to the side until he was lying down on a dirty sidewalk. When had he come to this? How did someone who was one of the most recognizable actors in the world come to be lying in a filthy alley next to garbage cans, while he tried to keep breathing through mind numbing pain?

"Sir? Sir, are you okay?"

Grayson kept his eyes shut. He could hear the voices around him, especially as they grew in number and worry, but he couldn't quite bring himself to answer them. His walk today had been a mistake. Even avoiding the sand wasn't quite enough. But was he supposed to stay in his rented home and never leave? He wasn't really a homebody, though he did enjoy his privacy. He liked to feel free and here where no one knew where he was, Grayson wanted to take advantage of it. If only his leg wasn't ruining everything.

"Sir, can you hear me? Do you want me to call a doctor? Or an ambulance?"

Grayson shook his head and forced his eyes open despite the pain still incinerating his leg. "No. I'm fine." Without his permission, his eyes squeezed closed again.

A loud gasp caught his attention. "Oh my gosh."

Grayson didn't need to look to know exactly who had found him. The beautiful woman he couldn't get out of his head was once again going to see him in his worst state. Life couldn't get any lower.

"It's okay," she said, obviously talking to the crowd. "I know him. I'll help him get home."

A small hand slipped into his and Grayson found himself squeezing tight. Her touch didn't do anything to take away the pain, but it did seem to help clear his mind. "I need them gone," he whispered hoarsely.

"I'm working on it," the woman assured him softly.

He could feel her lean back and when she spoke, her voice was directed at him. "It's okay, everyone. I've got this. He just overdid it in the heat. Thank you! I'll make sure that he gets home."

The thick air around him began to ease as Grayson felt the crowd slowly slip away, his mystery woman reassuring people over and over again that she had it covered. He didn't even know her name, but he was so grateful for her interference. He wasn't sure how he was going to handle it if he couldn't get them to leave. It's not like he could let them call an ambulance. His face would be plastered all over the place and his cover blown. Jude was going to kill him.

"Okay," her soft voice said just before her hand began to wipe the hair off his forehead.

He realized his hat must have fallen off when he went down and a spark of panic ran through him, momentarily interrupting the pain. He opened his eyes to tell her to back off, but the words died in his throat when he saw an angel leaning over him. Dark hair framed her beautiful face and hung down, creating a curtain around the two of them. Instant attraction sparked and Grayson once again found himself gritting teeth, only this time it wasn't in pain.

Now he was fighting the desire to touch her soft-looking cheeks and then pull her face down to see if the touch of her lips was as wonderful as the touch of her hand. "My phone," he murmured.

Her eyebrows pulled together over her sunglasses. "What?"

"I need my phone."

"Oh!" She backed off and began to look around on the ground. "I don't see it."

"It's in my..." *Ah, crap.* "My back pocket."

A severe blush ran up her neck and cheeks and Grayson couldn't pull his eyes away from it. "Are you asking me to get it?" she asked, swallowing hard.

He tried to nod, but even that slight movement had him groaning. "Please," he ground out.

"Okay," she muttered. "Just remember that you gave me permission," she said. "No yelling about it."

He huffed slightly, holding back a laugh. She had every right to be wary of him. But right now he was too grateful for her help and in too much pain to push her away. How she had known from the beginning that he needed the crowd gone, he didn't know, but he wasn't going to argue with the results. Saying she knew him might have been a stretch, but other than Jude, she was the only other person he'd spoken to...so technically it wasn't a lie.

He felt her shifting him and he groaned at the movement. The hard concrete was doing nothing to alleviate his pain. It only ticked him off even more that he couldn't enjoy the attention of a beautiful woman, even if she was just looking for his phone.

"Got it." She gasped, pulling it from his back pocket.

"Go to contacts," he whispered.

Her hand brushed his forehead again. "Just a second," she said.

The light dimmed and he realized she had propped his hat over his face.

"It's too hot for you to be uncovered." A loud breath could be heard. "Okay, now...who do you want me to look up?"

"Jude."

"What should I say?"

"Just type 911."

CHAPTER 5

Brook frowned, but followed his directions. An irritating trickle of jealousy was working its way through her chest. She barely knew this man and yet she had already imagined him as alone. But considering his looks, it shouldn't have surprised her that he was taken. She sighed and set the phone down. Her fingers itched to keep combing through his hair, but she'd already put the hat on his head, so between that and the fact that she was texting his significant other, Brook knew she had better keep her hands to herself.

She glanced down, noting that they were still holding on with one hand. The stranger's fingers were gripped tightly around hers and Brook couldn't bring herself to force him to let go. If his girlfriend or wife was upset about it, Brook would just explain that she was trying to help ease his pain.

"Has your leg calmed down at all?" she asked, trying to make conversation.

A slight shake of his head preempted another groan and Brook felt her heart flip-flop again.

"Okay, just don't move," she said hurriedly, then closed her eyes. What a ridiculous thing to say. Of course he wasn't moving. He was lying on the sidewalk of an alley. If he was able to move, he would have definitely done so already. "Should I try to distract you?" she asked, not knowing what else to do at this point.

"Sure."

His tone was low and rough with pain, and Brook found herself blinking back tears. She really was struggling to handle his situation. Who was this poor man who was amazingly handsome, but so wounded he could barely function? It seemed so unfair. He looked like someone who took good care of himself, yet he could barely walk. And she knew first-hand about all those muscles because she had had to handle him in order to get his phone. The thought of it brought a flush to her cheeks once more. None of it made sense. "I'm Brooklyn Howell," she said. "My friends call me Brook."

He huffed, then grimaced. Even behind his sunglasses, she could see his eyes pinched tight. "Is that an invitation for me to call you Brook?"

She patted the hand she still held. "I don't know. Are you going to be mad at me again?"

"Not this time," he murmured. "I'm... I'm sorry about before."

"It's okay," Brook assured him. "I could tell you wanted to be left alone." She could also tell he'd been in pain, but she didn't want to remind him of that. She didn't want him to focus on his troubles. This was supposed to be an intervention.

He grunted and shifted a little. After a moment, he took a deep breath. "I think it's starting to calm down."

Brook's shoulders relaxed, though she hadn't noticed that they were tense. "Good," she breathed. "Are you going to tell me your name?" He opened his mouth, but hesitated and Brook frowned. Was he really so private that he couldn't even tell her his name?

"You can call me Cord," he finally muttered.

Brook forced a smile. "Is that what your friends call you?" His unkempt beard pulled and she could tell that he was smiling. Somehow, she knew that if the hair wasn't in the way, that look on his face would have been glorious. *I wonder why he keeps his face covered up?*

"Something like that."

"Well...it's nice to finally know your name, but really, Cord...we need to stop meeting like this."

He chuckled before groaning.

"Sorry," Brook hurried to say, her panic from earlier coming back full force. "I wasn't really trying to make you laugh."

He took a couple of deep breaths. "It's fine. The concrete is part of the problem. You try shaking against it."

Without thinking, Brook brushed her fingers against the sweaty hair on the side of his head that wasn't covered by the hat. His hair wasn't long, but it definitely covered his ears, as if he were growing it out or just hadn't bothered to get a cut in a while. "I'll pass, thanks."

"Smart woman," he whispered, shifting again.

"What can I do?" Brook asked. She felt so helpless and the longer she had to watch him in pain, the more her chest hurt. She didn't like it at all, and it had nothing to do with his looks. She didn't like people being in pain at all. It didn't fit with the fairy tale, happy life she wished for all her friends.

"You already took care of it," Cord said. "Jude should be here any second."

"And she'll know what to do?" Brook asked.

Cord frowned. "Wha—"

"Of course I do."

Brook's head whipped around at the deep voice. Heat stronger than her earlier embarrassment enveloped her entire body. "Oh my gosh... Please tell me you're joking and that I didn't just call a man a woman."

The man, who Brook presumed was Jude, was standing with his arms crossed over his chest. He was thinner than Cord, but also very attractive and his smile was easily seen on his clean-shaven face. "I usually try to accommodate a beautiful woman, but I'm afraid in this case...I can't."

Brook slapped her forehead. "I'm so sorry."

Jude shrugged. "Don't worry about it. Happens all the time."

"Does it really?"

Jude shook his head. "Nope. I was just trying to make you feel better." He unfolded his arms and came over to squat next to Cord. "What happened?" he asked Cord.

Cord grimaced. "I was leaning against the building and when I tried walking away, the burning came back, buckling my knee." He shrugged as much as someone could when they were lying flat on the ground.

"How did you hurt your leg?" Brook asked.

Cord turned his head her way, but didn't speak.

Oops. Brook had the feeling she had pushed past a boundary with that question, though she hadn't meant to. It was natural curiosity.

"Is she?" Jude prodded.

Cord looked back at his friend and nodded.

"Ah."

Brook frowned. *Are they talking about me? Or his leg?* "Uh..."

"He didn't hurt his leg," Jude offered as he started moving Cord's body around. "He fell and hurt his back. He's got a damaged nerve from a bulging disc and this nerve goes down into his leg, causing weakness and pain."

"Oh..." Brook bit her lips between her teeth. "I'm sorry." Her eyes dropped to the handsome wounded man. "Cord, were you in the military or something? How in the world did you fall?" She paused, then gasped. "Oh my goodness, you're not like a mountain climber or something, are you? Did you fall off a mountain?"

Cord chuckled low again before grimacing. "No and no. I got hurt on the job."

"Oh." Brook waited for him to elaborate, but he didn't. She looked up at Jude to see if he would offer more, but the man was scowling at Cord and the two of them seemed to be having a silent conversation. "Did I say something wrong?"

Jude dropped their stare-down and shook his head. "It's nothing." He repositioned himself. "Okay, big guy. Let's get you home."

Brook knew she should leave now that Cord's friend was here, but she couldn't quite get herself to walk away and before she could stop herself, the words were out of her mouth, "How can I help?"

GRAYSON HELD BACK A snort. Brook looked like she was only about 5' 4" and she definitely was on the slim side. How in the world did she think she was going to help? Instead of telling her they were fine, however, he left it in Jude's hands. Grayson couldn't bring himself to turn her down.

Jude hesitated then shrugged. "Sure. Why don't you stand in front of him while I help lift from the back."

Grayson opened his eyes in shock and made a face at Jude, but his friend was ignoring him. *Unbelievable.* Like he needed to look like more of a weakling in front of Brook. She'd already been around twice when he was having trouble and probably thought he was a complete invalid.

You are.

He scowled at himself. Healing was going to kill him...in more ways than one.

"Uh...Cord? Are you okay with that?" Brook looked unsure and Grayson realized she thought he was growling at her instead of his thoughts.

"Yeah, *Cord,*" Jude said sarcastically. "Do you have a problem with Brook?"

Pinching his lips together, Grayson shook his head.

"Right." Jude moved behind his head and slowly lifted Grayson until he was sitting up.

The burning picked back up in his leg at the movement and Grayson hissed.

"Get him on his feet," Jude said over his head. "Being straight will feel better."

Brook took his hands and Grayson found himself holding on tightly as Jude got under his armpits and pulled him to his feet. He breathed heavily once upright, as if he had done all the work, though he was basically a limp doll at this point.

Brook squeezed his hands. "Hang on," she whispered. "We'll have you home soon. I'm sure you have some kind of medication that will help."

Grayson nodded curtly and locked his good leg as best he could so Jude could shift around to be under Grayson's left arm. Slowly they began walking until Grayson jerked a little when another body, this one small, dove under his other arm.

Brook looked up and Grayson could see her eyes from above her sunglasses. "I'm stronger than I look," she said with a grin.

He snorted. They were an odd group as they made their way down to Jude's SUV. It was painful once again to climb in the back so he could lie down, but Grayson was grateful his friend had brought his vehicle.

Brook stood outside the SUV wringing her hands as Jude shut the door. The two of them stood talking for a minute and Grayson wished he could hear what they were saying. He wasn't quite ready to be rid of Brook, despite the fact that he didn't like her seeing him like this. She had handled the situation with his collapse calmly and kindly and he found he enjoyed her company. Not to mention she was a much better view than Jude.

Knowing he shouldn't encourage her, though, Grayson laid his head back down and closed his eyes with a groan. "Let her go," he told himself. "Getting to know her will only bring trouble." The idea of walking away was harder than it should have been. In his world, there weren't very many people who were kind just for the sake of being kind. Everyone wanted something from him...but not Brook. She had come to his rescue like some kind of guardian angel, and had not once asked for anything in return. At least...not yet. She hadn't even tried to film the situation or ask someone to take a selfie of her good deed. "Incognito," he reminded himself. "You're lying low. A girl, even if only a friend, will ruin that."

The door to the SUV opened and Jude hopped up to Grayson's relief and disappointment. His emotions quickly shifted, however, when the passenger side door opened as well. Grayson lifted his head and saw that long, rich brown hair come into his vision. "What are you doing?" he asked sharply.

Brook looked over the seat and smiled sweetly at him. "Jude is being nice enough to let me help you get home."

"Why would you do that?" Grayson growled.

Her smile fell a little. "Because I wanted to make sure you were okay."

Grayson's head bounced a little on the seat as he dropped his head again. He ignored the tiny voice in the back that was rubbing his hands with glee at her presence. This was ridiculous. They were going to blow his cover if they didn't get away from her.

"I thought you might enjoy something other than my ugly mug while we wait for the meds to kick in," Jude teased.

Grayson scowled again, ignoring the fact that he'd had similar thoughts only a moment before. "Whatever."

"Ignore him," Jude said, obviously to Brook. "He gets cranky when he's hurting."

Brook made a noncommittal noise and Grayson felt shame for his behavior. This woman hadn't done anything to hurt him and hadn't even come close to exposing him. She'd been kind when he'd been rude and had helped him when he was at his lowest. He supposed he should act a little more grateful for her help. "Thank you." He grunted.

There was silence for a second, then Brook said softly, "Of course. I'm just glad you have someone to help you. I was worried you were all alone."

Jude laughed. "With all he lets me help, he might as well be alone."

"Are you two on vacation here?" she asked.

"Something like that," Jude responded. He sounded distracted and Grayson realized the car was turning around, telling him they were backing into the driveway. "We came here so he could heal," Jude continued once he stopped and shut off the car. "Thought the speed of life in this little town would be good for his recovery."

Their conversation continued outside the car once again and Grayson strained to hear what was being said. He didn't like being on the outside of what they were saying. That dark cloud that had clung to him for the last few weeks seemed to press down on him and an unfamiliar feeling slid down his spine.

Jealousy.

"No way," he muttered just as the door by his feet opened.

"Here we go," Jude said, holding out a hand.

Grayson pushed himself up and together they worked their way into the house. Brook was under his arm again, and Grayson didn't have the heart to tell her she wasn't doing much to help. He didn't dare lean any of his weight on her, but he was enjoying the fact that she was so determined.

A smile played on his lips as he glanced down at her, but he quickly got rid of it. This was no laughing matter. He needed Brook gone and he needed her gone now.

Slowly they made their way inside the house and down the hall to the master bedroom. Brook clung to his side as Jude maneuvered Grayson to a more comfortable position. It was a far cry from the concrete sidewalk.

"There," Brook said breathlessly, clasping her hands in front of her. "Now...what can I get you to make you more comfortable?"

Grayson pulled off his hat, but left on his glasses, worried his eyes would give away his identity. Instead of answering Brook, he looked at Jude and raised his eyebrows.

Jude gave him a sheepish grin, then put an arm around Brook's shoulder. "Actually, I'm going to get his pills in him and then insist on a nap," he said, steering her toward the door.

Grayson refused to admit how much he hated the fact that Jude's arm was around Brook. It should be his arm. *NO! It should be no one's arm. She shouldn't be here.*

Grayson squeezed his eyes shut and tuned out the quiet conversation, though after a moment he couldn't hear them anyway. This was not why he came to Seaside Bay. Pulling off his glasses, he chucked them across the room. Jude was right about one thing. A nap would do him good right now. He was in no mood to deal with people or explain Brook's help to Jude. Hopefully by the time he awoke, his leg would have calmed down and he'd have forgotten all about the beautiful brunette who had refused to leave Grayson's side.

CHAPTER 6

The smell of hot flowers hit Brook in the face as she entered The Hidden Daffodil. Her friend, Rose, owned the flower shop and tonight was their monthly flower arrangement night. It was this very class that had created the group of friends that Brook now called family.

The women in the class came from all walks of life and were all ages, but somehow, the young, single women had started to draw closer through their time spent together, and now they relied on each other for nearly everything.

Not too many are single anymore though.

Brook pasted on a smile, despite the sarcastic thought. It wasn't fair of her to be snarky about her friends' love lives. They were wonderful women and they deserved every good thing that was coming to them. For the thousandth time, Brook had to remind herself that she was just jealous and do her best to move on.

"Hey, chica," Charli said with a grin. She wrapped an arm around Brook's shoulders and gave her a tight squeeze. "What's happening in the movie world?"

Brook laughed softly. "Not much."

Charli snapped her fingers. "Oh, yeah. That guy you follow...he got hurt, didn't he?"

Brook pinched her lips together. She was trying to forget Grayson Cordova. "Yeah...something like that."

"I heard he was spotted on his property healthy and hale," Caro inserted as she came up to the other ladies. She winked at Brook. "Sounds like he might yet make his way to Seaside Bay to sweep you off your feet! Some paparazzi guy got a shot showing he wasn't hurt at all."

Brook shrugged. "I'm not holding my breath," she said.

"Reality stinks sometimes, doesn't it?" Charli sympathized.

"Ha!" Caro blurted. "My reality is fine, thank you very much." She fluffed her hair.

Brook's heart sank into her stomach. Caro was still a newlywed. Of course her reality was fine.

"I wasn't complaining about my reality," Charli argued back. "Just that it's always hard to realize our childhood dreams won't come true."

Now nausea was churning. The room began to feel too small as Charli and Caro playfully argued about whose life was better. Both had married the love of their lives, though Charli had been married a few months longer. As Genni, the first to marry and then Hadlee, the latest to marry, joined their bantering, Brook found herself stepping back.

For the first time since they'd all become friends...Brook felt like an intruder.

An imposter.

These women were her family, but Brook didn't belong.

A slim arm slid along Brook's back, startling Brook from her self-pity. She looked over and smiled sheepishly at Rose. The only other unmarried female in their group. "Sorry," Brook whispered thickly, though she wasn't really sure what she was apologizing for. But something in Rose's eyes told Brook that the beautiful flower shop owner knew what Brook was feeling.

But even Rose couldn't quite understand. She'd been married once. And she had a beautiful almost five-year-old daughter to enjoy, though the marriage had ended.

Brook was feeling more and more like she had no one.

"It'll all work out in the end," Rose whispered before giving Brook a tight squeeze. Then, with the same elegance she did everything, Rose walked away and called the room to order. "Good evening, ladies! Are you ready to put together a summer arrangement?"

The chorus of excited female voices helped calm the anxiety that had started to rush through Brook's chest. Taking a deep breath, she stepped up to her table and tried to lose herself in the fine art of flower-arranging.

"I'm sure some of you are wondering what our message is tonight," Rose said after a while. Rose seemed to have an obsession with the language of flowers and her arrangements always reflected a certain sentiment. Listening to them was one of the best parts of arrangement night. "Each of you has a couple of calla lilies in your bundle," Rose continued. "Those are symbols of new beginnings...rebirth... starting over or simply a fresh start."

She walked around the room, her beautiful red hair nearly glowing in the fluorescent lighting. "The yellow roses are one that most people are familiar with." She winked discreetly at Brook as she walked past. "They symbolize friendship in a non-romantic scenario." Rose continued on. "You might have found the chrysanthemums in your vases to be an odd choice." She smiled. "And I can understand why. They're not usually found in arrangements since they grow on bushes rather than in long stems, but I wanted to share them with you tonight. The word chrysanthemum literally means 'gold flower' in Greek, and it symbolizes a hope for the future."

Brook's fingers were shaking as she slid a chrysanthemum into place. What she wouldn't give to have that hope right now. She was lonelier than ever. Brendon still kept texting and the one interesting person in her life didn't even like her.

A self-deprecating chuckle broke free and Brook quickly hushed herself when her table partner eyed her sideways. "Sorry," she whispered.

Her future looked far from hopeful. In fact, it looked bleak...and lonely.

That was one of the biggest weights hanging over Brook's head. The loneliness. She wanted someone by her side and the dream man she'd contented herself with no longer was enough. Even worse, the man who *was* interested didn't create any interest in return.

I'm such a mess.

"Yours looks great," Caro said, coming over to Brook's table. Caro eyed her own creation with a critical eye. "Mine somehow got all scrunched on one side and now it looks like it fell on its face."

Brook snorted. "It looks beautiful, like always."

"Well..." Caro pursed her bright red lips and looked around. "As long as Jack doesn't laugh about it, it'll be fine."

"Jack wouldn't laugh at anything you did," Brook said, doing her best to hide the jealousy in her voice.

Caro barked a laugh. "Oh, yeah? You should have seen him the other night when I tried a new recipe. I don't think he got himself under control for a good five minutes."

"What in the world did you make?" Brook frowned. "Was it really that bad?"

Caro's nose scrunched and she leaned in. "Apparently plums and chocolate are a bad idea."

Brook blinked a few times. "Really? I thought chocolate went with most fruits."

Caro shrugged. "You'd think. But not plums." She tapped her lips. "And I'm not about to try prunes."

Charli made gagging noises as she approached. "Can't you just see it now? You could advertise your prune fudge for the over sixty-five crowd." She smirked. "At least it would be a tasty way to get the fiber you need."

"Speaking of fiber..." Genni said softly. The group stopped to watch her. She looked around nervously, making sure most of the other patrons had left before turning back to the group. "Okay, so fiber has nothing to do with it, but I wanted to share our good news." Genni's cheeks turned pink as she put a hand to her stomach.

Realization hit Brook like a ton of bricks and her jaw dropped open.

"Oh my gosh!" Caro squealed, grabbing Genni in a big hug. "You're going to be such a darling mother." She stepped back and winked. "And if that baby girl has Cooper's hair, then we'll have to put her in a glass cage, because every boy for miles around will be sniffing at your door."

Brook couldn't move. Even as Charli and Caro began to argue over what gender the child was going to be, she felt frozen. For some reason, this felt like the straw that broke the camel's back. It was yet another blow, a fierce one, that reminded her that everyone else was moving on with their lives...except her.

She was being left behind and with each step, the pain grew worse. *But what can I do? It's not like I can snap my fingers and make a partner appear in my life.*

Knowing there was nothing else to do, she blinked back her tears, put a smile on her face, and gave Genni a hug. It wasn't her friend's fault that Brook was struggling. This was her burden to bear. And she just hoped she was strong enough to handle it.

"DID SHE RECOGNIZE YOU?" Amelia shrieked with a gasp.

Grayson grimaced and pulled the phone away from his ear. "No. At least, I don't think so."

"She didn't!" Jude called out from the other room.

Grayson rolled his eyes. "Eavesdropping is wrong!" he shot over his shoulder. A snicker let him know Jude heard him, but didn't care.

"Wow…" Amelia said. "I can't believe you were talking to a young woman and she didn't see past that horrendous beard of yours."

Grayson scratched said beard. "It's not horrendous."

"It looks like a dead rat," his sister teased.

"Good. Then I won't have to worry about anyone getting too close."

"Somehow I don't think your new friend cared about the beard." There was a short pause. "Oh my gosh, she didn't see your eyes, did she?"

Grayson shook his head before answering out loud. "No. I kept my glasses on the whole time."

"Oh, good. Those baby blues are a dead giveaway."

Grayson huffed, but he knew his sister was right. The fact that he had light eyes against his dark features was one of his biggest selling points. At least, that's what the production studios thought. Most of his pictures were Photoshopped to enhance the contrast, making his grayish tones look more blue, and apparently women weren't put off by that at all.

"Did he tell you that he growled at her no less than four times?" Jude's voice was just behind Grayson and he glared over his shoulder at his friend.

"Growled? Are you serious?" Amelia screeched. "Gray…what the heck are you doing?"

"I didn't want her to get too close," Grayson said, defending himself.

Amelia's sigh was long and loud. "Yeah, but that doesn't mean you have to be mean to her."

He pushed a hand through his hair. It was longer than normal, but just like his beard, the purpose was so he didn't look like himself. So far it was working, but he still was worried that if Brook kept coming around, she would eventually see through the disguise. "I wasn't trying to be mean," he grumbled.

"I can hear right through that lie," Amelia shot back.

"How?"

"It comes with being a mother," Amelia said. As if on cue, there were cooing noises on the line.

Grayson smiled at the sounds. He was very happy to get out of California, but he had to admit he was missing his niece. She was so tiny and he wasn't happy to be missing all those first few moments of her life.

"See? Kaylee agrees with me."

Grayson chuckled. "Then tell me, O Wise One, what would you do? I can't afford to have her sniffing around."

"Gray!" Amelia said in exasperation. "She isn't sniffing around. From the sound of it, she was your guardian angel."

He shifted on the couch, knowing he had thought the very same thing when she'd come to his aid earlier that week. Suddenly he was desperate to change the subject. "How did 'Operation Fool the Media' go?"

Amelia blew a raspberry. "It worked...for now. Carson put a hat on and walked around your yard for a while and some snake got enough video to post. Luckily, it was fuzzy enough that they thought it was you."

Grayson nodded. "Good. Maybe that'll keep Richard off my back for a while. If nobody knows how hurt I am, then he can't complain about my future film prospects."

A snort came through the line. "That guy needs to worry about your health more than he worries about his pocketbook."

"His pocketbook is directly connected to my health, so ..."

"Gray, if he thought you wouldn't come back from this, that guy would be gone so fast, it would make your head spin."

Grayson sighed. He knew she was right, but he liked to believe that Richard was at least a semi-friend. Grayson didn't have a lot of people he could call friends and to turn away one on principle felt wrong. It seemed ridiculous that someone like him could be lonely, but it was true. He sometimes found himself surrounded by thousands of people, all of whom were calling his name, but not one of them was actually a friend.

Grayson worked hard to keep his work life and private life separate for this exact reason. The lights, the cameras, the screaming fans... It was all fake. The women who clamored for his attention wanted the attention of a movie star...not the attention of Grayson the man.

"Did he tell you he gave Brook a fake name?"

Grayson growled and shot another glare at Jude. "Man...would you shut up?"

Jude grinned unrepentantly. "What? She's the only interesting thing that has happened on this trip of ours."

"You gave her a fake name?" Amelia said with a laugh. "Well, I guess you couldn't really tell her your real one, but we didn't actually discuss that. What should I be calling you?"

"Gray. You should call me Gray." Grayson could practically hear his sister's eyeroll.

"Yeah, yeah, but what did you tell her your name was?"

Grayson huffed. "Cord."

"Cord?" Ameila snorted. "As in Cordova? How original."

"It was the first thing to come to my head," Grayson defended himself.

His sister laughed. "It's a good one. I like it."

Grayson shifted his body up, so he was slightly angled upright, though not fully, in order to keep his back from pinching the nerve. "Thanks for that ringing endorsement."

"You're welcome," she said, still laughing. "So...do you think you'll see her again?"

All humor fled. "I don't think I should." That was the correct answer, but it wasn't the one he wanted to give. Brook's kindness, despite his gruff behavior and how sweetly she had taken care of him, had Grayson craving to see her again. Yes, she was beautiful, but Grayson was surrounded by beautiful women all the time. It was her angelic nature that had him wanting more. She'd wanted to nurture and take care of him without asking anything in return and Grayson found a part of him, an empty part of him, that was screaming for more.

And that was exactly why encouraging her was dangerous.

"If she hasn't recognized you, then I think you're safe," Amelia said. Her voice was distracted. "I gotta run, but think about it. It wouldn't hurt to have a friend while you're there."

"I'll think about it," he said, knowing he already had been.

"Good. Okay. Love you! Gotta run!" After a couple of kissy noises, Amelia hung up, leaving Grayson once more with just his physical therapist.

"She's right," Jude drawled. "A friend wouldn't hurt."

"It's not a friendship that could last," Grayson said softly. He toyed with his phone, feeling restless.

"You don't know that. But even so, would a short friendship hurt?"

Grayson shrugged. "We'll see."

"It's not like we're here forever," Jude pointed out. "Enjoy her company for a couple months and then Cord, the tourist, can disappear with no one the wiser."

And that was the problem. Deep inside, Grayson knew it wouldn't be that easy. There was something different about Brook, something that called to him, and he knew that if he let them become closer, walking away would be close to impossible.

CHAPTER 7

"Thank you," Brook said with an easy smile as she took the ice cream bar from the gentleman.

The man nodded and then turned to the next customer.

Stepping away, Brook ripped off the wrapper and took a delicious bite of the chocolate and mint. It was her favorite combination and on a warm day like today, it was especially delectable. "Hmm..." She closed her eyes as the cool creaminess made its way down her throat.

"I'm not sure I've ever seen someone enjoy ice cream so much."

The rest of the bite slid down too fast and Brook began to cough. A muttered curse came from her right and she held up a hand while she caught her breath. "Ooohh..." she said, sucking in a lungful, then paused to make sure she wouldn't cough again.

"Are you okay?"

Slowly, Brook braced herself, then turned to look at the handsome newcomer. "I'm fine, thanks," she said, laughing lightly. "I didn't know it was possible to choke on something that melted." Speaking of which, she could melt completely at the moment. How could a man be so handsome when she'd never even seen his full face?

Cord chuckled and shifted his weight on his cane. "Thank you for testing that out for us. I'm sure the scientific community is grateful as well."

She snorted a laugh, relaxing a little. As much as she had wanted to see him again, Brook had been unsure of her welcome. The only reason he'd let her stick around last time was because he needed help. But having him approach her gave her hope that maybe she had found a new acquaintance. A very handsome new acquaintance. And one that did a good job of taking her mind off Grayson Cordova. *Probably because he reminds me of him...* "I'll eagerly await my letter of gratitude."

A slow smile pulled at that beard, making Brook's heart flutter.

"Are you all recovered from the other day?" she asked, glancing at his cane and back up.

Cord grew solemn. He followed her gaze and gave a pointed look to his cane, then back to her. "I think it might take more than a couple of days."

Embarrassment hit her in the stomach like lava, causing a flush in her cheeks and neck. "Sorry," she said softly.

He shrugged. "Whatever." He turned sideways and Brook could almost see his eyes. The hat and glasses which seemed to be a permanent part of him were keeping her from getting a good look, but she didn't know him well enough to ask to see behind the mask.

And she recognized that it was a mask. That and the snarky behavior. He was hurting and he had learned to put up a front to protect himself. Brook recognized it because she fought the same temptation, only her hurt was only internal instead of external and internal like his. "Can I buy you a treat?" she asked boldly. She hoped it would come across as some kind of a peace offering, but the fact that it would also keep him close by for a little longer was an added bonus.

He smirked and opened his mouth to answer when a group of teenage girls passed close by.

"It can't be," one of them whispered, their heads swiveling back and forth between Cord and Brook.

Brook frowned, wondering what they were talking about.

"He's got a cane," another whispered loudly. "That's not him."

"What in the world are they talking about?" Brook whispered mostly to herself. She looked to see Cord standing straight as an arrow, his every muscle taut.

"I think maybe I better get home," Cord said in a low voice. He started to turn, but Brook put a hand on his arm.

She ignored the tingling she felt from touching him. This wasn't about her attraction right now. It was about the fact that those girls were talking about his injury and it bothered him. "Don't listen to them," she said, stepping closer. "They're just a bunch of tourists."

He gave her a sad smile. "So am I."

Brook laughed softly. "Yeah, but you're not a ridiculous teenage girl who's still trying to develop her brain."

A snort, followed by loud laughter, broke free from the stoic Cord and he bent forward in his amusement.

Glancing around, Brook realized the girls had moved on, obviously not having found what they were looking for. She was grateful they were gone, since they were upsetting Cord, though she didn't quite understand why. "Come on," she encouraged. "Let me grab you an ice cream bar and we can get out of the sun."

"You want to buy *me* an ice cream?"

Brook wasn't sure why he sounded so shocked. Was he so old-fashioned that he thought only a man should purchase something? It's not like they were on a date. "Uh, yeah? They're really good," she added.

Cord grunted, but followed her back to the line. Ten minutes later, Brook was just finishing her treat while Cord was just getting started.

"Do you need to stay standing?" she asked as they walked away from the cart.

"It's better if I do." He huffed.

Brook cast her eyes around trying to find the closest place to let him rest. It was frustrating that he couldn't sit down, since that limited their options, but she was determined to help. "Over there." She nodded toward an awning on a storefront. "We can stand under that."

By the time they shuffled to the store, Cord's bar was half gone. He licked at his hand where the ice cream was dripping.

Brook laughed. "You look like a toddler." Even from behind his glasses, she could tell he was glaring at her, which only made Brook laugh harder. "Sorry," she said, getting control of herself. "You've tried to melt me with your eyes one too many times, I guess." She shrugged, feeling lighter than she had in quite a while. "You're not as intimidating as you obviously wish."

Grunting, Cord went back to finishing his snack. When he'd finally licked the stick clean, he gave Brook a grudging grin. "Thanks for that. It was nice in this weather."

Brook eyed the sky. "Yeah...we don't usually get so many warm sunny days. It's been really nice."

Cord nodded slowly. "I've heard it's usually a bit windier and cloudier."

"It usually is." Brook stuffed her hands in the pockets of her shorts and rocked back and forth on her heels. She wanted to ask him all sorts of questions and just enjoy his presence, but things were still awkward between them. She nodded her head, racking her brain for something to say. "So where are you visiting from?"

Cord's head snapped in her direction. "Why are you asking?"

Brook backed up a little. "Sorry. I was just curious." *Too curious, apparently.* She frowned. *Why is that such a weird question?*

Cord rubbed the back of his neck. "Sorry. You just...caught me off guard."

"It's okay," she said hesitantly. There was something up with this guy and Brook could not figure out what it was. He was edgy and rough, but also vulnerable and wounded. She could see he was defensive about his injury, but behind the pain she'd seen he had close friends like Jude, who obviously cared about him. Pinching her lips together, she decided maybe hanging out with Cord wasn't such a good idea.

He helped fill a hole she'd been struggling with, but he did it grudgingly, and Brook hadn't quite gotten lonely enough to grovel. "Look, maybe I better just go..." She pointed down the sidewalk to emphasize her point.

"No...wait." Cord deflated and pinched the bridge of his nose before looking back up at her. "I'm sorry. Can you give me a second chance?"

YOU SHOULD HAVE JUST let her go!

Grayson's conscience was torn. He knew it would be better for all parties involved if she left. He didn't want to get to know her more. He didn't want to be her friend. He didn't want to start to become emotionally attached...and yet he did.

He enjoyed her, even from the small interactions they'd had and knew that more time in her company would only lead to more enjoyable situations. Her smile lightened the weight in his chest and her perpetual kindness eased his grouchiness.

So it really wasn't a wonder that he'd stopped her, but it was definitely not the smartest thing he'd ever done.

"A second chance?" she asked with a huff. "I think we're past a second chance."

He made a face. "You're right. But I'm still sorry."

Brook shrugged and tucked a hair behind her ear. "It's all right."

"It's not all right," he said with a shake of his head. "But I'm grateful for your forgiveness."

She smiled and gave him a look. "Okay. If you say so."

Cord cleared his throat. "So...want to take a walk?"

"Are you okay to walk?"

Anger immediately blurred his vision, but he clamped his mouth shut before he could spout off something else rude. "I don't like to sit still too much," he said tightly. "I'm not allowed to sit down much, so walking or laying are my only options."

She nodded, looking embarrassed, and his anger was immediately gone. "Sorry. I just don't like seeing people hurt."

Grayson nodded and began to shift. He couldn't walk fast, but he could move okay. *As long as that burning stays away.* "So, Brooklynn Howell...tell me about yourself." He glanced at her sideways. "Are you a nurse or something? Is that why you're so intent on making sure no one is hurting?"

She laughed softly, her hands clasped behind her as they slowly strolled down the sidewalk. "You might regret asking me that."

"Uh-oh," he said dramatically. "Is this one of those 'If I tell you, I have to kill you' type situations?"

She laughed again and Grayson found himself straightening just a little bit more at the sweet sound. "Nothing quite so dramatic," she said as she calmed down, though a wide smile remained. "I'm really pretty boring if you want the truth of the matter."

"I doubt that," he said, urging her on. "I know you save idiots who push too far after injuries. That's pretty exciting."

Her smile softened. "You're not an idiot," she said. "It could have happened to anyone."

Grayson snorted and faced forward. "I'm still waiting."

Brook gave a dramatic sigh. "Well...I was raised in Cali."

He started to open his mouth to say he was as well, but quickly snapped it shut again.

"I'm the only child of Angela and Patrick Howell." She gave him a mischievous grin. "While that might have been boring for some kids, my mom and I were best friends, so it wasn't too bad." Her head tilted, letting that stray chunk of hair break loose and caress her cheek. "Do you have siblings?"

Grayson clenched his fist to keep from touching her skin the same way her hair was. He was normally a pretty suave guy when it came to women, though most of it was for the cameras, but right now he was completely off his game. "Yeah, a couple."

Brook nodded and faced forward again. "Good for you. Anyway, I grew up at my mother's knee in the land of glamor and silicone and couldn't help but be entranced by it."

Grayson jerked back a little. "Really? Then what in the world brought you up to Oregon?"

Her smile grew. "At first it was just money." She shrugged. "I've always loved Hollywood and the fashion that goes with it, so opening a fashion boutique was a no-brainer. However, opening one in California was stupidity at its best."

He chuckled. "I can see that. I'm sure the prices are sky high."

She nodded. "Yep. So I came north to find a place to get started. Portland looked good price-wise, but the more I thought about it, the more I knew I'd just get lost in a bigger city." She laughed softly. "I wanted my store to be a little more personal than that, so I downsized. I came to Seaside Bay because they didn't have anything like my boutique at all. And I do personal consultations with customers to help them find a style and fit that works for them."

"Wow..." Grayson said after a minute. "That's not what I expected at all." The voice that had warned him away from Brook was growing more insistent. If she was really that into Hollywood, how in the world had she not recognized him yet? His beard and glasses must be better than he thought.

A vision of the teenagers came rushing back and he automatically stiffened. *Or not...* They'd suspected something, but hadn't been sure. Apparently the way they were playing the media with Carson walking around Grayson's estate was helping.

"I know," Brook said with a sigh. "Most people don't get it." She shrugged. "But it really doesn't matter. I love it and the people around here love it. So it's a win-win."

He nodded. "That's great that you found your niche. Lots of people spend their entire lives looking for something that makes them feel complete." *Where the heck did that come from?* His words sounded a little too personal and Grayson panicked a little. He wasn't trying to lead her on. He just was enjoying her company. "I, uh, still would have pegged you for a nurse or something."

Brook rolled her eyes playfully. "There's no way I'd make it as a nurse." She leaned in. "The sight of blood makes me sick."

He grinned. "I can see how that would be a problem." They'd reached the end of the boardwalk and slowly, Grayson turned them around.

"Now it's your turn," she said, bouncing on her toes a little.

"What?" Grayson felt his eyebrows shoot up high.

"I told you my story. Now you need to tell me yours."

"Now wait a minute," Grayson said, retreating into himself a little. "I was just curious and somehow I doubt that you've told me everything."

Those eyes rolled heavenward again. "I told you the basics," she teased. "And fair is fair. You gotta give me something."

He pinched his lips together and thought for a moment. How much could he give her without lying too much and without sharing too much? He actually wanted her to get to know him, but could he do it without creating future heartbreak. "Uh...I told you I have two siblings."

She nodded.

"I'm the middle kid." He grimaced. "My sister is married and has a new baby, who is the most beautiful girl in the world."

"As all nieces should be," Brook said with a laugh.

He laughed with her and rubbed his warm neck. "My parents split when I was younger and we don't talk to them much."

"Oh, I'm sorry," Brook said, her tone becoming serious. "That had to be hard."

"Nah. We made it."

"Still..." Brook squished her lips to the side. "And your job? Your...injury?"

Here was where it got tricky. "I, uh, got hurt at work and needed a break from everything. So Jude agreed to come help. He's a physical therapist."

"That's nice of him," Brook said, looking equal parts disappointed and relieved.

Grayson knew she caught how he didn't quite answer her question, and hoped she wouldn't push it.

"It's always good to have a friend around."

"And do you? Have a good friend around?" Grayson could have slapped himself. What kind of a question was that? It was none of his business if she had a boyfriend or significant other. She wouldn't have come to his aid the way she did if she was taken, would she? *Yes. She would.* Grayson had to admit that Brook's giving nature meant she would have helped out no matter what. Still, he shouldn't have asked the question.

Brook had stopped walking and she looked upset, causing Grayson to hurry to try to apologize.

"Brook!"

Before Grayson could speak, they both turned at the new voice. A tall, lean man was heading their way and he didn't look exactly happy. *Well...crud.*

CHAPTER 8

Just what I need. Brook braced herself. Brendon didn't exactly look happy as he approached her and Cord. She could guess why, but it wasn't like Brendon had any say over what she did. She'd gone on one date with him. One. And had been politely saying no ever since. Apparently, being polite had kept him hoping for more.

"Hey, Brook," Brendon said with a tight smile as he arrived. His eyes flickered to Cord and back. "I didn't know you were off today."

"I usually get an afternoon or two off a week," she said simply. Clasping her hands in front of her waist, she tried to appear nonchalant. "Oh, uh, Brendon, this is Cord..." She frowned as she realized she didn't know Cord's last name. "Cord, this is Brendon Perkins. He teaches science at our high school."

The two men shook hands, but it was obvious they weren't excited about meeting each other.

"What's wrong with your leg?" Brendon asked bluntly.

"Brendon!" Brook cried. "That wasn't nice."

He shrugged. "Just curious."

"I hurt my back," Cord said in a low tone. "The damaged nerve runs into my leg."

"That sucks."

Brook gave Brendon another look. What was he trying to accomplish? She'd never known him to be so rude. Well, two could play that game.

"Did you need something in particular, Brendon?" she asked, tilting her head so she looked more innocent than frustrated. And she was frustrated. Brendon had no right to come in and be unkind. None whatsoever.

He cleared his throat. "No, I, uh..." His eyes flashed to Cord again. "I just thought you might like to take a walk, maybe get a drink or something."

Brook ignored the snort from Cord. Apparently, he wasn't going to play nice either. The worst part was, it wasn't like Brendon had anything to be jealous over. Cord barely tolerated Brook, even if she, herself, was attracted to the grump. She didn't want to tell Brendon that though. Maybe seeing her with someone else, no matter how innocent, would give him a clear sign she wasn't interested. "I'm busy" just wasn't cutting it.

"I'm already walking with Cord," she said softly. She didn't like hurting people and she knew that's more than likely what this would do.

"But..." Brendon snapped his mouth shut, sent a glare at Cord, then nodded. "Okay. I get it." Spinning on his heel, he hurried away.

Brook sighed and hung her head for a moment. She was sorry she'd ever agreed to that date. Yes, she needed to get over Grayson Cordova, and yes, she wanted to find someone to spend time with, but she'd known from the beginning that Brendon wasn't that person. There was absolutely no spark, no attraction at all...at least from her end. Using him to ease her loneliness had only given him hope when there was none. "I shouldn't have done that," she said softly.

Cord grunted and began to walk again. "I take it you aren't hung up on the guy."

Brook started forward, walking slow so they could stay side by side. "No, but he's nice. At least, most of the time."

"And you don't like nice guys?"

She made a face at Cord. "That's not it at all!" Sighing again, she faced forward. "I just...there was no...spark. No pull. He was sweet and kind and even funny sometimes, but I..." She kicked at a small pebble in her path. "Maybe I'm too picky."

"You want someone that you think about when you're not with them," Cord finished for her. "Someone who makes you ache for their presence, crave their touch, and holds you in the palm of their hand."

Brook put a hand to her chest, which was barely containing her racing heart. "Oh my gosh, yes! How in the world do you know all that?" *Please don't say it's because you've been in love like that before.* She held her breath, waiting for his answer.

Cord smirked. Or it looked like a smirk. It was awfully hard to tell with that beard of his. "Doesn't every woman want that? Their soulmate?"

Brook shook her head. "I don't know. But I suppose those of us who were raised on a steady stream of fairy tales and Hollywood glamor do."

The humor seemed to flee at her response and Cord's pace picked up slightly.

Brook kept pace. "Hey, you're the one who waxed poetic about it. Why did my answer upset you?"

Cord came to a slow stop before turning toward her. "It didn't."

"And yet you tried to get away from me."

She could feel the glare from behind his sunglasses. "I guess I just don't believe in the magic of movie stars. They're just people with the right camera angles and the right makeup."

"Maybe so," Brook agreed. "But that doesn't mean it isn't fun to enjoy the image they present."

"So you're holding out for...who? Some famous guy who tickles your fancy?"

Brook chewed her bottom lip and tucked a piece of hair behind her ear. "I wouldn't say I'm holding out, but if you're asking if I have a celebrity crush, then the answer is of course. Doesn't everyone?"

He gave her a wry look. "And just who is that? Anyone I know?"

She shrugged, suddenly feeling extremely young and foolish. There wasn't anything wrong with liking a movie star, was there? Women the world over liked to fantasize about handsome men and the characters they portray on film. Straightening her shoulders, she decided that his opinion didn't matter. She might be attracted to him, but that didn't mean there was anything romantic between them. She wasn't trying to impress him and even if she was, being someone she wasn't wasn't the way to do it. "Maybe. If you like action films."

He stiffened, but Brook pushed on.

"Ever heard of Grayson Cordova?" There was a pregnant pause between them and it made Brook nervous. Unfortunately, that meant that she kept babbling. "Actually, you remind me of him a little," she said, letting her eyes roam over his body. "You're similar in build and coloring, but—" *He's way nicer than you are.* She cut herself off before she could finish that sentence out loud. She might be rambling, but she had at least a little bit of control. Sort of.

"But what?" Cord growled. "He's got two good legs?"

The words felt like a slap in the face and Brook actually stumbled back a couple of steps. "I-I didn't mean it like that," she said, her voice hoarse. How did all this go so wrong? One moment they were talking about soulmates and movie stars, now she'd hurt his feelings by comparing him to someone who appeared to be healthy and whole. "I'm sorry," she said softly. "I was just making conversation. I really wasn't trying to hurt your feelings."

Cord's whole body seemed to deflate and he shifted his weight. "No. I'm sorry." He pinched the bridge of his nose. "Apparently, pain makes me cranky and I have been nothing but a jerk to you since we met." He looked up at her and even through his glasses and hat, she could see he looked embarrassed. "I'm sorry. I'm not usually such a bully. And it doesn't matter to me if you have a celebrity crush." One side of his mouth pulled up into a charming grin. "In fact, it's probably part of what makes you so sweet to everyone. My only explanation is that life has been difficult lately and I guess I'm not handling it well."

That's it. My mind is made up. Brook had been uncertain about pursuing a friendship with Cord. He wasn't going to be there forever and he wasn't always very kind to her, or anyone for that matter. She could admire his physique from afar easily enough. It didn't mean she had to be close to him to do so. But now that he'd been willing to apologize and she could see that there was an actual human being behind his rough exterior, she wanted nothing more than to break down those walls. This guy needed a friend. Someone who was willing to smile through his growls and help him get back to himself. And with nothing but a lonely future in front of her, Brook decided she was just such a person. "Don't worry," she said, resting a hand on his forearm. "I think it's totally understandable in your situation. And besides...who wants to hear someone gush about their fantasies?" She laughed softly. "No one. That's who." *Except...I might be willing to listen to yours. Somehow, I have a feeling they're pretty darn interesting.*

YOUR SITUATION. The words stung, even though Grayson knew they were meant to be kind. It was about the most polite way he could think of saying he wasn't quite normal. Her *friend,* Brendon, hadn't tried to mince words at all and yet they hadn't hurt near as much as knowing that Brook pitied him.

That emotion had become the bane of his existence. Well, that and knowing that Brook had a crush on his celebrity persona. What were the odds? She seemed so down to earth and sweet, and yet she had feelings for the guy he was on film. It had panicked him for a moment, especially after she'd said he reminded her of himself, but then she'd misinterpreted his frustration and had taken it all back.

Still, his behavior was unacceptable. She had done nothing to deserve his ire. In fact, she'd come to his rescue when he was at his lowest. The least he could do was humor her.

"I don't know," he drawled. "Sometimes fantasies are the reason we keep going." He tried to smile at her, but it felt stiff. Hopefully the dead rat on his face helped hide his real emotions. "Tell me why you like this Cordova guy."

Her face lit up. "Have you seen any of his movies?"

Grayson shrugged. "Maybe."

She blew out a raspberry. "How can you maybe see a movie?" Her smile was wide. "You seem like the kind of guy who enjoys action films. There's no way you haven't seen him."

Grayson nodded. "Okay, I've seen him. But I don't know what the big deal is."

Brook laughed easily and nudged him with her shoulder to get him walking. "Well, some of the appeal might be mostly for the female population."

"Oh, I see," he said, drawing out the words and nodding slowly. "So you're telling me he's handsome?"

Brook's cheeks turned bright red and it made Grayson want to chuckle. He knew that women found him attractive, most of his associates had never made any qualms about that. His parents had launched his career on that exact fact. But somehow, knowing that this wholesome woman blushed at admitting he was good-looking, it did funny things to his heart.

"Yeah...he's handsome," she said a little breathlessly.

"Sounds like guys like me don't stand a chance." He snapped his mouth shut. *What the heck am I doing?* He couldn't ask her things like that. It would sound like he wanted to be noticed by her, which he didn't, sort of. Grayson wanted to groan. He didn't know what he wanted. His mind was in turmoil. But he still knew deep down that it would be smartest *not* to push a relationship, whether friendship or otherwise, with Brook.

"Oh, don't think that way," she encouraged. "Grayson Cordova is a world-famous movie star. Admiring him from afar is a lot different than acknowledging someone real."

"You don't think he's real?" Someone needed to tape his mouth shut.

"He's real," Brook said, seemingly happy to keep talking about him. "But I'm not naive enough to think that what I see on screen is the same as he is in real life." She pursed her lips. "Although he doesn't seem to get in the same trouble as a lot of other celebrities do. He's really closed about his private life." She laughed. "Which is both awesome and frustrating at the same time."

A slow smile crept across his face. This woman really did pay attention to him.

Brook gasped and turned his way while they walked. "Oh my gosh, have you heard that he got in an accident?"

Okay, now they were getting too close to home. Grayson made sure he kept his face stoic. He was an actor after all, so he should have no trouble fooling her. "Oh?"

"Yeah. Something happened on the set of his last movie." She pouted. "Nobody seems to know exactly what happened though. Rumors are flying like crazy, but none of them are the same." She tilted her head a little and was quiet for a few breaths. "Someone climbed the fence of his estate and got some video of him walking around."

She was quiet again and Grayson grew curious as to her thoughts. Most people would probably think it weird that he wanted to urge her to keep speaking about himself, but maybe her thoughts on the matter would give Grayson a good understanding of what the public at large thought about the situation. "Sounds like maybe he wasn't hurt that bad after all."

She shrugged.

"You don't believe it?"

Brook glanced his way. "I don't know. The video was super fuzzy and the guy who was walking around looked thinner than Grayson." She laughed. "Listen to me. Talking like I'm some kind of expert or something." She shook her head. "Ignore me. I'm just being an idiot."

Grayson mulled over what she had said. Obviously she had kept close tabs on him over the years if she recognized that Carson wasn't him, but was it worth addressing? The media seemed to be buying the body double. *Best to leave it alone.* Yeah, it was probably smart to just let things go and move onto something else. Besides, the end of the sidewalk was close, they'd been walking for quite a while, and Grayson was getting tired. He probably should head back to the house and take a nap before doing another session with Jude for the day.

"You're not an idiot," he assured her. "Sounds like the whole thing is a mystery." He cleared his throat. "So who runs your boutique when you're gone?"

"I've got a great store manager," she said with an easy smile. "We work our schedules so that I'm there when she's gone and she's there when I'm gone. It works great and nobody gets overwhelmed since we're open almost every day of the week."

"Sounds like you've got this all figured out."

Brook laughed. "I'm in retail. There's no way to have it all figured out." She turned his way, her straight white teeth flashing in the sunlight. "As soon as you think you do, something weird will happen to throw off your balance."

Grayson stopped and blinked when he felt something hit the top of his hat.

"Oh!" Brook put a hand over her head. Glancing up, she grimaced. "Stupid cloudbursts."

Another couple of pops hit his cap. "It's raining?" Grayson asked, glancing at the spots on the sidewalk. How could it be raining when it was sunny? He squinted, looking up, and immediately looked back down as more heavy drops hit his face.

"Come on," Brook urged, grabbing his arm. "Let's duck back here."

Within seconds of them making it to a small alcove, the rain cut loose, drenching anything not covered.

"What the heck is that?" Grayson asked, wiping off his arms. "It's still sunny."

Brook laughed softly and gathered her hair up into a ponytail. "It's a single storm cloud. When they open up like this, it's called a cloudburst." She grinned. "It'll let up in a few minutes, disappearing as quickly as it came."

"Huh." Grayson eyed the sky, then turned his attention back to his company. He really did need to get back to the house, but at the moment, he couldn't quite remember why. Brook made him feel lighter and happier, plus he was enjoying her company more than he should. Maybe, just maybe, it wouldn't be quite so bad to become friends with her. He certainly wasn't upset at being stuck with her for a bit longer than he'd planned. And when more people crowded into their spot seeking shelter, he had to admit that he didn't mind getting closer physically either. And that might be more dangerous than anything else.

CHAPTER 9

"So he's a total invalid?" Caro asked, popping a carrot in her mouth. She grimaced and looked at her lunch. "Why do carrots have to taste so...carroty?"

Brook laughed softly. "Probably because that's what they are. What do you want them to taste like? Chocolate?"

Caro raised her eyebrows consideringly. "That would certainly help me eat my vegetables."

Brook rolled her eyes. "I suppose it's a show of self discipline."

"Something I do not enjoy at all." Making a few smacking sounds, Caro set her lunch aside and leaned back in her chair. She had come to eat lunch with Brook during their meal breaks since her shop was just down the street from Brook's. It was a great way for the women to catch up, especially since Caro was now married and Brook didn't see her as often. "But you didn't answer my question. Are you telling me this...Cord...is completely helpless?"

"No." Brook dropped her friend's gaze. "He's not helpless. He's just injured."

"And he collapsed on the sidewalk?" Caro shook her head. "This guy sounds like he needs to be in the hospital."

Brook shrugged. She was poking at her salad rather than eating, since her appetite was nonexistent. She couldn't quite explain her draw to the stubborn and grouchy man. At least, not in a way that Caro would understand. How did she tell her friend that she was lonely and didn't want anyone else to feel the same way? That the stranger in town intrigued her because she suspected he was hiding a heart of gold beneath his growls and scowls? That she felt a desperate need to help him get better, not only physically but emotionally?

Caro would think Brook was nuts. Even Brook wondered it about herself once in a while. It made absolutely no sense. He was just a tourist. Albeit, a handsome tourist. Who didn't always welcome her company. That should have anybody running for the hills and not looking back.

Caro leaned across the desk and put her hand on Brook's twitching fingers. "Brook. I know things have been different lately. Everybody's been getting married and we don't spend as much time together as we used to, but don't jump into something that's only going to cause you grief, huh?"

Brook looked up, not sure whether to be upset or grateful at those words. Did Caro think so little of her that she thought Brook would pounce on the first handsome man to walk in her path? Or was she just a concerned friend who wanted to help but didn't know how? "You're right," Brook said, her chin high. "Things are different. But I'm not jumping into anything." She leaned back, twirling her fork in her fingers. "But I need something to keep me occupied and this guy could use a friend."

"Just a friend?" Caro questioned.

"Yes," Brook said dryly. "Just a friend." Not that she would be opposed to more, but she wasn't so far gone that she would start a relationship with a tourist.

"Didn't you say he's staying with a physical therapist? Why can't he be his friend?"

Brook threw down her fork. "Why are you so against this?"

Caro pinched her bright red lips together and looked away. "I'm just...I just don't want you hurt," she said softly. "You told me a long time ago that you were lonely and wanting to find someone, and since it hasn't happened yet, I just don't want you to grasp at straws."

"I already told you this wasn't about anything but friendship," Brook defended, shoving her salad away. "Why can't you believe that?"

Caro smiled and laughed quietly. "Because I know you too well. You like to feel needed and you always seem to fall for guys who need 'fixing.'" She put her fingers up to emphasize the word.

Brook opened up her mouth to argue, but stopped. There was some truth to those words. She liked to be helpful. It was a trait that served her well in the shop, but this extended beyond that. She liked to build others up and feel like she was accomplishing good things. But did she really only fall for guys who needed help? That didn't seem quite right.

Caro must have read her mind because she scowled. "Don't you remember a few years ago when you dated Preston What's-His-Face?"

Brook rolled her eyes. "How could I forget? I didn't know men had eight arms."

Caro nodded with pursed lips. "You thought he needed lessons in dating etiquette."

"Yeah, but that's not why I dated him."

"Then why?" Caro pressed.

"Because..." Brook cut off. Okay, so maybe she had felt sorry for him. He was interested in her and she thought she could help him if they went out a few times. It didn't work. Instead, Brook had spent the entire time trying to contain his very flexible arms.

"Or the lumber mill dude?" Caro scoffed. "I don't even remember his name."

"Doug," Brook said softly. She had to hand it to Caro. She certainly could remember the weirdos.

"Didn't he have some kind of lisp or something?"

Brook nodded. "Yeah."

"That wouldn't have been so bad, if he wasn't so shy," Caro groaned. "You hoped to bring him out of his shell."

"Okay, okay," Brook said, putting her hands in the air. "I get your point."

"No, I don't think you do," Caro said, leaning on the desk again. "Here you are, yet again with someone who needs help." She shook her head. "When are you going to spend time with someone because there's an attraction, Brook? Not because you want to fix something?"

"Maybe when someone actually is attracted to me," she shot back. As soon as the words left her mouth, Brook felt bad. "I'm sorry. I shouldn't have said that."

"No, it's a fair point," Caro said softly. She sniffed. "I blame it on the small town. The men here are just idiots."

"Caro," Brook drawled. "The guys we're friends with aren't idiots."

"Maybe not, but they're also too much like brothers," Caro said. "You can't date your brother."

Brook gave an exaggerated shiver. "Absolutely not. Can you imagine kissing Benny?"

Bright red nails covered bright red lips. "Don't make me sick." Caro moaned. "That's just wrong."

Brook laughed. "Someday, someone won't think so."

"Well...that day has not yet come and when it does, it won't be you."

"True enough." Brook relaxed in her chair. Caro was right about her trying to fix people, but Brook couldn't help but think that wasn't such a bad thing. So she was a nurturer? That was a good thing, right?

"Speaking of men..." Caro pumped her eyebrows. "Have you noticed what the rags are saying about Grayson Cordova?"

Brook stiffened. How was she supposed to get over the guy when everyone kept bringing him up? "No."

"Well," Caro leaned in and dropped her voice as if imparting a secret, "there are a couple of news stations that are convinced the video of him is fake. They think he's more hurt than the movie people are letting on."

"So...what? They think he's still in the hospital?" Brook's curiosity was getting the better of her, but what was she to do?

Caro shrugged. "No one knows. But there's a rumor that he's not in California anymore."

"Huh." Brook slumped back. "But that doesn't make sense. Why would he leave home if he's hurt?"

"No clue." Caro threw her hands in the air. "But at least trying to figure out lover boy's moves will keep us entertained, huh?"

Brook chuckled and shook her head. "I suppose so," she admitted.

"THEY WHAT?" GRAYSON shouted into the phone.

"Whoa, man! Calm down!" Jude came running into the room.

Grayson had been lying down, but now he was sitting up as every muscle clenched in anger. He squeezed his eyes shut and pinched his nose. "Does my security do absolutely nothing?" he asked. "I thought I was paying for the best in the business."

Jude's hand pushed against Grayson's shoulder and Grayson let himself be pushed back down, but he still was tense.

"We seem to have a leak somewhere," Carson said with a huff. "I don't know who it is yet, but there are rumors running around that you're not here and the video is a plant."

"I'll bet Richard is having a heyday," Grayson muttered.

"You should have heard some of the words he came up with," Carson said with a chuckle. "I didn't know there were that many curse words in the English language." He sighed. "I'm sorry, Gray. I don't know who's been bought out, but if these rumors continue, it's going to be hard to keep you safe up there."

Grayson didn't say anything for a few moments. He wasn't sure what to offer to his brother. "It's not your fault," he finally responded. And it wasn't. It wasn't even Carson's responsibility to help keep the press off Grayson's back, but his brother had been helping anyway.

"Still, I'm sorry it's happening. I know you needed the break in order to heal."

Grayson nodded even though his brother couldn't see it. "I know, thanks."

"What are you going to do?"

Grayson pinched his lips together. "I'm not sure. Is there even anything I can do?" He huffed. "I should probably call the security company and have them fix it. If they can't do their job, then I'll need to get them replaced."

"Easier said than done," Carson grumbled.

Grayson nodded again. His brother was right. All the paperwork and non-disclosure agreements made switching security companies a pain in the tush. But if it afforded him more time here in Seaside Bay, then it would probably be worth it. A small smile pulled at Grayson's mouth. He hadn't expected to enjoy his time here quite so much, but he had to admit that he was. And there was one very specific reason why.

"So...meet anyone interesting?" Carson asked.

Grayson stiffened. "What?"

Carson groaned. "Seriously? You think you can tell Amelia about that woman, but not me? What am I? Chopped liver?"

"You're competition!" Jude shot out from the opposite couch.

Grayson glared, but Jude just shrugged and went back to his phone.

"Oh, ho, ho!" Carson crowed so loudly that Grayson had to pull the phone away from his ear. "Is big brother worried I'll steal his new girlfriend?"

"No," Grayson growled, only to close his eyes and sigh. "She's not my girlfriend."

"Suuuure," Carson pressed. "You have a girlfriend every time you turn around."

"That's not true," Grayson defended himself. Could he help it if women threw themselves at him? He didn't encourage them or date any of them. They were just there.

"Okay, maybe it's not. But still. It's not like you're ever lacking for female company."

"It's only for the camera," Grayson insisted. "You know I haven't had a girlfriend in over a year."

"Ah, yes. Ever since Victoria decided the producer would be better for her career."

Grayson rolled his eyes. He hadn't been heartbroken at all when the model had shifted her attention to someone else. In fact, it had been a relief. So much so that Grayson hadn't bothered to replace her because he enjoyed his solitude more than he'd enjoyed being part of a couple. The media, however, had determined that he'd been too in love with her to move on. It was ridiculous.

"Are you going to tell me about her?" Carson asked.

"There's nothing to tell." That goofy smile pulled at him again.

"I can hear you smiling."

"What? No, you can't!" Grayson's eyebrows nearly flew off his forehead. How in the world had Carson known he was smiling?

Carson laughed hard. "I couldn't...until you just confirmed it."

If a couple of Richard's favorite words slipped from Grayson's mouth, no one could blame him.

"Come on, Gray. Tell me about her."

"Why do you want to know?"

"Because I'm currently quarantined in a massive house all by myself and I could use something to fantasize about."

His words almost made Grayson laugh out loud. It reminded him of Brook's fantasies about him. It was too funny. As long as she never figured out who he really was anyway.

"She's a boutique owner and we're friends, I think."

"You think?" Carson scoffed.

"Yeah. I think."

"That doesn't sound very promising."

Grayson shrugged. "No one said it had to be. Don't forget I'm incognito at the moment. It's not like it could go anywhere." *Not that it wouldn't be fun to let it. Being close to a beautiful woman is rarely a bad choice.*

"You're boring."

"And you're jealous," Grayson shot back.

"Whatever." Carson huffed. "I'm out. If you don't have anything juicier to share, I'm gonna go use that massive TV you have in the pool room. Maybe I'll put on *Jaws*."

"You're going to watch *Jaws* while you're in the pool?" Grayson's eyes opened wide. "You're weird."

"Like I said, you're boring."

"Have fun, I guess."

"I will. See ya!"

And just like that, Carson was gone. Grayson shook his head and threw his phone onto the coffee table. His brother was awesome, but also a handful. He had to be busy all the time, which made him a great lawyer, since his mind was always churning with some case, but right now he was taking a leave of absence to help Grayson out, so it made sense that Carson was bored out of his mind.

Jude shut off his phone. "You ready to do some exercises?"

Grayson took a deep breath. His leg hurt just thinking about what was coming, but he was desperate to see some progress. Even lifting his leg to move his ankle was proving almost too much for Grayson to handle and that never put him in a good mood. *You'll never get better if you don't keep trying.* Pulling on the same self discipline he used to claw his way to the top of the movie charts, he pushed himself upright. "Let's do this."

CHAPTER 10

Brook tapped her pen against her desk. It was almost closing time and she found herself struggling with the idea of going home. Her apartment seemed dark and empty, especially after spending some time with Cord a few days ago. He'd finally started to relax a little and they'd had a fun conversation, despite Brendon's interference.

She blew out a breath. Brendon hadn't texted again since they saw each other on the boardwalk, for which Brook was equal parts grateful and sad. She knew his feelings had been hurt, and she wasn't happy about that, but he simply wasn't gettin her hints.

How else could I get across that I wasn't interested?

She shook her head. There had been no other way. She'd turned him down politely multiple times, but he still kept coming back. Now he thought there was something between her and Cord, which got him off her back, but made Brook feel guilty.

"Let it go," she told herself. "Just let it go." Maybe if she kept herself busy tonight, she could ignore the tiny voice in the back of her mind that kept calling her mean names.

But what could she do? Her friends would all be home with their husbands, Rose would be home with Lily, and the only other single friends she had were guys, and she wasn't interested in a one-on-one with them.

Again, she came back to Cord. He would be fun to hang out with...maybe...but could she be the one to initiate something? Would he bite her head off for suggesting it? Or would it be like a few days ago when he smiled and laughed with her? "Ugh." She let her forehead thud onto the desk. "How am I supposed to know which Cord I'm gonna get?"

Her mind continued to churn. If she went to his house, what excuse could she give? Having a real reason would be much better than "Hey, I was lonely. Wanna spend time together?" Nothing said "let's be friends" like desperation.

Brook's phone buzzed, momentarily distracting her from her maudlin thoughts. She grabbed it and opened the text.

You have to try our new dipped shortbread. It's to die for.

"Oooh..." A slow smile crept across Brook's face. Caro and Jack had started to merge their two different culinary delights now that they were married and their shops were in the same place. Not that they had to work hard. Cookies and chocolate were no stranger to each other. But it seemed like every week Caro was inviting Brook to come try some new creation. So far all of them had been delicious.

"That's it," she whispered. *Sassy Sweets*, Caro's storefront, was a local and tourist hotspot. Doubly so, now that Jack's famous Cookies Up! baked goods were there as well. Nothing would welcome Cord and Jude, of course, to Seaside Bay like bringing them a box of treats. Her thumbs flew over the keyboard.

How late are you open tonight? I'd like to get a box. She didn't have to wait long for the answer.

For you? As late as you need.

Brook laughed softly. Caro might spend most of her time with her new husband, but that didn't mean she wasn't loyal to her friends. Nothing seemed to break that woman's confidence.

Be there in an hour.

A thumbs up emoji was her answer and Brook threw herself back into her paperwork. She didn't want anything hanging over her head when she went to Cord's tonight. If everything went as she hoped, she would be spending a pleasant evening with a handsome man and his physical therapist. It would be wonderful in comparison to her dreary apartment. But first, work.

The next hour flew by, but Brook shut down her computer with a happy sigh. She was free. Grabbing her purse and keys, she went out front. "Good work today, ladies!" she called out as she headed for the front door. "I'll lock this one behind me. Please do the same for the back door."

"Consider it done," Ainsley called from where she was vacuuming near the back.

With a quick wave, Brook was out in the cooling evening air. She shivered, more from the shock in temperature than from the actual cold. Her office was quite warm during the day, with the setting sun beating through the back window. But now the sun was almost gone, letting the nearby shoreline bring down the warmth in the air.

Rather than grab her car, Brook walked briskly down the street to Caro's shop. It would be quicker than trying to find a parking spot anyway. When she was done, she'd take her car to Cord's house.

"Well, well, well," Caro teased as Brook came through the glass door. "Just the person I wanted to see."

Brook's eyebrows shot up and she stopped. "Uh-oh. That always means trouble."

Jack came from the back just in time to hear Brook's comment. He chuckled. "Trouble and Caro are synonyms."

Caro whacked his arm with the back of her hand, then smiled prettily up at him. "You just wait 'til we get home, buster."

"I look forward to it," Jack whispered, but Brook heard it and felt a harsh blush come racing up her neck and into her cheeks. Her skin tanned quite nicely in the sun, but dang if she'd ever been able to hide her embarrassment. It was a curse most of the time.

Brook cleared her throat when the newlyweds continued to stare at each other. Maybe stopping here wasn't such a good idea.

Caro laughed. "Sorry," she said, her smile wide and goofy. "Got carried away."

Brook rolled her eyes good-naturedly. "I think that's a permanent state of mind for you at this point."

Jack snickered again until Caro glared at him. She turned back to Brook and folded her arms across her chest. "Come to try the shortbread?" She winked. "You're in luck. I saved some for you."

Brook returned the smile. "I'd love to try it, but I also want to put together an assorted box."

"Oh?" Caro grabbed a couple of pink boxes, offering Brook different sizes. "What's the special occasion?"

Brook's eyes darted to Jack, who was busy with the inventory, and back to Caro. "I thought it might be nice to introduce Cord to some of the local stuff," she said softly.

Caro's eyebrows shot up. "I see."

Brook held back a sigh. Caro was obviously still concerned, but Brook wasn't going to worry about it. Caro had never met Cord. She didn't know that he needed a friend and that Brook did as well. Nothing romantic would probably come from it, but at least it would ease Brook's loneliness for a little while. That would make it worth her time, wouldn't it? "What should I take him?"

"Him?" Jack finally caught up to the conversation. "Brook, do you have a date?"

Brook shook her head. "No. Just a new friend." She shrugged. "I thought he'd enjoy a sweet treat."

Caro's face had gone serious, but she began moving down the display case. "Well, let's send him the classics and then you can choose a couple of specialty items, okay?"

When Caro's blue eyes met Brooks, they weren't excited, but neither were they condemning...more like resigned. Caro offered a small smile letting Brook know she wouldn't stand in her way. If this is what Brook wanted to do, Caro would be here.

Brook smiled back and nodded. "That sounds wonderful. Thank you."

A KNOCK AT THE DOOR had Grayson jerking from his spot lying on the couch. "Who the heck could that be?" he murmured. His eyes went to Jude, who shrugged and held up a finger for Grayson to be quiet.

He watched his friend go to the front door and peek through the hole. The relaxing of Jude's shoulders told Grayson it wasn't the media, but still...who in the world would be coming by late in the evening when they were tourists?

"Hey, Brook," Jude said from the other side of the door.

"Brook..." The name was out of Grayson's mouth before he could stop it. When he realized how breathy it had been, he snapped his teeth shut. He hadn't seen her in several days. Not since their little trip down the boardwalk when she'd had to tell that Brendon guy to get lost.

Grayson rolled his eyes at himself. Brook definitely had *not* told the guy to get lost, but it had been implied in the fact that she wasn't willing to leave Grayson to go with him. It had been a proud moment for Grayson, though he probably shouldn't have taken so much joy in it. It's not like there was anything between him and Brook and there never could be. As long as he ignored the fact that she was quickly getting under his skin with her kindness.

"Hey, G-Cord," Jude said, his eyes widening in momentary panic. "Look who came to visit us tonight."

Brook was standing, looking unsure of herself in the foyer. "Hey," she said, waving a hand at Grayson. "I just finished work and thought you two might enjoy trying a local treat." She held up a pink box. "My good friend and her husband are the best sweets makers in town."

Grayson raised an eyebrow. "Please tell me that doesn't contain saltwater taffy."

She laughed and came farther into the open sitting room. "None whatsoever." She tilted her head. "You don't like taffy?"

Grayson groaned in jest. "I hate how it sticks to my teeth. Even as a kid, I hated it."

"That's funny," Brook said with a laugh. "Grayson Cor—" She stopped, blanched and swallowed. "Sorry. I, uh, did *not* bring you taffy. I think it's okay, but Caro and Jack's stuff is much better."

Ah, crap. His aversion to taffy had been printed in multiple interviews when he was a teenager. If Brook really had been following him for years, then she had probably read those. He held his breath, doing his best not to look at Jude and give away the fact that he was worried she would eventually put two and two together.

"Can I set them there?" she asked, sounding even more unsure than before.

Grayson forced his face to relax. She was probably worried he was going to throw her out. It wasn't like he'd been exactly warm during their couple of times together. "Oh, yeah. Have a seat." He gave her his best smile. "Forgive me if I don't get up," he joked. "I'm afraid this couch and I have a growing attachment to each other."

She laughed as he'd intended and the anxious atmosphere of the room lightened. "No worries," she said, putting the box on the coffee table, then sitting across from him. "You stay lying down." Her smile was pure innocence. "We want you to get better so I think you're allowed to lie down on the job."

"Oh, ho!" Jude crowed a little too loudly. He cleared his throat, obviously aware he was being slightly awkward. "I'll have to remember that one," he said with a wink at Brook.

Grayson found his fist clenching when Jude sat next to Brook. *Knock it off,* he told himself. *She's not yours.*

"So what did you bring?" Jude rubbed his hands together.

Brook turned that beautiful smile to Grayson's friend, furthering the jealousy churning in his gut. "Well, my friend Caro dips chocolates and her husband bakes some of the best cookies I've ever had." She turned back to Grayson. "He used to drive a cookie truck up and down the California coastline, surfing and working." She leaned forward to open the box. "Last year he ended up here with a broken truck and the rest, as they say, is history."

"Wait, are those cookies from Cookies Up!?" Jude gaped.

Brook paused. "Yeah. How did you know that?"

Grayson's throat went dry and he broke into a coughing fit. He hadn't told Brook where he was from and definitely didn't want Jude sharing.

"Uh..." Jude looked at Grayson with wide eyes before going back to Brook. "I've heard of this guy. He's all over social media, right?"

She relaxed a little. "Yeah. He is." She shook her head. "I guess it's a small world after all." She paused before lifting any of them out of the box. "Have you eaten any?"

"No..." Jude hedged. "Just heard of him."

"At the risk of sounding like a cliche," Brook said with a laugh, "you're in for a treat." She took a napkin out of the box and picked up a cookie, handing it to Jude. "Give this one a try. It's one of Jack's classics."

Grayson recognized the famous cowboy cookie. He'd had more than a few in his time, but he couldn't say anything since Jude had managed to distance them from the food truck's home base in California. He knew exactly what Jude was tasting right now and it was heaven in a cookie.

"Are you ready for one?"

Grayson blinked, coming out of his thoughts. "Of course. I've never turned down a good dessert."

"Any allergies? Which one do you want?"

Grayson shook his head.

"Wait, what?" Jude put a hand to his chest in affront. "You didn't ask me about that before giving me a cookie! How come he gets to pick his own?"

Brook's cheeks were so red Grayson was worried she would burn on the spot, but he couldn't help but chuckle. The jealousy he'd been struggling with only moments before mysteriously disappeared. Okay, it wasn't mysterious. Brook had obviously given herself away that she had a little more affection for Grayson than Jude. And Grayson wasn't upset about that at all. "Got chocolate chip?" he asked, deciding to ease Brook's embarrassment.

"Of course!" she chirped, her cheeks still flaming. She got another napkin and pulled the massive cookie out of the box. She rose from the couch and brought it to him. "Do you want to stand?"

He shook his head. He was wiped out from therapy today. "Nah. I'll just have to risk the crumbs running down my neck."

Brook laughed. "I'm sure we can help you get cleaned up if we need to." Their eyes met and stalled.

Jude and his loud chewing faded into the background as Grayson found himself caught in her hazel eyes. Tonight the green was more dominant, probably due to the green shirt she was wearing. Or maybe it was because the light was behind her, putting her face in light shadow. The bright green in her irises seemed to stand out, and Grayson found he couldn't look away.

The air grew thick and began to spark with electricity. All his amusement fled and Grayson felt his eyes widening. In this moment, Brook was stunning. He'd thought she was beautiful from the start, but the more time they spent together, the more he saw beneath her physical beauty, the more Grayson was finding himself trapped. The shift in the air at this moment let him know his intrigue wasn't one-sided and he found his hand slowly raising, as if to touch her face.

"Oh my gosh," Brook breathed softly. "I think this is the first time I've ever seen you without your sunglasses."

Grayson froze. By the time he was able to speak, every curse word known to man, including some that hadn't even been invented yet, had run through his brain. "They're contacts."

CHAPTER 11

Brook blinked and shook her head. What was she doing? Cord's long dark hair was framing his face and his beard covered the bottom half of his face, leaving only his eyes open for inspection. And what eyes they were. Bright gray, almost blue. Against his dark hair, it was an amazing contrast and was remarkably reminiscent of Grayson Cordova. He also had blue eyes and dark hair, but they were a true blue, not like Cord's gray. If she hadn't looked at the news just this morning of another sighting of the famous actor at home, Brook would have entertained the thought that the two were one and the same.

"They're... contacts?" she asked, not quite grasping what Cord was saying. She frowned, trying to break free of the attraction haze she was currently caught in in order to process his words. "Oh... Oh!" She wanted to smack herself at her stupidity. "You mean your eyes." She peered closer. "Contacts? Really?"

Cord pressed back into his pillow and Brook jerked back at the indicator she had gotten too close.

"Sorry," she murmured, wringing her hands in embarrassment. This was definitely not the evening she had planned. Twice now she'd given away the fact that she was attracted to Cord. How ridiculous could she look? It was a miracle he hadn't kicked her out yet. "I was just trying to see the lenses."

Cord nodded, still looking too tense for her comfort.

Apparently, he didn't feel the same pull she did. Brook had thought he'd felt the moment they'd had earlier. *I guess it wasn't really a moment if it was only one-sided. I'm more pathetic than I thought.*

Cheeks flaming, she darted back to her couch, folding into herself a little. Maybe it was time to go.

"He's always had a thing for messing around with his eye color," Jude said with a laugh. He acted as if he couldn't feel the weird vibe that had descended upon the room. Maybe he couldn't. At this point, Brook had no idea what was going on. Her obsession with everything Grayson Cordova seemed to be infiltrating her life in a way it never had before. She was seeing him all over the place, and just when she was trying to get over him. Ugh.

"That's interesting," Brook said, trying to smile, but knowing she failed. "Anyway...I hope you enjoy the cookies and chocolates." She nodded and slapped her knees, then stood back up. "I probably should get home and leave you to your evening."

"Have you had dinner yet?"

Brook stopped and slowly looked back to Cord. The look on his face said he was just as surprised as she was that he'd asked her that. "Uh, no. I came here right after work."

Cord worked his jaw for a moment before meeting her gaze. "Would you like to stay and eat with me? I mean, us?"

The tiniest flicker of hope fluttered in her chest. Maybe he had felt something when they were looking at each other. For her, time had stood still, and to think he didn't feel it was enough to break any-one's spirit. "I..." She glanced at Jude.

"You might as well," Jude said with a grin as he wiped his fingers together to get rid of the crumbs. "Mrs. Flores always leaves us some-thing good and enough to feed an army."

Her eyebrows went up. "You have a cook?" Her head swiveled back to Cord. "Really?"

Cord huffed. "Even if I could cook, I can't move around enough to do it. And Jude here can't do anything that requires more than a microwave."

Jude shrugged. "Guilty as charged. You wouldn't want to eat my food."

Despite her embarrassment, a small giggle slipped through her lips. "I don't want to intrude." *Yes, I do. I really don't want to go home and be by myself.*

"It's not intruding when you're invited," Cord said with that brilliant smile of his. "Besides, you already brought dessert. Providing dinner is the least we can do." He started to struggle to sit upright and Brook dashed to his side.

"Here, let me help." She reached around his back and together they had him standing in a couple of seconds. Once she was sure he was steady on his feet, she carefully let go and started to back up when she looked at his face again. Like a moth to the flame, she once again couldn't look away. A weird desire to grab a razor so she could see the bottom half of his face nearly had her knees shaking. His eyes and brow were so handsome. She could only imagine that a strong jaw would enhance what little she could see.

"I'm starving," Jude interrupted their stare-down and came up, holding Cord's cane.

"Thanks," Cord murmured, taking the cane and walking away from Brook.

She chewed on her cheek, trying to hold back her disappointment. *You're not here for romance,* she reminded herself. *Friends. We both need friends. That's all this can be.*

"Are you coming?" Jude asked from the kitchen entrance.

"Yeah, thanks," Brook said. She walked slowly so that she didn't close the gap between her and Cord too much. He wasn't extremely fast at the moment and she didn't want to pass him or walk on his heels. She couldn't be trusted when she got too close, apparently. When she finally entered the kitchen, she took a moment to appreciate the view. The home they were staying in was absolutely gorgeous. It wasn't the biggest mansion on the beach, but it was close.

Brook and her friends, more than once, had taken walks along the water just to imagine what it would be like to live in such a place. And now that she'd seen the inside, she suspected she could easily get used to it. The hardwood floors gleamed, along with antique white cupboards. White granite sparkled in the lights, making it look like there were stars in the room, and the stainless steel appliances had absolutely no fingerprints. It was amazing. Especially against the greige walls, which held just enough color to show off everything else.

A chuckle snapped her out of her admiration and that darned heat flooded her face once more. "Kitchen envy?" Jude teased.

Brook huffed a laugh and smiled at him. "Something like that. I'm not even that big of a cook, but man... I could do some damage in this place." She came in a few more steps. "I think your kitchen is bigger than my entire townhouse."

Jude grinned and opened the fridge. "I think Mrs. Flores left a salad in here." He rummaged around and brought out a bowl. "Normally we would just leave it in there, but since we have a lady in our midst..."

"What is it with men and vegetables?" Brook scolded, putting her hands on her hips. "It's no wonder women live longer than men. If left to your own devices, you'd all die of heart disease in your thirties."

Cord lifted the foil off a baking dish and took a deep sniff. "Ah, but what a way to go, huh?"

Brook laughed. The feeling in the air no longer seemed like it was choking her. In fact, it was fun. Both of the men were cracking jokes as they brought the food to the table and Brook found herself joining in the banter. This was exactly what she had been hoping for. With her other friends caught up in their own lives, she needed something like this. Others who simply wanted a light, carefree evening, no strings attached.

Now if she could just convince her traitorous heart that's the way it needed to stay.

GRAYSON WASN'T SURE he had laughed so much in the past year as he had tonight. Dinner had been delicious, as usual, but if he was being honest, it was the company that had him smiling like a fool and feeling better than he had in months.

"You can't be serious." Brook gasped, her mouth gaping at Jude's latest story.

Jude put his hands in the air. "I swear. She was completely sincere." He laughed. "She even had a bottle of WD-40 in her purse so that she could show me exactly what kind she used."

"Oh my goodness." Brook laughed, putting a hand over her mouth. "I probably shouldn't laugh at her, but that's crazy."

Jude nodded. "It was difficult to convince her that it was not meant for human joints, but I was afraid she'd end up poisoning herself or something if I let it go."

Grayson watched Brook's face light up with smiles and laughter as Jude continued telling his best physical therapy stories. She really was like an angel. Her eyes practically glowed with humor and kindness, and small wrinkles appeared at the side of her eyes when she was really tickled. It was so endearing and so real. He came from a world where wrinkles were a death toll and everyone went to insane extremes to keep their bodies from showing any signs of use. But it was Brook with her wrinkles, snorting laughter, and embarrassing slip-ups that had him entranced.

Before dinner when she'd put her arm around him to help him to his feet, a strange jolt had burst through his system. It was like nothing he had ever felt before. And without his permission, he found himself wanting more. He had secretly hoped that while they were walking to the kitchen, she would catch up to him and see fit to "help" him again, but apparently Jude's interruption had embarrassed her enough that Brook had stayed back, not even coming close to touching him again.

Right now she was sitting across the table and Grayson had no chance of touching her without being totally obvious. It was frustrating. He wanted to see if the situation was a fluke. Maybe it had only happened because he was feeling claustrophobic in the house. Or maybe it was because she was the only woman he'd had any contact with in the last few weeks.

The only other explanation was dangerous, and he wasn't sure he was ready to entertain the thought quite yet. He'd just had a life-changing event and didn't think he could handle another one right now.

Brook stood up, her plate in her hands. "Let me grab these," she said, picking up everyone's plates.

"No way," Jude argued, standing and taking the stack from her hands. "You're a guest."

"But I helped make the mess," she pointed out, trying to reach for the plates again.

Grayson grinned as he watched the two argue over who should do the dishes. Finally, he stood up. "Come on, Brook," he said, stepping around the table to grab her hand. *Not a fluke.* That tingle from earlier shot straight up his limb and brought his heart into hard cardio mode. He probably should have let go, but his hand stayed right where it was. "Let Jude do it. He never does dishes." Grayson leaned close to Brook, getting a noseful of her sweet, fruity scent. "Besides, if he's busy with dishes, we can sneak the box of cookies out onto the deck and eat it all before he's done."

"I heard that!" Jude said from the sink.

Grayson shrugged when Brook smiled.

"And I can still move faster than you," Jude shot out. "You might have to fight me over those cookies."

Grayson tugged on Brook's hand. "I'll take my chances," he called back. Tilting his head toward the sitting room, he and Brook walked. His fingers still held tight to hers, even though it was slightly difficult as he shifted his weight with the cane. The hum from their touch continued to flow, however, and he just didn't want it to stop. The sensation was so much better than the heavy weight of his situation.

He was starting to worry that he wasn't seeing the progress he had hoped for. Jude kept telling him to be patient, but the burning and weakness in his leg just wasn't letting up. It seemed like there should be some hope by now, but it wasn't there. His leg was just as bad as it had been when they'd shown up in Seaside Bay several weeks ago.

"Ohh," Brook cooed as they walked out the glass doors to the deck. "Oh my gosh, the view is so gorgeous out here."

Grayson huffed a quiet laugh. "You're acting like you've never seen it before. I thought you lived here." Brook let go of his hand to walk forward and rest against the railing. No one would ever get Grayson to admit how bereft his hand felt at the loss.

"I do," she said. Her awe was evident in her low tone. "But I've never seen it like this."

Grayson frowned and shuffled to her side, glancing up and down the beach. "It's the same beach we walked along earlier this week."

Brook shook her head. "No. That was one full of people, noise and ordinariness."

"Ordinariness?" Grayson snorted. "What exactly is that?"

Her multi-colored eyes flashed at him over her shoulder. "It just means that it was the same as always. Right now, however..." She waved an arm at the ocean. "It's more magical. It's quiet and peaceful and the moonlight is shining just right." A small shiver rocked through her upper body. "It's perfect."

Grayson didn't respond. He hadn't thought anything of the view. It was similar to the one he saw everyday at home. It should have been similar to what Brook saw everyday from town, if not from her house. So why was it different?

He took a deep breath and shifted his weight. Silence fell between them, only interrupted by the breaking of waves against the shore. The sharp smell of salt trickled into his nose, followed by a subtle perfume that he recognized as Brook's. Closing his eyes, Grayson tried to relax and let his senses take over.

As if a switch had been flipped, he realized there was much more going on than simple waves. Crickets chirped, mosquitoes buzzed, waves rolled, and the air became charged with that same hum from before. Even without his eyes, Grayson could feel Brook's presence next to him. His fingers twitched, wanting to take her hand again, but he refrained. He needed to do this without her touch interfering.

"Do you feel it?" she whispered in a voice so light it seemed to carry on the breeze.

Grayson opened his eyes and turned to her. The moonlight highlighted the planes of her beautiful face, making her lips fuller and her cheekbones higher. How he had ever thought her beauty was like so many others, he didn't know. She outshone any woman he'd ever known.

And yet you can't have her.

The words were like a splash of cold water and Grayson forced himself to step back from her spell. "Yeah. It's something special, all right." He didn't dare meet her eyes again, afraid of what he would see. Mentally he shook his head. He really needed to get control of himself before someone got hurt.

She was sweet and wonderful, but friends were all they could ever be. He didn't live here and she didn't know his true identity. The risk was definitely not worth the reward.

CHAPTER 12

When Cord stepped backward, it was like a splash of cool water on Brooklyn's face. She did her best not to wince at his retreat. For a split second it had felt like they were having a moment again. She had felt a draw to him before, but in the romantic glow of the moon, with the waves hitting the shoreline behind them, it had been stronger than ever.

Cord's gray contacts had flashed, looking anything but false, and Brook had had the craziest thought he might kiss her. Even more insane was the fact that she wouldn't have stopped him. She barely knew him, though they had spent some time together. It wasn't like they'd ever gone on a date or had even hinted at some kind of romantic relationship between them. Most of their time together had been spent with Cord growling and Brook ignoring his grumpiness.

"So..." Brook pursed her lips, looking for some way to break the awkward silence. "Where did you say you and Jude were visiting from?" Cord stiffened slightly and Brook remembered that had been a taboo topic before. *But why? Why would that be a big deal?*

"Uh...south."

"Oh." Brook frowned. She wanted to press, wanted to pin him down and know more, but didn't like the idea of grilling a wounded man. Even if his behavior made no sense.

He scratched at his beard and shifted his weight.

"Do you need to lie down?" Brook stepped in his direction, suddenly worried he'd been on his feet for too long.

Cord shrugged. "I'm okay for a few more minutes."

"I don't want you overdoing it," she said.

Cord grinned. "You sound like a mother."

Brook laughed uncomfortably. "Sorry. I wasn't trying to boss you around. I'm just worried that you won't heal the way you need to if you push too hard."

Cord threw his head back and groaned. "You've been talking to Jude."

Brook's eyebrows rose high on her forehead. "Uh, nope. No insider track here." She smiled. "Just common sense."

He brought his chin back down and gave her a playful glare. "Are you saying I don't have common sense?"

Brook shrugged in a flirty gesture. "You said it."

He chuckled, slowly turning into a full laugh. "I can honestly say that people don't usually say those kinds of things about me. At least, not to my face."

"Well, maybe if they did, you wouldn't have a job that nearly gets you killed," Brook pointed out.

He huffed another laugh. "True enough."

"Is there anything I'm allowed to ask you?"

Cord frowned. "Excuse me?"

Brook turned back toward the ocean, feeling slightly foolish about the question, though it was a legitimate question. She was thinking it, but probably shouldn't have said it out loud. "You visibly stiffen each time I ask you a personal question." She glanced over her shoulder for just a second to see how he was taking her bluntness. "I thought we were becoming friends and it seems natural to want to know about you. But I feel like I'm committing a crime each time I try."

Cord shuffled to the railing and stood beside her, his face looking toward the ocean. "It's nothing personal," he hedged.

"Nevermind," Brook huffed. "It doesn't matter." *This was a stupid idea. He doesn't even want me here, let alone to be friends.*

"I'm serious, Brook," Cord said, his voice edged with frustration. "It really is nothing personal."

"But?" she pressed when he didn't say anything more.

Cord's shoulders drooped. "But I can't tell you what's going on. It could cause problems."

"Problems?"

He nodded.

"Telling me where you're from and what your job is could cause problems?"

Again, he nodded.

Brook stared at him hard for a moment, but couldn't detect any signs of deceit. His answers were vague and she couldn't figure out any scenario... Her eyes shot wide open. "Oh my gosh. You're not... I mean...are you?" Brook snapped her mouth shut.

It had finally come to her. What kind of job would require a person to shy away from relationships and keep their personal details a secret?

He's got to be CIA or FBI or a spy or something.

Her eyes dropped to his leg and back up. *That would also explain how he could get such a serious injury at his job. Oh my gosh, how did I not see this before?*

"What?" Cord asked, stepping closer. "What are you thinking?"

Brook pressed her lips together. Since he was so worried about sharing anything, it made her hesitant to say it out loud.

"What, Brook?"

She shook her head and looked at her feet. "Nevermind. It doesn't matter." She was not about to press him to admit the truth. She didn't want to even come close to blowing his cover, or at least giving away his location when he was being so careful to keep it all a secret.

"No, it's not nothing. You've obviously decided you know something."

Ha! I'll bet people-reading skills are part of his spy job.

She looked up from under her lashes to meet his intense gaze. "I just figured out what kind of job might require you to be so secretive." She kept her chin ducked, but didn't look away from his eyes. Hopefully, all those crazy skills he had probably learned could help him read what she didn't want to say.

"Oh." Cord leaned slightly closer as if he truly could read her thoughts.

Brook held very still, even when a chunk of hair broke free and tickled her nose.

Cord's hand caught the hair too quickly for Brook to notice he'd moved. His eyes never moved from hers as he rubbed it between his fingers. "Your hair is really soft," he whispered.

It was back. The intense charge that seemed to come to life every time she and Cord got close was pulsing between them like a charging lightning bolt. She knew that if she actually touched him right now, the shock would be enough to knock her off her feet. *Or maybe the better word is sweep.*

Slowly, Cord tucked the hair behind her ear. Brook's lungs stopped working as his fingers grazed her skin. His was softer than she would have imagined, no noticeable calluses on his fingertips as he ran his touch along her jawline. Once he was below her chin, he slowly tilted her head back until she was facing him fully.

Her heart was going to break out of her chest any moment. She was positive that it had never raced this hard in her life, not even when running track in high school. Her breathing was short and fast as his face slowly came closer. With his knuckles under her chin, a warm thumb caressed her bottom lip and Brook was sure she was going to faint with anticipation if he didn't actually kiss her soon.

"You have really nice lips," he whispered.

It was an odd compliment, but Brook couldn't find it in her to be put off by it. "Thanks," she managed softly.

He leaned even closer. "I think maybe I need to..."

Oh my gosh...please do!

HE SHOULDN'T DO IT. He should let her go and step back. He should ignore the charge in the air and the chemistry pulling them closer. He should think of the fact that he was hiding and he wouldn't be here forever.

Every rational thought was lost, however, as soon as he had touched her. Grabbing the windblown hair had been an automatic reaction. He'd had the silky strand in his fingers before conscious thought had caught up to him. Tucking it behind her ear had led him to caressing her skin and at that point, there was no turning back.

She was looking up at him with a pleading gaze as if she needed this just as much as he did. Brook was a bright spot in his life, even if she had no idea who he was. He wasn't quite sure what revelation she'd had, but he was positive that if she'd figured out his real identity, she wouldn't be so reluctant to say it. So, for the moment, he was safe.

Actually, I might be in more trouble than I've ever been in before.

He could feel the warmth of her breath as he brought their lips to within millimeters of each other. A last-second thought had him pausing a second before actually kissing her.

She deserves better.

He felt a tug on his shirt as her hand rested on his chest and she lightly gripped the fabric. That was the last bit of encouragement he needed. He gave her a feather light kiss, and it was enough to send a jolt through his body. His weak leg jerked and Cord pulled back slightly, grunting in a mixture of pleasure and pain.

Before he knew what was happening, Brook stepped up into him and wrapped her arms around his torso, helping hold him up. *In that case...* He had no desire to let his leg stop him from giving her a proper kiss and if she was willing, he wouldn't argue.

Sliding his hand from her chin to the side of her head, he went in for more. The touch was firmer this time, and the explosion of feeling followed suit. His chest warmed and a shiver ran through him. His grip on his cane tightened and so did her arms.

Tilting his head to the side, he asked permission for more and on a shaky sigh, she granted it. Time became irrelevant. He'd never felt more complete than he did in this exact moment. No acting award or standing ovation had ever touched all the corners of his soul the way Brook's eager kiss did.

He wasn't quite sure what made her so special, and he was afraid that digging too deeply might ruin everything. Like pulling the curtain back on a magician's show. There was something unique, special, and mystical about their connection and Grayson wanted more of it.

Just as he was about to back her into the railing, their lips broke for a split second and she whispered his name in a dreamy tone.

"Cord…"

There was no better way to bring him back to reality. Sucking a deep breath in through his nose, he pulled his lips from hers. His mouth ached, along with his heart, as he watched her. Those dark lashes stayed down against her cheeks for a few extra seconds before she opened her eyes. The hazy, hungry look was almost more than he could take.

But she didn't know who he was.

He had no right to take such liberties when she didn't even know him. It just wasn't right. Despite the reputation of most actors, Grayson was not a playboy or philanderer. He and his siblings took family seriously, probably because they'd seen what happened when their parents forgot what was most important. He, Carson, and Amelia had promised each other that they would always keep each other grounded. They would marry for love. They would put the important things first. And his career wasn't on that list, though it had been a blessing in many ways. Without it, Grayson would never have been in the position to help his siblings get away from their difficult upbringing.

All of that was why Brook's word was more than he could handle. He, Grayson Cordova, was kissing her. And she was crediting someone who didn't exist. He was pushing a romantic connection built on a lie.

She deserves better.

The words now came back to haunt him. He should have listened to them in the first place, but she had been so tempting. So beautiful. So...perfect.

"I'm sorry," he rasped, stepping back. "I shouldn't have done that."

Brook blinked, the dreamy gaze disappearing. Even in the dim light, he could see the red flush rush up her neck and cheeks. Her tan skin did little to hide her embarrassment. "Yeah..." she said hoarsely, then cleared her throat. She ducked her head and, with shaking hands, tucked that same piece of hair behind her ear. "I, um, sorry. I didn't mean to—"

"No, no, no," Grayson hurried to say. He reached out, and barely stopped himself from touching her. Man, that was going to be tough. Now that he knew what it was like, avoiding their chemistry would be harder than ever. "This isn't your fault," he assured her. "It was mine. I crossed a line." He tried to smile, but it felt brittle. "You're a beautiful woman, Brook. I got caught up in the romantic setting, I guess."

"Oh." She nodded jerkily. "Right. Got it." She stepped back even farther. "I should have known that..." She shook her head. "Sorry. I just...I should have known..."

Grayson wanted to stop her rambling for her, but he wasn't sure what else to say. Which was ridiculous when he thought about it. He got paid a lot of money to use words to entertain people, and right now he had none of them. Where was a good script writer when he needed one?

She was still backing up and each step sent a sharp pain through Grayson's heart, but he kept himself from saying anything. "It's getting late." She finally managed a complete sentence. "I should get home." Her smile was anything but genuine. "I do have a store to run, you know."

"I know," he said softly. He didn't want her to go. Which is exactly why she needed to. He had a sinking feeling in his gut, however, that this might be the last time he saw her. Grayson did his best to memorize her features. He might regret that she didn't know who he was, but he would never regret that kiss. It was amazing. Earth-shattering. And eye-opening. He hadn't realized just how much of him needed that connection. He spent so much of his time trying to hide from people like the media that he had forgotten that somewhere along the line, he still needed a close connection or two.

"Okay, well..." She paused as if giving him a chance to say something.

Grayson bit his tongue so hard, it made his aching leg fade to the background.

"Good night."

He watched her hair spin in the air as she turned quickly and darted down the deck. "Good night," he whispered, though there was no way she could hear him at this point. A car started and headlights flashed across the side of the home. She was gone and he had no one to blame but himself.

"Come on in, man," Jude said from the sliding glass door.

Grayson didn't even have to ask how much his friend saw.

"You look like you're going to collapse any second."

Grayson nodded and started to walk inside. He was drained, and for the first time in a long time, it had nothing to do with his leg.

CHAPTER 13

Brook did a good job of keeping herself away from Cord for three days before her desire to see him began to outweigh her good sense. That restlessness was back and nothing she did seemed to shake it.

She liked Cord. A lot. But he obviously didn't feel the same. No one with any sort of romantic feelings could have come out of that kiss untouched. He had drawn her in like the moon pulling the tide and Brook had felt helpless to resist, though if she was being honest, she hadn't tried very hard.

His touch had been just as electrifying as she had suspected. If he hadn't broken the moment by apologizing and looking at her with pity in his eyes, she would have said she was a changed woman. But somehow, knowing that he had only been caught up in the moment sent her plummeting back down to earth with no one to slow her fall.

It had done more than just sting her pride. It had smashed it to smithereens.

Which was exactly why she had tried to stay away. But it was proving much harder than it should have been. Her sense of self preservation was obviously flawed, because despite the pain, she wanted to see him again.

"He probably isn't allowed to have romantic interludes in his line of work," she whispered to herself as she folded a table of jeans. "Or, at least, not long-lasting ones."

The idea of a short, noncommittal relationship hurt worse than him pulling away with pity the other night. That kind of lifestyle was not for Brook. She took on friends for life and when she fell for a guy, it was going to be for good, not a few weeks.

"Brook?"

Her head snapped to the side. "Hey, Ainsley. Did you need something?"

Ainsley gave her an awkward grin. "No. You just seem to be talking to yourself, so I wanted to make sure you were okay."

"Oh!" Brook laughed, hoping it wasn't as shrill as it sounded to her own ears. "No. I'm fine. Just working out a problem."

"With the store?"

"Nope." Brook smiled widely. "The store is great."

"Oh, good." Ainsley put a hand over her heart and took a deep breath. "I was afraid I was doing something wrong and you were just afraid to tell me."

"Goodness, no." Brook stepped over and gave Ainsley a quick hug. "Sorry if I've been distant. I've just got a lot going on."

Ainsley's grin turned mischievous. "Please tell me it has something to do with that gorgeous lumberjack you were walking with last week."

"Lumberjack!" Brook burst out laughing.

Ainsley huffed and put her hands on her hips. "Don't tell me you haven't noticed the bushman beard," she scoffed. "It's enough to hide a groundhog in."

Brook continued to chuckle as she wiped her eyes. "Yes, if you must know, it has to do with Cord. But I'm pretty sure he's not a lumberjack."

"Pity," Ainsley said as she walked away. "I could watch that body swing an ax all day long."

Brook snorted and the laughter began again. "Oh my gosh, Ains. That's hilarious."

"Just calling it like I see it!" she sang over her shoulder.

Brook's smile was easy and felt good after the last few days of stress. "Lumberjack," she whispered with a few more giggles. She shook her head. She'd never thought of him in that light. It was a far cry from the CIA or spy career she figured he was in.

Her amusement slowly deflated as she considered what life must be like for him. He was probably going stir-crazy in that big house, forced to slow down and lie down half the time. No wonder he had been so grumpy when she'd first met him. Between needing to stay off the radar because of his job and being held back from something he loved, it would make anyone go crazy.

She sobered further when she considered how few friends he probably had. It made her feel bad for staying away for so long. Back home he more than likely had a few close friends, those who were "in the know" on his career. But here? He had no one. Not friends, not family, and not any kind of decent activity.

"Shame on you," Brook scolded herself. She should never have let her own pride keep her from being a friend to someone in need. But was it too late to fix that? Could she just show back up at his house and say "Hey! Remember me?" Would that be too weird? Maybe he was grateful she hadn't shown up again. It saved him from having to cut off their relationship later.

Or maybe he's as lonely as you are.

She pinched her lips together. Was more pain worth the risk? If she put herself out there and he turned her down, could she survive it?

You have a one-hundred-percent survival rate thus far. I think you can handle it.

With that decided, now she needed to figure out how to approach him. She didn't want to make it weird. Maybe if she just acted like nothing was wrong, he would follow suit and they could just forget that the kiss ever happened.

Brook rolled her eyes. He could forget, but she'd never be able to get it out of her head. She'd never had one so good and she was positive she never would again. Her poor future husband had his work cut out for him

Grabbing her phone out of her pocket, she opened up a text before she could chicken out. She wasn't quite ready to meet him by herself. But maybe if she met him in town, she could introduce him to a few of her friends and help him enjoy his time here a little better.

Want to meet the guy who made those cookies I brought you?

The phone immediately went back in her pocket so it was out of sight. If she didn't focus on something else, she knew she would obsess about it until he answered. If he answered.

To her surprise and delight, her phone buzzed within moments.

You sure you want to share that secret? It might not be good to give me that type of information.

She snickered. His words made her even more sure of his career. Gathering information was what he was built for. Though she hoped he usually did it without the beard. Her mouth had been painfully raw from beard burn after their insanely good kiss.

I'm pretty sure it's okay. There are enough cookies for everyone.

If you say so. Where and when should I meet you?

Brook glanced at the clock and then the job she'd been working on before answering.

Main street. Sassy Sweets. One hour.

I'll be there with bells on.

Brooke scrunched up her nose. **Please don't. That won't be conspicuous at all.**

Right. Incognito it is. See ya then.

She sent him back a smiley face and put the phone away. Her heart already felt lighter. Even if she ended up broken-hearted when he left, she would know that she'd done a good deed in helping give him a friend during his stay. And who didn't need a friend? From what she could tell, Cord needed a few. And she knew just the people for the job.

GRAYSON'S HEART WAS pounding way too hard for a simple meet-up. He hadn't heard from Brook in three days and he'd been sure she was gone for good. Her invitation that afternoon had caught him completely off guard and he'd jumped at the chance to see her again, despite the wall between them. If she wanted to act like nothing was amiss, he would be more than willing to play along.

"Looks like this is it," Jude murmured, ducking his head to look at the sign on the store front.

It seemed weird to bring Jude with him, but Grayson's leg wasn't doing well that day and he couldn't walk from the house. He also couldn't drive, so that left having Jude bring him. It was probably smarter to have him there. It would give Grayson a buffer between him and Brook, though deep down, he wanted there to be no barrier at all.

She'd gotten under his skin and that kiss still replayed in his mind every time he closed his eyes. Even now, his fingers twitched with the desire to run through her hair and feel that porcelain soft skin. Yeah...the more he thought about it, the more he was sure it was smart to have Jude play chaperone.

Jude put the SUV in park and started to climb out. "Hang tight and I'll be right there."

Grayson grit his teeth, but stayed still. He was leaning back as far as he could go in order to ride in the vehicle and it was difficult to get out of the position. But waiting for help made him feel like an idiot. He hated how useless this situation made him feel.

And yet you still got a kiss out of it.

"Ready?" Jude pulled open Grayson's door and leaned in. He helped Grayson sit up, then stand and lastly, get his cane situated.

"Thanks," Grayson mumbled.

"Don't mention it," Jude said. "Dude. I think you've gained weight." He laughed when Grayson made a face. "Just kidding. You're just as muscled as ever. I obviously need to do some more lifting if I'm gonna keep this up."

Grayson smirked. He was proud of his body, usually. He'd worked hard to get it as in shape as possible and it had nothing to do with surgery.

"You made it!" Brook was quickly walking their way when Grayson's head came up.

An automatic smile tugged at his mouth. "Hey, Brook. Long time no see." *Why the heck did I say that?* He wanted to smack himself. She was a busy, independent woman. Just because he had too many hours at his disposal didn't mean she did. She ran a business for heaven's sake.

Her cheeks turned red and she gave him a sheepish smile. "Yeah...sorry about that." Her eyes darted to Jude, who stood in an easy stance to the side. "I've been busy at work."

"That's great," Grayson said too cheerily. "I'm glad to hear the store's busy." *Could I sound any more stupid?* He was overcompensating and he needed to cool down. Next time she wouldn't leave because he'd hurt her feelings, she'd leave because he was an imbecile.

Brook nodded. "Yep. That's always a curse and a blessing." She looked over her shoulder, then back. "Ready? You guys will love Jack and Caro."

Grayson kept his mouth shut so he wouldn't say anything else stupid and nodded instead. He shuffled along, his leg burning the whole time. He was probably pushing it by being there, but no one could have stopped him from seeing Brook. He'd needed it, more than he was willing to admit.

Brook came to his side land wrapped her arm around his back. "Lean on me," she said softly. "I'll help."

"Thanks," Grayson said just as softly. He didn't need her help. The cane took his weight well enough, but he did need her presence. It felt good to have her so close. His memories hadn't done the situation justice.

"I'll get the door," Jude said, darting ahead. He stood with his back to the glass door and Grayson and Brook worked their way inside.

There was a large group in the small shop. Adults and children alike walked along the bakery cases, their noses practically pressed against the glass. The place smelled like sweet sugar and cinnamon, and Grayson's stomach growled in anticipation.

Brook laughed quietly. "Hungry?"

"Guess I should have had a snack before I came," he said with a grin.

"Nah. Coming to a sweet shop hungry means you can eat more."

"Exactly the problem," Grayson quipped.

Brook laughed quietly and the sound was perfect. Grayson's heart seemed to jolt in her direction. It was so hard not to just tuck her under his arm and claim her as his. Only the fact that it wasn't fair for her to live a lie kept Grayson from doing just that. Some lucky dog would get that privilege after Grayson was gone, one who didn't hide his identity, and he could only hope the guy was worthy of it.

"Brook!" a petite blonde waved from behind the counter. Her blue eyes studied Grayson and her smile slipped a little before her eyes went back to Brook. "Hang tight and we'll get you taken care of."

"Thanks!" Brook answered. She pointed to the woman. "That's Caroline, or Caro as we all call her. She makes the chocolates." Her finger went to a tall, athletically built man with shaggy, blond-streaked hair. Grayson had seen him before, but carefully omitted that fact. "That's her husband, Jack. He makes the cookies."

Grayson chuckled. "That man is not who I would have pictured as a baker."

"I know," Brook said with a laugh. "But we love him anyway."

They waited another ten minutes before the other crowd was gone and it was just Grayson, Brook, and Jude in the space.

"Whew," Caro said, wiping her forehead dramatically. "That was a rush!"

Jack came up behind his wife and wrapped an arm around her waist before leaving a kiss on top of her head. "Rushes mean good business."

"True," Caro conceded. "Now." She put manicured nails on the high counter. "Whatcha need, Brooksy?"

Brook tugged Grayson forward, still helping him walk. "First, I want to introduce you two to Cord and Jude." She nodded at each of them in turn. "Cord is here to recover and Jude is his physical therapist."

Caro and Jack waved. "Nice to meet you," Caro said, though her tone was slightly wary.

"You too," Grayson said. "We enjoyed the box Brook brought out the other night. You're both amazing at what you do." His words must have been the right thing because Caro preened under the praise. She fluffed her hair and put a hand on her hip. "We're the best sweets shop on the coast."

"The whole coast?" Jude asked. "That's a pretty big claim."

"I never say something I don't mean," Caro said with a sickly sweet smile. Jack just shook his head behind her, smiling indulgently at her head.

Grayson had a feeling he knew exactly where the name of their little shop had come from. "Do you mind if we get another variety box?"

"Not at all," Jack said quickly, grabbing the pink cardboard. "Pick away. Any friend of Brook's is a friend of ours."

Grayson's smile widened. It was obvious Brook was well taken care of. "Thanks," he said.

Jude stepped up and started picking out different items, leaving Grayson standing idle. He didn't care. It all looked good. Grayson was mostly here to see Brook again anyway. His ears perked up when Brook stepped up to the counter to speak to Caro.

"Just invite him," Caro hissed.

"He can barely walk," Brook said in exasperation.

Those words hurt. He knew it was because she was worried about him, but he still hated being told he couldn't handle something. Call it pride, call it vanity, it really didn't matter. But as soon as Brook said those words, Grayson reacted without thinking. "Invite us where?"

The women both spun in his direction, that delicious flush running up Brook's skin. "Uh...we like to have a bonfire on Fridays," she said timidly. "But I was worried it would hurt your leg to walk that far on the sand."

Grayson looked down then back up. "Would you be willing to help me walk again?"

Her eyes opened in shock. "Of course," she breathed. "Any time."

Grayson nodded. "Then I think it sounds fun."

A slow smile spread across her face and Grayson felt that weird twitch in his heart again.

"It's a date," Caro said with a slap on the counter. "We'll see you Friday."

CHAPTER 14

Jude is cooking. Want to risk being poisoned with me?

A laugh bubbled through Brook's lips as she looked at her phone. Last night it seemed like something had changed between her and Cord. She was so glad she had decided to push past her embarrassment and restart the communication between them. Even if he never felt for her what she was starting to feel for him, it would be well worth it to have a friend, if only for a little while.

Her smile tried to falter with the remembrance of the fact that he wasn't a true resident, but she pushed the worries away. Time didn't matter. He needed support and she needed a purpose. This was perfect.

I'm not big into hospitalizations...

Not even if your roommate is a grouchy invalid?

More laughter broke free and Brook had to cover her mouth with a fist to try and control it. Ainsley was giving her a weird look from her place at the front counter, but Brook waved her off. She took a moment to finish going through the inventory she was working on, then headed back to her office before answering him. Apparently, she couldn't control herself enough to be in public.

I have to admit that's tempting, but...

Come by and we'll throw in a game night.

Brook paused. She chewed her bottom lip. He was playing hardball now. She adored games. Not that Cord knew that, but once she got started, Brook knew she had a problem with getting a little...competitive. She really should say no, but she didn't want to.

Sold. Store closes in forty-five minutes. I'll be there.

I'll count the minutes.

Warmth flooded her system. She knew he was just flirting for fun, but man, it tugged at her heart strings. She was going to spend a month crying her eyes out and eating gallons of ice cream when he finally left. But deep down, she knew she wouldn't miss this experience for anything.

It still didn't seem quite fair that her friends were all finding their "happy ever afters" and Brook only managed to find a "friend for now," but he helped fill a hole inside her. He helped the part of her that was so lonely and feeling like the odd man out. She finally had someone in her life. That was all she was willing to focus on for now.

Time dragged on like a tired sloth, but closing finally arrived. It had been slow enough at the end of the day that Brook probably could have left early, but she didn't want to appear too eager. Their relationship was already off kilter since she was totally falling for him. She didn't want to make it worse by becoming a crazy stalker lady.

She pulled into his driveway, grabbed the tray of smoothies she'd picked up from Mel's shop, just in case dinner was inedible, and headed up to the front door. Brook shifted everything in her hands so she could knock, though it almost cost her her keys to do it.

"COME IN!"

She laughed under her breath and did her best not to drop anything while she opened the door. "I don't think it's very safe to invite strangers into your house!" she called out as she entered.

"If you were a stranger, I wouldn't have invited you in," Cord said from his place on the couch. He had raised his head to look at her, but the rest of his body was lying down.

"Maybe not, but how could you be sure it was me?"

He smirked and held up his phone. "Camera."

Brook returned his smile and walked over, setting all her stuff on the ottoman.

"What in the world did you bring?" Cord asked. "I thought we were feeding *you* dinner."

Brook made a point of looking toward the kitchen, then bending down closer to Cord. "I brought some of my friend Mel's famous protein shakes, you know, just in case."

Cord snorted. "Nice. Better sneak those into the fridge."

"On it." Brook left the rest of her things, but took the cup carrier to the kitchen. She didn't bother trying to hide herself, knowing that Jude wouldn't be offended. "Hey, Jude," she sang.

Jude, whose back was to her from his place at the stove, threw back his head and groaned. "If I had a penny for every time someone sang that..."

"Only a penny, huh?" Brook said as she put the smoothies in the fridge. "That would take a while to add up."

"Not if you knew how often people said that to me," he shot back. He was grinning at her and Brook returned to greeting.

"Sorry," she said, not meaning a word of it. "I couldn't resist."

"You and half the population," Jude grumbled. He nodded toward the fridge. "What did you bring?"

"Protein shakes from my friend Mel's smoothie shop."

"Good thing," Jude grumbled, making a face. He turned back to the stove. "We might need them."

Brook wanted nothing more than to go spend time with Cord, since he was all by himself. Time alone with him was wonderful and torturous all at the same time. But Jude's dejected stature kept her from leaving. She walked up to look over his shoulder. "Ummm..."

Jude pushed a hand through his hair, causing it to stand up in spikes. "I know." He moaned. "But I'm not sure what I did wrong."

Brook grimaced. "I'm not an expert, but I'm gonna say your pan was too hot."

"What?" Jude sighed. "I thought pancakes were supposed to be foolproof."

Brook couldn't take her eyes from the black hockey pucks that were oozing uncooked batter and soon she couldn't hold back her laughter. "I'm sorry," she said, putting her fingers against her lips, but nothing stopped her amusement. Soon she was bent over, gasping for breath as she continued to laugh.

"It's not that funny," Jude grumbled like a pouting boy. It only served to have Brook laughing harder.

"What's going on in here?" Cord's smooth baritone came from the doorway.

Brook straightened, wiping tears and pointing to the stack of ruined pancakes. She tried to speak, but more laughter came out, so she shook her head instead.

"Dude," Cord said, wrinkling his nose. "It stinks in here. Did you burn something?"

Jude threw his spatula on the counter. "I'm done! Fix your own dinner!"

"Come back," Brook said as she slowly got herself back under control. The wide grin on her face, however, refused to budge. "Pancakes don't take very long. I can help you fix it."

Jude sat on a bar stool and folded his arms over his chest. "I don't want to."

Cord had shuffled over and he slapped Jude on the back. "You sound like you're a toddler."

"Why don't you see if you can do better?" Jude shot back. He gave Cord a challenging look.

Cord looked at Brook and that charge she always felt began to hum. "I'm willing to teach you too," she said with a shrug. "It really won't be that hard to fix."

Cord kept eye contact with her as he came forward. When he was fairly close, he leaned in a little. "I've always enjoyed one-on-one lessons."

Her heart sped up and her stomach flip-flopped. *I'm in so much trouble...but what a way to go.* "Wash your hands," she whispered. "And we'll get started."

GRAYSON HAD GOTTEN really good at pushing the logical voice in the back of his head into silence. He shouldn't be encouraging this situation with Brook, but he couldn't seem to help himself. He didn't *want* to help himself. He enjoyed her company. He enjoyed her lightness and kindness. He enjoyed her smiles and laughter. And most of all, he enjoyed her kiss. If he wasn't so worried about hurting her, he would make it a goal to enjoy that last one more often. As it was, he hated deceiving her. She deserved to know the truth and he wanted to give it to her, but he couldn't do it. His recovery wasn't complete yet, wasn't even close to being complete. And until that was taken care of, he couldn't risk anyone else getting wind of his location.

"You coming?" Brook asked.

She had stepped up to the stove and Grayson followed. He put them shoulder to shoulder, letting them touch each time one of them moved. He could hear her breath catch a couple of times and it only spurred him on. Not to mention how much he enjoyed his own body's reaction to the brief contact.

Brook stuck her pinky in the batter and sucked it off. She nodded. "Your batter tastes good," she called out to Jude, who was still pouting at the table.

"Well, at least I didn't screw that up," he grumbled.

Brook laughed under her breath and threw a conspiratorial glance toward Grayson. He grinned and winked.

"He never did like to lose," Grayson said softly.

"I heard that," Jude snapped.

"All right, boys," Brook said. "Enough." She took the skillet from the stove and walked over to the sink. "The biggest problem is that your pan was too hot." She turned on the water and stuck the pan under, creating a hiss and steam that nearly filled the room.

"Whoa," Jude said, his jaw slack.

Grayson's eyebrows were high when Brook came back. "I take it hotter isn't better?"

"It is if you want the outside cooked, but the inside raw," she explained. Her eyes looked more brown than green today as she looked around the kitchen. "Where can I find a different pan?"

Grayson moved and opened a cupboard. "I think they were down here."

After securing the right one, Brook put it on the stove and then turned it on to just below medium.

"That's going to take forever," Grayson said, scrunching his nose. He held back a smile at the fact that Brook had stepped up next to him with their shoulders touching again. Apparently, he wasn't the only one who enjoyed it.

"Do you want the pancakes cooked or not?" she asked, turning to put her hand on her hip.

Grayson's hand seemed to move of its own accord as it reached out and rested just below her own. "I don't know. Do you have other suggestions to satisfy my hunger?" His body was completely out of control. This was not what was supposed to be happening. *What in the world is she doing to me?*

That dreamy haze from the night of their kiss came back into Brook's eyes and he felt a shiver go through her body. When he squeezed her hips, she obeyed by taking a step forward.

"I don't think PDA is the way to cook pancakes," Jude said dryly.

Brook jumped at the interruption and put enough distance between them that Grayson's hand fell to his side. His favorite reddish/pink color shot up her skin and he almost stepped forward so he could touch the heat.

"Though you two might be hot enough to cook them without the use of the stove," Jude continued.

Grayson rolled his eyes as Brook turned away from them both, presumably to gather herself from being embarrassed at Jude's comments. Grayson, on the other hand, turned to his friend and glared, doing his best to melt Jude with the heat he had been talking about.

Jude smirked, his arms folded over his chest. He shrugged. "Sorry, not sorry. I'm hungry."

"So was I," Grayson said in a snarky tone.

"I'll bet you have enough leftover crumbs in that beard to help you out."

Brook snorted and Grayson looked her way. Her shoulders were shaking as she tried to hold in her laughter.

"Are you telling me you have a problem with my beard too?" Grayson asked her, an indulgent grin on his face.

Brook straightened and gave him an impressive innocent look. "Oh, no. Your beard is...fine."

"You hesitated," Jude said.

"No, I didn't," she said too quickly.

"Yes, you did," Grayson inserted.

Brook rolled her eyes. "Let's change the subject, shall we?" She spread her hand and held it above the pan. "Feels like it's ready to go." She grabbed a ladle that was hanging from the ceiling. "Okay, boys, pay attention." She poured a spoonful in the pan, which immediately sizzled and filled the air with the slightly sweet smell of breakfast.

Grayson stepped up closer. He might not be able to kiss her right now, but that didn't mean he couldn't be close. The pancakes would be fine. "How do you know when to flip it?" he whispered in her ear.

Brook's skin turned red again and he had to resist the urge to kiss just below her ear. "See the bubbles?" she asked, her voice squeaky. She cleared her throat. "When the bubbles are all over the circle, then it's time to turn it over."

"I see," he said just as softly. He leaned down just enough to let his nose brush along the edge of her ear. His grin was inevitable when he watched goosebumps form on the side of her neck. There was something so satisfying about knowing that the woman he was interested in was just as affected by him as he was by her.

But you shouldn't be interested in her.

He sighed and backed off...but only a little. It seemed like a waste to not enjoy his time with Brook. But he needed to be careful. She was different. She was special. Grayson had a niggling suspicion that given the right circumstances, Brook could be *the one.*

But how would that work when she didn't even know who he was?

A slurping sound caught his attention and Grayson turned around. He could feel Brook do the same.

Jude was sitting at the table, doing his best to get every last drop out of one of the protein shakes Brook had brought with her. "This is so good," he said around a mouthful of smoothie.

Brook laughed, the tension between them thoroughly broken. "Mel is awesome at what she does. I'll tell her she has a new fan."

Jude reached for the next one.

"Hey!" Grayson said. "That's mine!"

Jude smirked, kept eye contact, and took a long drink. "I think you already got your dessert," he said.

"Oh my gosh," Brook whispered.

Grayson grinned at her. "If only he was right."

She looked at him from under her lashes. The look was purely seductive, yet he didn't think she knew it. "If only," she said breathlessly.

CHAPTER 15

"Well, that does it," Jude said, dropping his fork on the table. Brook raised her eyebrows. "What does what?" She bent forward slightly to put her last bite of dinner in her mouth. She probably had a little more syrup than was polite on her plate and she didn't want to drip it on her lap. But could a girl be blamed for satisfying her sweet tooth where she could?

And her sweet tooth was screaming tonight. Cord was in a mood and he'd been super flirty. So much so, Brook was almost ready to believe he had feelings for her as well. If he hadn't apologized for kissing her, she would have given into the hope that he wanted to kiss her again.

Luckily, Jude had stopped her before she grabbed Cord's shirt and pulled their mouths together. The man was a temptation unlike anything Brook had ever experienced before. Maybe it was the fact that she'd been in love with a fake persona her entire life that had kept her from experiencing these types of feelings for a real, breathing person. But no matter what, she was loving it. Even with the inevitable train wreck that would come, she was loving it.

Brook had never felt so alive and so annoyingly giddy. It made her feel young in a way she had missed. Now she totally understood why Caro and all her other friends had become hormonal teenagers when they were falling in love. It was fun and ridiculous all at the same time.

"These are the best pancakes I've ever made," Jude said with certainty.

Cord snorted. "You didn't make them." He stuffed the last piece of bacon in his mouth.

"I made the batter," Jude pointed out. "You wouldn't be enjoying them unless I did that."

"I'm pretty sure Brook could have handled making the batter," Cord said with an eye roll.

"Oh my word," Brook said. "You two are ridiculous. Just stop!"

Both men looked at her like she'd lost her mind. A slow smirk formed under Cord's unruly beard. "Are you sure you want me to stop?" He winked.

Brook glared. "That won't work on me, buster."

Jude burst out with a barking laugh. "I don't think I've ever seen a woman not fall for that," he said between breaths.

Cord gave her an unimpressed look. "You're hard on a guy's ego, you know that?"

She gave him a saccharine sweet smile. "Get used to it."

Jude's laughter turned into a cough and soon he was gulping the rest of his water, trying to get it to calm down. "Oh, man. That was so worth enduring you guys making googly eyes at each other all night."

Darn that blush. Brook could feel the heat on her skin once more. It seemed like it happened way more than usual right now. Every time she spent time with Jude and Cord, she found herself embarrassed in some way. But she wouldn't change it for the world.

She stood and began to gather plates and dishes. Cord grabbed her arm. "What do you think you're doing?"

She gave him a look. "Cleaning up."

He shook his head. "Nope. That's Jude's job." His thumb jabbed in his friend's direction.

"What?" Jude said indignantly.

Cord smiled at Jude. "You're the only one who didn't cook."

"Oh, like you did so much?"

Brook shook her head and started taking the dishes away. Those two were worse than Benny and...well, anybody. She smiled, despite their silly arguments. It was nice to know that Jude and Cord were such good friends. The more time she spent with them, the more Cord seemed to come out of his angry shell. Brook was willing to wager that this type of banter was more like how they acted when they were at home, which was exactly what she was hoping for.

"Come on," Cord said, his warm hand cupping her elbow. "Let's go to the sitting room."

Brook blinked in surprise. She hadn't heard him approach, which was a testament to where her mind was since he wasn't exactly quiet when he walked at the moment. "I don't mind helping," she said, holding back slightly.

He grinned. "Maybe not, but Jude and I have it settled."

"Yeah, yeah," Jude said, his hands waving them away. "Get on with you. I've got work to do."

Brook laughed softly. "What's he giving you to do those?" she asked.

"Wouldn't you like to know?" Jude said with a wink.

Cord growled very softly, but it was enough to have Brook's heart racing. She really could get lost in him if she let herself. His actions all said that he wanted to spend time with her, and that was a boon to her ego.

"I'm coming," she said to Cord, happily tripping after him. Their walk slowed when they were shoulder to shoulder and Cord's hand drifted down to take hers. "You promised me a game," she said, trying to keep the conversation light. Each time he touched her, a small part of her heart seemed to break off, landing firmly in his hand. Too much more of this and she wasn't sure she'd ever be able to put herself back together again.

"I did," he said with a nod. He glanced at her sideways. "Are you sure that's what you want to do?"

Brook raised a single eyebrow, giving him a challenging look. "What's the matter? Chicken?"

He chuckled. "No, but I don't lose very often."

"People also don't tell you no very often," she pointed out.

"No, they don't," he agreed.

"But I do."

His grin grew. "Yes, you do."

"Then how do you know that I won't beat you in a game as well?"

Cord squeezed her hand, then brought it up and kissed the back of it. "I guess we'll just have to find out, won't we?"

"Challenge accepted," Brook said, hoping he couldn't hear how breathless her voice was. One look, one touch, and she was complete putty. It was so interesting how one person could be so different from another. No other man had caused this reaction in her and part of her worried no one else ever would. For the first time ever, she was letting go of Grayson Cordova and enjoying someone else. More than enjoying, she was falling for him. It reminded her of the first time she found a pair of jeans that were perfect on her frame. She felt more alive, more attractive, more womanly all because something was just right for her.

Cord was just right for her.

But she wasn't just right for him.

If he really was a spy of some kind, no woman was probably just right for him. Long-term relationships would be nearly impossible. The thought made her sad for herself, but doubly sad for him. And only served to reiterate her desire to see through this friendship, no matter how much his eventual leaving would hurt.

"UNO," GRAYSON SAID with a frown. "You really want to play Uno?"

Brook grinned mischievously at him. "I told you you were chicken."

He rolled his eyes. "I'm not chicken. I'm just not a fan of card games."

She tapped the deck on her knee. "Well, then, what do you want to play, Mr. Hotshot?"

Grayson relaxed in his recliner. "I don't know. Risk? Monopoly? You know. Something that requires strategy."

She narrowed her eyes at him. "I hadn't planned to be here until midnight."

He chuckled and shifted his weight around. "I'll give you that. Those games definitely require some time."

"I guess we could start a game and not finish it, but..." She chewed her lip, looking uncertain.

"But what?"

"But I hate leaving things unfinished." She made a face.

He laughed again. He always felt so light and free when she was around. It was amazing. "Okay. Tonight we do cards. But next time, we're pulling out the big guns."

"Deal." She began shuffling, then handing out the cards. "You know, this isn't going to work. Hang on." Standing up, she pulled the coffee table to the side of his chair and then her own seat. It prevented Grayson from having to lean forward every time he wanted something.

"Smart," he murmured, enjoying that ever present flush. It seemed to happen frequently around him and he liked it. A lot.

"You're left of the dealer," she said.

"I'm the only other person besides the dealer."

"True enough."

The game began quietly at first until Grayson laid a card forcing Brook to draw two extras.

"Oh!" she cried good-naturedly. "I see we're pulling out the artillery." She grinned. "You just wait. I'm still warming up."

"Better do it quick," Grayson teased back. "I'm gonna be out before you can do anything about it."

"Don't you worry," she said. "It's not going to be over until I win."

Grayson had to give it to her. Apparently her feisty side came out over cards. He tossed another card down that skipped her turn. She grumbled under her breath, making him chuckle. "Still feeling confident?"

Brook stuck her nose in the air, then ruined the effect by laughing. "Sorry. I just get really competitive."

"I'm pretty competitive myself," Grayson admitted. "It's how I got to be...good at my job." He had almost said something he shouldn't have. Brook made him so comfortable that one of these days he was going to slip up.

She nodded sagely. "I would imagine that you're good at just about anything you do." Her eyes darted to his, then back to her cards as if worried she had said something too bold.

"Thank you," Grayson said sincerely. It was nice to have someone give him a compliment that wasn't followed by some kind of request. Especially a compliment given strictly based on who she thought he was as a person. That same warm feeling he often got around her began to swirl in his chest.

They laughed and teased for the next few minutes while the game played itself out, but Grayson's mind was distracted. Every time he looked at her, he saw her lips, and the desire to kiss them was quickly turning into a need. He wanted to surround himself in her sweetness and light. He wanted to hold her in his arms and shield her from the world, keeping her all to himself.

He jerked a little, taken back by how fiercely he meant those words. She was so innocent compared to the world he came from. Whether he was a partaker or not, he saw enough of the hidden side of life to know that people like Brook were rare. He never wanted her to change, but even if they were somehow able to get past the fact that he lied to her about his identity, taking her back to his life would ruin her.

Better just enjoy what time I've got.

Uno was definitely not how he wanted to spend their limited time together. Throwing his cards on the table, he began to struggle to get out of the chair.

"Cord? What's the matter?" Brook went from flirting and laughing to concerned and helpful in an instant. It almost made Grayson laugh, but he bit the inside of his cheek to keep from doing so.

"Nothing. I'm just done," he said.

Her arm went around his back, gripping his side as she tried to help him get up without bending any more than necessary.

"Couldn't handle the loss, huh?" she said as they began to shuffle forward.

Grayson re-gripped his cane and shifted his weight until he was steady. "Maybe I was just saving you the humiliation," he said, taking her hand. He pulled her forward so she wasn't helping him anymore. While he appreciated the effort, he didn't like the way her help made him feel like an invalid. He wanted to be strong and whole when he was with her, or at least as close as he could get.

"You wish, buddy," she quipped.

He brought her hand up and kissed the back of it. "Come on. Keep me company on the deck."

Brook sighed and opened the sliding glass door. "I'll bet the ocean does wonders for your stress and healing."

He bit that same spot on his cheek again to keep from correcting her. It was going to be swollen to the size of a cantaloupe before the night was out. Grayson had a personal physical therapist. Appointments with the best doctor in Oregon. A beachside mansion with a personal cook and cleaning lady. And the best thing for his recovery was the woman at his side. None of his other resources had done anything to lift his spirits or heal his emotional needs the way she did. He hadn't even recognized that they needed to be healed until she pushed her way into his life.

"It certainly has been nice," he said just to respond to her. He led her to the lounge chair that he often laid on and worked his way to reclining in it. He was just upright enough to look forward and admire the water. When Brook tried to go to the chair, he tugged on her hand. "Will you sit by me?" he asked softly.

It was no wonder he had kissed her the last time they were out here. The sounds of nature were soothing and he felt his blood pressure immediately lower. His heart rate, however, did the exact opposite. The feel of her hand, the look in her eyes... It was enough to let him know she felt the exact same way about their location as he did.

"Okay," she whispered. Gingerly she rested a hip on the edge of the lounge chair.

"Yeah, that's not going to work," he said. Scooting himself to the side, he patted the spot next to him. When Brook swallowed hard, he grinned. He knew he was giving her mixed signals. Last time they were out here, he'd pushed her away. But those three days of distance had been enough to tell him that he couldn't do it. He knew he'd regret it later, but keeping a barrier between them would be worse than falling in love and then losing her. *It is better to have loved and lost than to have never loved at all.*

The words came back to him with a strong ring of truth. Brook didn't know he was falling in love. She didn't need to know, it would only make things difficult. But if she was willing, he had every intention of taking advantage of their time.

Slowly, she leaned down and rested on her side next to him. Her eyes said she was wary and unsure, so Grayson helped ease her concerns. He put his arm around her and tugged her into his chest.

"That's better," he said, his voice having gone husky.

Her hazel eyes glittered in the light as she looked up at him, hand resting on his chest. "Are you sure?"

Grayson leaned forward and rubbed his nose against hers. "I think I've figured a few things out in the last few days," he whispered.

"When I get better, I can't stay here, but while I'm in town, the idea of staying away from you is more than I can handle." He pulled back to look her in the eye. "Although I'll do it if you say so." He dropped her hopeful gaze. "I don't know exactly when I'm leaving, or even if I'll ever get better, but—"

She rose up on her elbow and put fingers to his lips, stopping his words. "None of that matters to me," she said, her fingers trailing down his beard. She reached up and began to run her fingers through his hair and he closed his eyes to enjoy the sensation. "I know you can't make any promises, but I don't want to lose this time either."

He opened his eyes and that dang pulse of his skyrocketed at the sincere look on her face.

"You should stop wearing colored contacts," she said with a soft smile. "I'd love to see what you look like for real."

He gulped. "I've... I only have these."

She shrugged. "That's okay. You look handsome either way."

He shouldn't do it. It was hitting him again, the regret of lying to her. It wasn't fair for someone like her to—

Brook cut off his thoughts when she leaned over and brought her lips to his. Grayson's response was automatic and immediate. His arm tightened around her back and he reciprocated the offered affection. All concerns and worries were lost in the buzz of electricity that began to pulse through his body. Vaguely he still knew that there would eventually be a reckoning for his lies, but right now there were more important matters, and Grayson intended to give them his full attention.

CHAPTER 16

Brook waited patiently for Jude to park the SUV before she slipped to the passenger side to help Cord. Well, she pretended to be patient. Inside, however, her heart was racing and even the cool evening breeze did nothing to help with the sweat forming on the back of her neck. She had already introduced Cord to Caro and Jack, so it wasn't like she was keeping him a secret or something. But it felt different to bring him to a bonfire.

For Brook and several others in the group, this was the equivalent of meeting the family. Each of her married friends had brought their significant others to the gatherings, and they had all become permanent fixtures.

Brook already knew that wouldn't happen with Cord. No matter how sweet he had been a couple nights ago. No matter that he admitted he liked her. No matter that she was falling head over heels in love with him. It had been stated upfront that they had an expiration date. Eventually he would heal, and then he would leave. At that point, Brook would go back to mooning over a man from afar, only this time she suspected it would be much more difficult to handle than a celebrity crush.

"Hey," she said as she opened Cord's door.

"Hey, yourself," he answered with a grin. He was wearing tinted glasses that made his gray contacts look nearly brown. It seemed odd that he would wear them at night, but she shrugged it off. He had seemed self conscious about his contacts from the beginning, so maybe he was trying to hide how unusual they were.

Before she could do much to help, Cord had used a strap to pull himself upright, then twisted so his legs were hanging out of the SUV.

"Whoa. You're getting good," she said with an encouraging smile.

Cord grimaced. "Learning how to maneuver around doesn't mean my leg is improving."

She leaned in to make sure he was paying attention. "Maybe not, but any progress is progress."

He chuckled. "You sound like one of the inspirational posters they hang in the high school hallways."

Brook shrugged and helped him get down to the ground. "Hey, they got me through that awkward stage. Don't see why they can't help now."

Cord shifted his weight until he was where he wanted to be and then took Brook's hand. "You? Awkward. I don't believe it."

She laughed, walking slowly beside him as they started toward the beach. "You better believe it. Braces, frizzy hair, pimply skin...I had it all."

"The real question is, do you have the pictures to prove it?" he asked.

Brook shook her head. "Nope. My mother does."

"She keeping them for future blackmail purposes?"

"I sure hope not." Brook shivered dramatically. "If I ever bring a guy home, she'd scare him off within minutes."

They reached the sand and Cord worked to find stability for his cane.

"Gotcha," Jude said from Cord's other side.

A blush hit Brook's cheeks. She had been so caught up in Cord that she hadn't even said hello to Jude. "Hey, Jude," she said with a small laugh. "Sorry. I wasn't trying to ignore you."

"Yeah, it's okay," he teased. "I know it's hard to see anything when bear man is around."

She snickered when Cord growled. "Between the beard and his constant growling, I think that's an apt description," Brook said.

Cord shook his head. "Lots of men have beards," he grumbled.

"And lots of men can't get a date to save their lives," Brook shot back.

He laughed at that. "True." He looked over at her, still smiling. "Luckily, I'm not one of them."

"Don't start," Jude snapped. "I can't leave the room this time."

"There they are," Brook said, pointing ahead to the fire, grateful for the easy change in subject. She didn't need anything else to be embarrassed about at the moment. She blushed around Cord too often as it was.

Cord whistled low. "That's a big group of friends."

"In the last couple of years, several of them have gotten married," Brook said, her voice having dropped automatically. "So we've nearly doubled in size. In fact," she plastered a smile on her face, "Genni and her husband Cooper just announced a couple weeks ago that they're expecting."

Cord glanced at her before facing forward again. "You're not happy for them?"

"What?" Brook gasped. "Of course I am! She's the first one to have a baby." A small laugh slipped through her lips. "In fact, that baby is probably going to be smothered in love from all its aunts and uncles."

Cord's smile looked melancholy. "Must be great to have such good friends."

"It is," she said brightly. "Not all of us have family to pull on." She shrugged. "So we rely on each other."

"Brook!" Caro shouted and rushed to meet them. "Hey, Cord. We're so glad you made it. You too, Jude."

Jude smiled. "Thanks for having us."

"Same," Cord said.

Caro turned to Brook. "We set up chairs for you guys and I made Jack carry one that reclined so Cord wouldn't be sitting upright."

"Caro, you're the best," Brook gushed, letting go of Cord to give her friend a hug.

"I know," Caro said with a laugh. She let go of Brook and winked at the men. "Come on, gentlemen. Let's get you settled and then we'll get you fed."

"As much as I'd prefer those in the opposite order, I'll take what I can get," Cord joked.

"Men and their stomachs," Caro said with a snort. "We'll be lucky if they ever figure out they've got brains as well."

"Caro," Brook said, shaking her head. "I doubt Jack would appreciate that."

"Eh, he's used to it," Caro said, smiling at her husband, who shook his head.

He wasn't within earshot of their conversation, but odds were he knew his wife well enough to know she was up to something.

"Need some help?"

Brook smiled at Ken, who was walking around the circle of people to their side. "Hey, Ken. This is Cord and Jude." She nodded to each in turn. "They're here while Cord is recuperating from an injury."

Ken was the largest of their group with height and width to his name. He shook hands with the men. "Good to meet you," he said politely before facing Cord. "I'm assuming the recliner is for you?"

Cord grimaced. "I've got a damaged nerve that runs into my leg. Sitting is difficult on it."

Ken nodded. "Gotcha." He gently shifted Brook out of the way. "Excuse me, Brook." Then he helped Cord get settled.

Brook stood to the side feeling helpless, but grateful. She felt a certain sense of propriety when it came to Cord and wanted to be the one helping him, but she couldn't deny that Ken was better suited to the job. Truth be told, Brook was probably more of a liability, but that didn't stop her from wanting to be involved.

As soon as Ken was done, she scooted her chair over and sat down.

NO SOONER HAD GRAYSON been seated than he noticed the attention of the entire group was on him. He was used to having people watch him. His entire career depended on it. But right now, the attention made him squirm in his seat. Coming to the bonfire might not have been his best idea. He'd been trying to get closer to Brook, but now he realized just how risky it was. What if someone recognized him? What if they pressed about his family or his career? Or even his injury? It had been easy enough to toe the line of honesty with one person, but doing it with an entire crowd was a whole different deal.

"You might want to pull out those award-winning acting skills right about now," Jude whispered.

"You should have stopped me from coming," Grayson said as quietly as possible as he nodded and smiled at the group.

"You wouldn't have listened," Jude shot back.

Grayson glared at him, but had to admit he was right. Grayson made most of his decisions at the moment based on his feelings for Brook. Tonight he was seeing just how foolish that was.

"Everyone," Brook said loudly, "I'd like you all to meet Cord and Jude." She smiled at him. "They're tourists," she made a face, causing Grayson and the rest of the group to chuckle, "but are sticking around long enough for Cord to heal from a work injury." She turned to Grayson and Jude. "Want me to introduce everyone? No one will expect you to remember all the names."

"Says you!" a man with messy blond hair called from the other side of the circle. "I'm giving a quiz at the end of the night." He grinned. "Winner gets the last of Jack's cookies."

"You play for high stakes here," Jude called back.

"Go ahead," Grayson said to Brook. He was pretty good at memorizing, since he'd had years of practice. Maybe he could finally impress her with something other than being able to sit up in a car.

"Okay, you asked for it," she teased. Her finger started just to her left. "You've already met Caro and Jack and know they own a sweets shop."

"Nice to see you again, Jack," Grayson said.

"You too," Jack responded. He reached out and took his wife's hand, resting it against his thigh. "We're glad you guys could make it tonight."

"Next is Captain Felix and Dr. Hadlee Mendez." She turned to Cord. "Felix owns a fishing charter and Hadlee is working at an aquarium up north. If you have any questions about oceans or fish, these two will know more than you need."

Grayson's eyebrows rose up. "Fishing charter?"

Felix wasn't smiling, but he nodded.

"Do you catch anything big?"

Felix smirked and folded his thick arms over his chest. "Big enough," he boasted.

Grayson grinned back. "When I can walk without tripping, I might have to give it a whirl. I love a good fishing trip. Caught myself a decent-sized marlin off Hawaii once." Grayson snapped his mouth shut. He shouldn't be revealing stuff like that. It would only lead to questions.

Felix's mouth softened into a smile. "You let me know when you're ready."

"Will do, thanks." There was no way to describe the amount of relief that flooded Grayson's system when Felix moved on without asking for details.

"You met Ken," Brook continued. "He's our police captain, so don't speed if you see him around."

"Crap," Jude said. "Someone should have warned me."

Soft laughter broke free in the group again. "I'll tell you the same thing I tell everyone," Ken said with an easy smile. "The first pullover is a warning. After that, you're fair game."

Jude wiped his forehead. "Good to know. I'll be sure to keep an eye out for you."

Ken chuckled and settled deeper into his chair.

"Next are Mel and Jensen," Brook said. "Mel runs the smoothie shop and Jensen teaches at our high school."

Hello's were murmured from both sides.

"And lastly, we have Genni and Cooper." Brook's look softened, bringing Grayson back to their earlier conversation.

He believed Brook when she said she was happy for her friend, but there had been something else there as well. He was pretty sure Brook was envious. She wanted what Genni and the rest of the women did.

"They own a bed and breakfast..." Brook trailed off. "Where's Scottie?"

Genni groaned and rolled her eyes. "*His* dog," she emphasized, "shredded my bed of daylilies, so she didn't get to come tonight."

"Scottie is their Australian Shepherd mix," Brook said softly to Grayson.

"Ah," he responded before speaking a little louder. "That breed is notorious for being destructive."

"Tell me about it." Cooper sighed. "She messed with everything."

"Have you had her trained?"

"A little," Genni said. "Not a professional class, just us looking stuff up online."

"Shepherds are really intelligent," Grayson said. It was knowledge he'd picked up from a movie he'd done. "If they get bored, they get destructive. You might find that good training would go a long way in learning how to keep her occupied."

Cooper's eyebrows shot up and he laughed a little. "Good to know. Thanks."

Grayson could feel Brook's stare and he gave himself a second before looking at her.

"Are you a dog lover?" she asked with a curious smile. "You seem to know a lot about them."

Grayson shrugged, feeling stupid yet again. Twice in only a few minutes, he'd said things he shouldn't have. If no one knew who he was by the end of the night, it would be a miracle. "We had a dog growing up." Which was true, but it wasn't a Shepherd. He didn't need to share that little tidbit.

"Oh." She looked slightly disappointed at his answer, but turned back to the group. "We're missing a few tonight, but now you know everyone here."

"Thanks for having us out," Grayson said politely. If they were missing some, then the group really was bigger than he could have imagined. His support group seemed so small compared to what they were sharing in this tiny town.

"Can I get you something to eat?" Brook whispered.

Knowing he needed to offer her something, though he wasn't quite sure why he'd hurt her feelings, he reached out and took her hand. "Who wants to get better with someone as beautiful as you waiting on them hand and foot?"

She laughed just as he'd intended. "And who would complain about catering to someone so handsome?"

Man, he wanted to kiss her. He'd thought it would be good to get to know her more, but now he was regretting the crowd. It wouldn't be appropriate to pull her to his chair like he'd done the other night. But it was oh, so tempting. Instead, he forced himself to be content to kiss her hand. He adored how she blushed every time he did. "I'd love some dinner, thank you."

She gave him a shy smile and stood. "Anything I should know about allergies or..."

Grayson shook his head. "Nope. I'm good with anything." He glanced at Jude. "As long as it isn't Jude's pancakes."

"I heard that," Jude said wryly.

Grayson grinned at his friend and shrugged.

Jude gave him a soft punch to the shoulder, then stood. "Come on, Brook. Let's grab plates and I'll show you what...Cord enjoys."

"In other words, do the opposite!" Grayson called out after them. He chuckled when Jude shot him a look. Settling back into his chair, a sense of contentment trickled through him. Who'd have thought that in this tiny, podunk town, Grayson Cordova, world-famous actor, would have found not only a woman who made his pulse race, but a group of people who were as warm as the fire burning merrily in the middle of the circle. If he wasn't careful, he could definitely get used to this.

CHAPTER 17

The bell above the shop door rang and Brook looked over to greet her customer, but she stopped. "Cord?"

He smiled at her from under his baseball cap and glasses. "Hello, beautiful."

She smiled back and shook her head, that dang heat climbing her neck as always. "What brings you here?" She noticed that her employees were watching her and she hurried over in order to bring down the volume of their conversation.

Cord chuckled. "Actually, I have a favor to ask."

"Of course, anything," she said.

Cord's smile grew. "You don't even know what it is yet."

Brook tilted her head to the side and gave him a look. "You know I'm happy to help."

"It's a biggie," he warned.

Brook put her hands on her hips. "Are you going to tell me or keep me in suspense?"

"I need a ride to my doctor's appointment."

Brook nodded. "That's not a big deal. I can do that."

"In Portland."

Brook paused. "Whoa. That changes things."

Cord grimaced. "I'm sorry to ask, but Jude got an emergency call and you were the only other person I knew that I was willing to spend so much time in a car with."

She put her hand on her chest. "You sure know how to flatter a girl."

Cord stepped a little closer and took her hand, pressing his lips to the back of it. It was a move that Brook loved. It always sent a tingle of warmth up her arm and straight into her heart. It felt intimate and sweet and made it difficult not to hope for a more long-term future. "Brooklyn Howell, I'd like to request your presence on a trip to Portland for a doctor's appointment. Afterwards, I will treat you to a romantic dinner at The Melting Pot for just the two of us." He winked. "Whaddya say?"

"The Melting Pot?" Brook said, her jaw dropping. "That place is super expensive." She knew very few people who had gone to the swanky restaurant, but those who had still boasted about how good it was.

Cord rubbed the back of his neck, looking sheepish. "You're worth it," he said simply.

She struggled with the idea of him spending so much on her. Who knew what his finances were like after his accident? He wasn't working and the hospital bills had to be astronomical. "I feel funny letting you spend that much on me."

He kissed her hand again. "I promise I'm trying to show off and I'm not putting myself in debt to take you out," he said with a smirk. "Please."

His last word melted her reserve. He was an adult. He would know if he could afford such a luxury or not, so she chose to trust his word. He'd never lied to her before. "Okay," she whispered. "When's your appointment?"

He glanced at his watch. "We need to leave in fifteen minutes to make it there on time."

"What!" she screeched. "Why didn't you tell me?"

He gave her an embarrassed grin. "Sorry. I told you Jude had an emergency. Up until a bit ago, I was planning on him driving me."

"How did you get here?" she asked, trying to look out at the streetside parking.

"Jude dropped me off on his way to deal with his stuff."

Brook's eyebrows were surely going to climb right off her forehead. "You were that sure I would say yes?"

One side of his mouth raised up. "I was hoping."

"It's a good thing I like you," Brook scolded. She gave him a light smack on his chest. "And that my boss is usually a pretty nice person."

He chuckled. "I'll be sure to thank her."

Brook pointed a finger at his nose. "You owe me."

Cord grabbed her finger and gave it a warm squeeze. "I'll look forward to paying you back."

Smiling, Brook went to get things settled so she could leave. Luckily, both of her employees were there, which made leaving easy enough, though she hoped they didn't have a big rush this afternoon. Sometimes the bigger family groups would swarm her shop and create a roadblock.

Ten minutes later, they were in Brook's green sedan, heading toward the highway. "You doing okay?" she asked. Cord was laying as far back as he could in the passenger seat.

He reached over and began to play with her hair. "Just fine," he said.

"You keep that up and I might crash," she teased, loving the feel of his touch.

"Might be worth it if we were in the hospital together."

"Cord!"

He laughed and dropped his hand. "Sorry. You're just so tempting."

"I could say the same about you," she murmured as she merged onto the highway.

"Sounds like we're the perfect pair, then."

Brook's heart did a flip-flop. There was absolutely no way to deny her feelings at this point. She was unequivocally in love with this man. She loved his company. She loved his smirk. She loved when he teased her. She loved his touch and she actually found herself craving his kiss. The majority of her thoughts and dreams were focused around a man with an unruly beard and a slightly gruff personality. He never seemed to imagine that anyone would ever tell him no and was surprised when Brook stood her ground. She enjoyed shocking him and helping bring his ego back to earth.

But even with his faults, Brook wanted to be with him. She wanted to see him heal and go back to the man he was before his accident. She wanted to know all about his past and his future. She simply wanted to be a part of his life forever.

And yet she knew it would never happen.

They had clarified that from the beginning and since she was fairly certain of his line of work, Brook couldn't blame him for his convictions. Being married to a spy or government agent would be a difficult life. She wasn't sure she could handle always wondering where he was or if he was safe. That would test anyone's loyalty and love.

"What are you thinking about?" he asked, pulling Brook from her thoughts.

"Sorry," she said, glancing at him with a smile. "Got lost in my thoughts."

"They didn't look like they were happy thoughts."

She shrugged. "Not all thoughts are. But it was no big deal." She smiled at him again, hoping he would let it go.

It was a moment before he responded, but she relaxed when he said, "If you say so."

A few moments of silence passed between them. "Tell me about your dog."

"What?"

Brook laughed. "You said you had a dog when you were young. Tell me about him."

Cord shook his head while he chuckled. "You never forget a thing, do you?"

Brook shrugged. "I try to pay attention." She would never admit that she had been hurt when he'd spoken about dogs at the bonfire. It just seemed like something that he could easily have told her about his past, since he was so vague about the rest of his life. If he could share it with her friends, surely he could have shared it with her at some point.

"And I love that about you," he said. "But wow, it's been a long time since I've thought about Fido."

It took Brook a moment to get past his first words, but she finally managed to stutter. "Fido? You really had a dog named Fido?"

"What's wrong with that?"

She laughed. "I don't know. It just seems so cliche."

"Hey," he defended. "That's what you get when a seven-year-old names your pet."

"All right, all right," Brook said. "Go ahead. Tell me about Fido."

THE TRIP WENT TOO FAST for Grayson's liking. When Jude had had to fly out for an emergency back down in California, it had opened up an opportunity for him to spend more than just an evening with Brook. After the first few minutes of awkwardness, they had settled into a comfortable routine. He'd answered as many questions about his childhood as he could without giving anything away as to his real identity.

He had bet on the fact that she knew nothing about his years before being on television and it had paid off. Stories from when he was a teenager or later were a risk, but she seemed content to hear about his antics as a youth and everything that went along with being the middle of three kids. Grayson had a dozen stories of stupid stuff he and Carson had done when they were younger that had left her in tears of laughter. It had been perfect.

But now they were at the hospital and Grayson had to figure out how to get her to wait in the car so she wouldn't hear his real name.

"Your check-up is at the hospital?" she asked in confusion.

"Yeah. I'm seeing one of the surgeons for a post-operative check-in."

"Ah, I see." She nodded sagely. "Okay. Well, give me a minute and I'll come help you."

"No." As soon as the word came out, he knew he had spoken too quickly. It had been a panicked reaction, but for Brook it would sound like he was being harsh again.

"You don't want me to come in?" Her words were halting and unsure. The corner of her lips turned down and even an idiot could see she was hurt, exactly as he knew she would be.

Grayson reached over and picked her hand up off the steering wheel, bringing it to his lips. She seemed to enjoy the flirty gesture and he needed everything on his side at the moment. "Sorry. I just think maybe it would be better if you waited here or maybe on the grounds or something," he explained.

"Can I ask why?" she asked. "You asked me to bring you here, and now you want me to wait in the car like a little kid?"

"No, it's not like that," he assured her. *It's exactly like that.* "But I might have to talk to my doctor about...sensitive stuff...in regards to my injury and I'd—" Pulling out an old move, he rubbed the back of his neck, showing rather than telling her he was uncomfortable with the topic.

"Oh... Oh!" she said, her eyes widening. The green was back in her eyes today and Grayson decided it was his favorite. The color was deep and looked like a bottomless pool found in a cave somewhere tropical. "Yeah, I can see how that would be awkward." She laughed uncomfortably. "I guess I'll walk around the grounds, then. Good thing it's a nice day."

"Sorry," he said. "I promise I wouldn't do this if I could—"

"No, no, no...it's fine," Brook hurried to reassure him.

He opened his mouth to keep arguing, but snapped it shut again. He didn't deserve this woman. She was so trusting and sweet, and he was a dirty rotten scoundrel. His feelings for her were real, but who would ever believe that after leading her on like this? Sighing, he nodded. "Thank you," he said softly. Cupping her cheek, he leaned in for a feather light kiss. The guilt churning in his gut kept telling him this might be the last one he ever got, but he fought against the prophecy. He still had a long way to go in his recovery. He'd have Brook to himself for a while yet.

Turning, he opened his door and worked his way upright. Brook came around the car and made sure he was steady. "I'm going to find a bench somewhere," she said as they walked out of the parking garage.

Grayson nodded. "Perfect. I'll text when I'm done."

Brook nodded but didn't speak. A few minutes later, she left him at the side entrance he had been instructed to show up at and waved a cute goodbye. With a grin, she disappeared around the corner.

"Mr. Cordova."

Grayson turned to see a security guard opening the door.

"We're glad you could make it, sir." The man looked around. "Where's your security?"

Grayson shook his head. "I'm under the radar at the moment. A bodyguard attracts too much attention."

The man nodded. "Understood." He backed up, holding the door with his shoulders. "If you'll come on in, sir, we'll get you taken care of."

"Thank you," Grayson said as he shuffled past the man. The man's name tag said "Owen." "Owen?"

"Yes, sir?"

"Have you ever been to The Melting Pot?"

"Yes, sir."

Grayson wanted to roll his eyes at the formality. It was getting old fast. No one had given him any kind of preference in almost two months and he'd forgotten how much he hated being fawned over. "Would you mind calling me in a reservation for this afternoon? And put it under the name Cord."

"Cord?"

Grayson nodded. "Cord."

Owen made an *if you say so* face and nodded. "Consider it done."

"Thank you." Sometimes there were perks to being famous, like a security guard being willing to play secretary.

"Right in here, sir," Owen said, pushing open an exam room door. "If you'll have a seat, Dr. Maughn will be with you momentarily. Meanwhile, I'll be guarding the door to maintain your privacy."

"I appreciate it. Thank you." Grayson shuffled inside and found a low exam table, perfect for him to lie on as he and the doctor talked. He immediately walked over and laid down. It felt good to lay flat. The car ride hadn't been crazy long, but it was enough to have his leg burning again. The sensation was growing stronger the longer he stayed on his feet. He had enough experience at this now that Grayson knew if he didn't lie down, his leg would give out on him and he'd have another episode like he had back at home.

Home.

Grayson shook his head. Seaside Bay wasn't home. California was home. Man, Brook was more than under his skin. She had him thinking things that could never happen. His entire career was in California. He couldn't just up and leave it.

Unless your leg never heals.

"Mr. Cordova?" Dr. Maughn poked his head in the room and smiled. He fully entered and held out a hand. "Good to see you, Grayson."

Grayson shook his head and waited for the doctor to pull his stool out from under the desk.

"So..." Dr. Maughn's eyes were on his tablet. "Tell me how your progress is going."

Grayson sighed and closed his eyes for a second. "To be honest, Dr. Maughn, I don't feel like it's progressing at all."

Dr. Maughn frowned. "Well, that doesn't sound good." He set down his tablet and scooted forward. "Why don't we just take a look, huh?"

CHAPTER 18

"Wow." Brook's jaw was slack as they were led into the restaurant. The entire place was dim, even though it was still bright and sunny outside. It almost felt like they had walked into a dark basement, but the soft music and the cushy booth seating told her otherwise.

Cord chuckled from behind her. His hand went to her lower back. "Come on," he said softly. "Let's get seated."

"Oh, yeah. Sorry." They followed the hostess to a booth in the far back of the restaurant. Lots of eyes followed them as they walked through and Brook felt slightly uncomfortable when a group of women near her age all twittered as they walked by. Brook surreptitiously touched her hair, worried she was a windblown mess.

"Thanks," Cord growled as they arrived at their booth. It was a voice Brook hadn't heard in awhile, and told her he was grumpy with the situation. The hostess eyed him warily, then nodded and darted away.

Brook sat down and scooted in so Cord could sit next to her. "You didn't have to bite her head off," Brook said dryly. "She hardly talked to you."

Cord shrugged and worked his way into the bench.

"Are you going to be okay sitting up for this long?" Brook fussed over him for a moment until he was seated as comfortably as possible. "Maybe we should go somewhere else and get it to go so you can lay down in the car."

"I'll be fine," he said through gritted teeth.

Brook leaned back. Something was obviously wrong. But she wasn't sure if it was because something bad had happened at his appointment, or if he was just in severe pain. He had been tight-lipped ever since coming out of the hospital. She studied him for a moment and noticed that his eyes kept going back to the aisle they had walked in on. "Cord," she said softly, resting a hand on his forearm. "What is it?"

Cord seemed to shake himself, then looked at her with a smile, but it was stiffer than normal. "Nothing. Are you ready to have an amazing dinner?"

"Sure," Brook said softly. If she was braver, she would press him on the issue. But Cord had a tendency to just clam up when she tried to find out more information. She wasn't looking forward to a ride home if he was angry the whole time. This was the first time they'd had more than a few hours together and she didn't want to spend it fighting.

Cord set down the menu and took her hand. "Do you trust me?"

"What?" His question caught her off guard since she'd just been thinking about how much he was keeping hidden from her.

"Do you trust me?" Cord asked again. "To order for us?"

"Oh," Brook laughed softly. "Of course," she said. Her smile was mostly genuine as she continued. "I'm so excited for this." She waved a hand at the built-in stove top on the table. "I've never done anything like this before."

"It's pretty good," Cord said with a nod. "I've done some extensive traveling, so I wouldn't say it's the best thing *ever*, but any time I'm in the area, it's a go-to."

"You've done a lot of traveling?" Brook tried to sound nonchalant as she asked. His words fit right in with what she suspected of his past. If only she could get him to confirm her thoughts! It would certainly be nice not to have to just guess, but to have actual knowledge about the man she was sort of dating. By normal standards, Brook would have called him her boyfriend. But since they both knew this was short-term, she hesitated to put any kind of a label on it. He must have felt the same way since he avoided talking about their relationship at every turn.

Cord grunted a noncommittal sound. A clear sign that he didn't want to talk about it.

"Cord." Brook pulled away from his touch and folded her hands in her lap. "I want you to be real with me."

His eyebrows disappeared under his hat. In the dark light of the restaurant, she could barely see his eyes at all since it was pulled so low on his forehead. At least he had taken his glasses off. His eyes might not be quite as striking as Grayson Cordova's blue ones, but the light gray had its own appeal.

"What do you mean?" he asked, his shoulders stiff.

"I mean with what happened today." She leaned in, resting her forearms on the table. "Did you get bad news from the doctor?" she whispered.

He dropped her gaze and shrugged. "It was the same old stuff I always get," he said, though his tone let her hear his disappointment. "I just need to keep doing what I'm doing and hope my body heals."

"I'm sure that's frustrating," Brook said compassionately. She couldn't imagine having her life upended so heavily.

"I'll live," he said, still keeping his eyes on the table.

"Cord, look at me," Brook urged. When he finally raised his head, she cupped his cheek as best she could against his beard. "I'm sorry things aren't going the way you want. Was there no good news at all?"

He pressed his hand to the outside of hers, holding it to his face. "Of course," he said lightly. "I get to spend more time in Seaside Bay."

"Are you two ready to order?"

Both of them jerked a little when their waiter asked the question. Brook pulled back her hand and cleared her throat. She had been so caught up in Cord's pain that she hadn't heard the man approach. "I think we are," she said, plastering a wide smile on her face. Then she looked to Cord, waiting for him to order.

Cord kept his head down, not even looking at the waiter while putting in his order.

Brook bit her tongue until the waiter was gone before leaning in toward Cord. "You could have at least looked at him. I promise he wasn't scary-looking."

Cord chuckled and grabbed her hand once more. "Are you sure about that? I got a definite vibe from the guy."

Brook rolled her eyes. "Cord. You can't go around being rude all the time. People are going to hate you."

"Why would I care?"

She huffed. "Because you aren't someone people should hate." Brook shook her head in exasperation. "I've seen you with Jude. I know you're capable of being a good friend. And you've shared a little with me about your family, so I know you've been taught how to get along with others." She grinned. "Speaking politely and looking people in the eye is called common courtesy. You should try it sometime." Her heart began to pound as Cord brought her knuckles to his lips. Any scolding she had left died on her lips.

A clicking sound caught her attention and Brook looked over to see a woman darting away from them, cell phone in hand.

Cord must have noticed too, but his reaction was much more dramatic than Brook's. A curse slipped from his mouth that had Brook gaping. "That was not what I was talking about," she said.

"Come on." Cord started to get out of the booth, fumbling with his cane.

"What? Why?" Brook scrambled after him. "Does this have to do with that woman?"

"Just come on," Cord snapped.

Brook felt like she had been slapped. She pressed her lips together and kept her words to herself. No matter how much she loved

Cord, he was going too far at the moment. Maybe it was time they got home and she got a little distance from him.

On their way out, she flagged down their waiter and canceled their meal. Just because Cord was being rude didn't mean Brook had to be. The walk to the car was silent and for the first time, Brook had no intention of being the one to break it.

GRAYSON'S CAREFULLY built world was crumbling under his feet. He should never have taken Brook to Portland. He knew it had been a risk, but he'd been managing in Seaside Bay well enough that he'd figured a bigger city would be a breeze. He'd never been more wrong.

Brook was silent as she drove, and for the moment that suited Grayson just fine, though he knew it wasn't a good sign. He'd been rude when he'd rushed her out of the restaurant and he would need to apologize, but first he had to do damage control.

He fired a text off to Jude, Richard, and Carson, warning them that a woman had taken his picture and it would probably show up on social media somewhere. After cursing him out, Richard said he would contact the Mendelssohn Agency, who did PR for Grayson. Carson and Jude promised to be on the lookout and Jude said he'd be back late that night.

Knowing there was nothing else he could do at the moment, Grayson let himself relax back into the seat. His stomach growled loudly, reminding him how he'd drug Brook out of the restaurant. He needed to say something, but he wasn't sure how to start the conversation. Especially without telling her the truth. He was so tired of lying to her, but at this point, he didn't know how to get out of it. If she ever found out what was really going on, he knew Brook was going to be heartbroken...and so was he.

"I'm sorry." Brook didn't answer him right away, though she glanced in his direction. The silence sat heavy between them, but Grayson was determined to wait her out. He was trying to offer an olive branch, but he couldn't force her to respond. And truthfully, he wouldn't blame her. He didn't deserve to be forgiven, no matter how much he was falling for her.

"It's fine," she finally said, but her voice was small.

"No..." he pressed. "It's not." He cleared his throat. "But I'm asking for forgiveness anyway." He deflated into the seat. "I was harsh and rude," he admitted. "And I shouldn't have bullied you around the way I did."

"Yeah...you seem awfully used to having your way," Brook grumbled.

The situation was far from funny, but Grayson had a hard time not laughing at her comment. If only she knew how far people were willing to go to please him. He loved the fact that she wasn't one of them. "It's true," he continued. "I'm used to being in charge and getting my way, but that's no excuse for treating you badly."

"Or the waiter and hostess," Brook said, giving him a significant look.

"Or the waiter or hostess," he drawled. "I wasn't prepared to be stared at and treated like a freak, so I'm sorry that I didn't handle it well."

Brook visibly softened at his words. "I don't think anyone treated you like a freak..." She frowned and pursed her lips. "Although it's weird that that woman took your picture." She snorted. "You'd think she'd never seen a guy walk with a cane before."

Grayson turned to look out the window. That dang conscience was beating his head with a hammer right now. He didn't know how much longer he could keep this up.

If you tell her the truth, you're going to lose her.

That thought was enough to have him steeling his resolve. He wasn't ready to lose Brook. She was the best thing to happen to him ever, and the idea of being without her hurt worse than his injury.

"It doesn't matter," he murmured.

Brook reached over and patted his thigh. "Just forget about it," she soothed. "That lady was also being rude and had no right to do that, but it's no reflection on you." She smiled brilliantly at him. "I like you just the way you are and I can name quite a few others who feel the same."

Grayson huffed a laugh and took her hand, enjoying the delicate, feminine feel of it in his own large palm. He would dream about touches just like this when he eventually went back to California. His stomach growled again and Brook laughed.

"Would you like to grab something to eat on the way?" She looked in her rearview mirror. "It's not The Melting Pot, but I'm sure we could find some fast food somewhere."

"That'd be great, thanks." He held back from saying anything else. He desperately wanted to promise her he'd take her to the restaurant another time. She'd been so excited and in awe of the atmosphere and one moment had ruined it all. But he had no idea if the chance would ever come again. Dragging her away wouldn't be nearly as bad as making a promise he couldn't keep. He settled for something a little more vague. "We'll have to plan another date soon."

Brook looked at him again with a soft smile. "I'd like that."

The tone of adoration in her voice had Grayson's heart beating against his chest. It would be the perfect moment for a sweet kiss if he wasn't lying back like an idiot. He cursed his situation once more. One that was ruining his life. Yes, coming to Seaside Bay had brought him Brook, but their relationship was based on a lie and he wanted it to be real. He also wanted to present himself as whole, instead of always being needy around her.

"There's an exit a couple miles up the highway. I'm sure we can find something there."

Grayson smiled, but it was a struggle. "Perfect. Thank you." He meant it for far more than just helping him get dinner, but she didn't know that. And if they were able to curb the situation with the photo, she would never know.

The thought both depressed and relieved him at the same time.

CHAPTER 19

Brook was feeling better by the time they rolled into Seaside Bay. They had talked and apologized and worked things out, and it felt much better than sitting around, stewing in anger. She pulled into his driveway with a sense of relief. The day had been an emotional roller coaster, and as much as she enjoyed Cord's company, it was nice that it was almost over. A hot bath and a good book sounded like heaven at the moment.

The only thing that would be better would be an evening of Cord's kisses, but that might be asking too much after today.

"Here we are," she sang, putting the car in park. Frowning, she looked around the driveway. "It looks like Jude is still gone."

"Yeah. He said he'd be back in the middle of the night." Grayson opened his door and began to pull himself upright.

"Hold on, I'm coming." Brook rushed around and got her shoulder under his arm.

"You do realize that you're way too small to help me, right?" Cord gave her a mischievous grin.

She scowled at him. "I'm stronger than I look. Who do you think regularly hefts the boxes of inventory in the back of the shop?"

"One of your employees?"

She gave him a look. "Just because I hire a stock boy doesn't mean I don't help."

He chuckled. "Well, then come on, Wonder Woman, and walk me inside." He swung his arm around her shoulders and they started for the front door.

Cord punched in a code and opened the door before pausing. "Would you like to come in?" he asked. His tone had softened.

Brook loved it when he spoke like that. It made her legs feel like jelly and her heart did a little dance in her chest. She smiled at him. "As tempting as it sounds, it's getting late and I probably shouldn't tempt fate."

He reached out and cupped the back of her neck. "Then maybe I should make the next few moments count, huh?"

"I always knew you were smart," she whispered right before his lips met hers. Oooh...she hadn't had a good Cord kiss in a few days. It seemed to reach into every corner of her, shedding light and happiness and love everywhere it went. She stepped into him and carefully wrapped her arms around his neck. She wanted closer. She wanted more. She wanted—

A series of clicks came from behind them. The sound reminded Brook of the woman in the restaurant and she quickly stepped away from Cord, gasping as light began to penetrate the darkness.

"Mr. Cordova!"

"Grayson!"

"What are you doing in Seaside Bay?"

The shouts grew louder and the flashes completely blinded Brook. She couldn't wrap her mind around what they were saying. Why were they calling for Grayson Cordova? She put a hand over her eyes and tried to open her mouth to respond, but no words came out. The shouts and questions were coming much too quickly for her to answer any of them.

She barely noticed Cord moving behind her before she was yanked backward into the house. She stumbled, catching herself on the wall of the foyer as Cord slammed the door shut and turned off the porch lights.

"What's going on?" she asked breathlessly. Her heart was racing and it wasn't all from Cord's kiss.

"We have to get out of here," Cord growled.

"We have to…" She looked at him like he was crazy. "Are you kidding me? Where would we go? This town is tiny and that mob out there thinks you're Grayson Cordova." Brook scoffed and shook her head. "I mean, you remind me of him, sure, but I'm not sure why they're here. Grayson is down in California recovering from his…" She trailed off as pieces of a weird puzzle began to slip into place in her mind.

Cord wasn't paying any attention to her as he shuffled through the house to the back doors. Brook didn't speak as she trailed him. Her mind was running at a hundred miles an hour and she wasn't sure how to stop it. He couldn't be…could he? No…Cord wouldn't have lied to her about something like that. He'd been purposefully vague, sure, but outright lying? About something as big as being a celebrity? Maybe as a spy, he'd impersonated Grayson once?

She grimaced. That didn't make any sense either. None of it did. The media wouldn't be here if they didn't think Grayson was around, and Cord wouldn't have lied about who he was.

"This way," Cord hissed, breaking into her thoughts.

"I don't understand why we're running," she whispered back. "Why not just stay in the house?"

"Because they'll eventually figure out a way in."

"What!" she screeched.

"SHHH! Keep your voice down," Cord pleaded.

"You can't tell me that you really think those people will break into the house?"

Cord sighed and pinched the bridge of his nose. "They won't necessarily break in, but they'll sure find a way to take pictures even if they aren't physically in the building."

"But *why* are they taking pictures of you?"

Cord turned away, not answering her question, and Brook found herself growing impatient. She was usually a pretty easy-going person. She didn't like confrontation and she didn't like arguing, but right now she was starting to feel pretty steamed.

"If we hurry, we can sneak out the back before they realize we're gone."

Brook pinched her lips together, refusing to answer.

Cord glanced over his shoulder and the look on his face said he knew he was in trouble. "Just give me a few minutes," he said, regret thick in his tone. "And I'll tell you everything."

She still didn't respond. There was nothing to say. Unless she wanted to brave the circus out front, she was stuck with Cord, or whoever the heck he was, until they escaped.

Slowly, Cord pulled the sliding glass door open. "We cannot be this lucky," he said in an almost inaudible tone. He stepped onto the deck, looking in every direction, even above his head, which Brook thought was insane. "Come on," he whispered, waving his non-cane hand at her.

Brook stepped behind him, closing the glass. Slowly, they shuffled across the deck and she helped Cord down the steps toward the sand. There really was no cover out here, so she wondered just where he was going. All it would take was for one person to come around the corner of the house and they'd be spotted.

Luckily, the moon was almost nonexistent, making it hard to see anything. Brook was tempted to grab her phone out to have a flashlight, but Cord would probably shout at her if she did.

"Are you going to tell me what's going on now?" she hissed at him.

"We need to get into town first," Cord shot over his shoulder. He paused. "Do you think you could call Ken? He was the police officer, right?"

"You want me to report that people are trespassing?"

He shook his head. "No. I want them to take us in for safe keeping."

"What in the—"

"There they are!"

Another set of curse words came bubbling out of Cord's lips. "Hurry."

Brook had to bite her tongue. She didn't think it was her that was slowing them down. Despite her anger, however, she didn't want Cord to get caught up in whatever media storm was about to descend. Setting aside her own feelings, she wrapped an arm around his waist and did her best to speed him up without hurting his leg.

"There's a field up ahead," Cord panted. "If we can lay down in the grass, we might be able to hide from them."

Brook glanced over her shoulder. She could barely see the outlines of the crowd, but from the noise, it was clear that they were hot on their trail. "We need to split up," she said with sudden clarity. Cord would never make it. He couldn't walk fast enough and even with her help, she knew the field was several more minutes down the beach.

"Not a good idea," Cord said tightly. "I don't want them anywhere near you."

"It's our only chance," Brook snapped. She strained her eyes in the dark. "There." She steered them to the left where there was a sandy outcropping. Without warning, she pushed Cord, causing him to stumble and land behind it. "Stay put," she commanded.

"Don't you dare," Cord growled, trying to get up.

"It's our only chance," she repeated. Glancing back, she could see a few silhouettes that were close. "I'll be back for you." Without waiting for his response, she hurried away, breaking into a light jog. Just enough to keep her ahead of the media, but not so fast that they would figure out Cord wasn't with her anymore.

Please let this work, she prayed. She pictured the beach in her mind and hoped her memory was enough to help her navigate without any light. She had a distinct advantage over the photographers, and right now she needed every bit of it.

GRAYSON WAS LIVID. He had been sitting in this sandy cove for close to an hour, left behind by Brook as she played decoy for his own stupidity. How he thought he could ever out-navigate the hungry paparazzi, he didn't know. Maybe his brain hadn't been working right after kissing Brook. But whatever the reason, she was now in possible danger, all because he had screwed up. If the sharks had managed to corner her, she wouldn't have a clue as to how to defend herself or what her rights were when it came to getting rid of them.

For the thousandth time, he considered trying to go after her, but what kind of help was he? He could barely walk. Even if he could find her, how could he protect her? Growling under his breath, he hit the sand. It was a good thing this area was soft, or he would have been hurting something fierce when Brook pushed him down. He'd even been able to semi lay down in order to keep his leg from becoming useless. It meant that his clothes were filled with sand and he'd probably have to shower to get rid of it all, but that was a small price to pay for his sins.

And sins they were. The cold recognition in Brook's eyes when she realized there was something going on, bigger than she could have ever imagined, haunted him. She would never forgive him. He was absolutely certain of that. And yet with each pulse of his heart, he was realizing a different devastating truth.

Grayson Cordova had fallen in love.

His feelings for Brook had been more sincere and deep than he'd ever had before, but it wasn't until now, when he was completely helpless and his only thought was for her protection, that he realized it had turned into love.

He would give anything, even the recovery of his leg, if it meant he could keep her safe. Unfortunately, it was his leg that was keeping him from protecting her. He buried his face in his hands, regret and shame pouring through him like hot lava. Everything in him ached and hurt and it had nothing to do with a damaged nerve.

"Please be okay," he muttered. "Pleeeease be okay."

"Cord?"

He snapped his head up. The voice was a man's, but the fact that it was his fake name and not his real one, gave him hope. He waited to see if they would speak again, slightly worried about offering up his location so easily.

"Cord? Are you around here? It's Ken, Brook's friend."

Grayson let out the breath he'd been holding. "Over here," he called. He sat up and waved an arm in the air, even though it was probably too dark for Ken to see.

"He's over here!" Ken's voice called out to someone else.

Grayson could hear footsteps coming his way and eventually a flashlight hit him in the face. He covered his eyes.

"Sorry," Ken said, tucking the light lower. "You all right?"

Grayson nodded. "I'm fine, but is Brook?"

Ken hesitated, then answered. "Yeah. She's fine." He stepped up to Grayson's side. "Let's get you out of here, huh?"

Another body came to Grayson's other side and began helping. Grayson squinted as he was raised to his feet and realized that Bennett was helping as well. "Thank you," he muttered, feeling completely humiliated at needing so much assistance. "But where's Brook?"

"She's at the station," Ken said.

"Was she hurt?"

"Not physically."

The words were a physical blow. He was quiet as they climbed the hill and began walking toward the parking lot. "Should I be worried you two are going to take me somewhere and leave me to rot?"

Bennett chuckled, but it was Ken who answered. "Not yet," he said. "I'm still trying to piece together exactly what's going on, and I figure I need you in order to do that."

"And after?" Grayson ventured.

"After?" Ken snorted. "I might do my best to make sure you never see this town again."

"I wouldn't blame you," Grayson muttered. They got to Ken's patrol car and the men helped him lie down in the back seat.

"Don't worry," Bennett said with a grin. "Ken's bark is worse than his bite." The easy-going man sobered. "But Brook is like family and you need to know where our loyalties lie."

Grayson nodded. "Just where they should."

Bennett gave him a nod and shut the door, climbing into the front with Ken. The ride to the station was only a few minutes long and Grayson was grateful he didn't see any large groups of photographers hanging out on any sidewalks.

Getting inside the station was a breeze and it was only then that Grayson realized that Ken wasn't in his uniform. Brook must have had to pull him from his house. "Thank you for coming to get me," Grayson said. "It looks like you were probably at home."

Ken shrugged. "It's my job," he said, leading Grayson toward the back where the offices were. He ushered Grayson inside. "I've got a couch to the right if you want to lie down."

"I'd rather stand for a while if it's all the same to you," Grayson responded. He'd been lying most of the day and needed to use his muscles a little.

"Suit yourself." Ken walked around the desk and sat down, with Bennett taking one of the chairs.

Grayson looked around. "Where's Brook?" He stepped forward. "You said she was here."

Ken raised an unimpressed eyebrow. "Brook is here. Just not in this office. Now...why don't you tell me the whole story."

"Not without Brook."

Ken leaned back and folded his arms over his chest. "I don't think it's a good idea to have her in the same room as you."

It was another gut punch, but Grayson knew he deserved every bit of it. He didn't want to hurt her more than he already had, but he also wasn't going to break his word. "I promised her an explanation." He narrowed his gaze. "Now, I can give that to her while we talk and you and Bennett are here to run interference, or I can find a way to pin her down by herself. Which would you prefer?"

Ken glared, but nodded at Bennett. "Go get her, will ya?"

Bennett gave his friend a salute and headed back out the door.

The two men left continued to try and dominate the other with their eyes until Bennett returned. "Got her, boss." He led Brook to a couch and they sat down together, leaving Grayson steaming, but impotent.

Ken grumbled. "I'm not your boss."

Bennett's laughter felt completely out of place in the thick tension of the room. "You order me around like you are."

Grayson heard little of what was being said. He was too busy drinking in the sight of a dirty and disheveled Brook. She looked exhausted and ready to collapse, but her chin was high and her jaw set. Her strength was just another part of her that he loved.

"Are you okay?" he asked, hoping she would at least look at him. He was rewarded with a split-second glance.

"Fine, thank you," she said primly. Her eyes quickly went back to Ken.

Sighing, Grayson walked to the couch. "Maybe I will lie down."

CHAPTER 20

Brook sunk into Benny's side as she watched Cord or Grayson, or whoever he was, shuffle to the other side of the room. He looked like he was hurting more than usual and was hunched over his cane like an old man. It hurt Brook's heart to watch. Almost every part of her wanted to jump to her feet and go help, but she held herself back.

She might have been willing to help them escape the paparazzi, but now they were safe and everything was hitting home. He'd lied. He'd played on her sympathies. He'd toyed with her emotions and made her fall in love, knowing that he wasn't who he said he was.

How many other things did he lie about?

Without her permission, her mind went through everything he'd ever said. All the times he'd mentioned how beautiful she was. When he'd said he needed her help or said how much he liked her. All those sweet words now tasted rotten.

Nausea churned in her stomach and Brook dropped her stare. She couldn't look at him. He had betrayed her in every sense of the word and she felt like a fool. How many red flags had she ignored? The slips of tongue, his egotistical view on things, the fact that few people told him no. Even the fact that he was renting one of the largest mansions on the beach and had a personal physical therapist and cook. How many people could afford that? And his eyes. Those felt like the biggest sign of all and one which she should have caught right off the bat.

True, his eyes weren't quite the same color as she saw in the movies, but still, how many men had such dark features and such light eyes? *Contacts.* The lie made her want to snort in derision. He'd been in such a panic when she saw his eyes and it was no wonder. They were his signature feature. But like a dope, she'd believed him. She'd thrown out her own intuition and assured herself that he was honest, just like she assumed most people were. Brook was of the opinion to think well of everyone until they gave her a reason not to.

He had definitely given her a reason not to.

"Where do you want me to start?" Grayson said softly from his place on the couch. He was slouched backwards, but not quite laying down.

Brook dropped her eyes again when his met hers. He didn't need to see how much he'd hurt her. It would only make her look more pathetic than she already did.

"How about the beginning?" Ken snapped. The muscles in his arms were tight and he looked ready to throttle Grayson if given the chance. Brook knew that he was protective of their entire friend group, so this situation had become personal for the police captain.

"Yeah..." Grayson pushed a hand through his hair. "I guess that's the best place." He sighed heavily and glanced at his watch as if he were waiting for something. "Jude is due back in town in another hour," Grayson said. "He'll be wondering where I'm at and probably freaking out about all the media."

Ken pursed his lip, but nodded. "I'll send someone to watch for him at the house."

"Thank you." Grayson sounded sincere, but Brook wasn't willing to buy it. He'd sounded sincere the entire time they'd been together as well. He was an actor after all. At least, she thought he was. He hadn't actually confirmed anything yet.

"My name is Grayson Cordova." He paused and looked uncertainly at Brook.

Her cheeks were hot enough to melt a piece of chocolate on. And she could absolutely use a piece of Caro's chocolate right now. Maybe it would help her cope with the humiliating situation.

"I'm from California. I got hurt on the set of my latest movie." He waved at his leg. "In medical terms, I tore the annular tissue of my L5-S1 disk."

"And in layman terms?" Ken said wryly.

Grayson nodded. "In layman terms, it means I have a bulged disk in my back, which is putting pressure on a nerve that runs down my leg. It creates pain, weakness, and general instability of the leg. Sometimes it aches or burns, sometimes the whole leg gives out." He glanced at Brook again. "It's not something I can control. The doctors have all said I simply have to wait it out."

Benny whistled low under his breath. His hand was rubbing up and down Brook's arm in a soothing motion. "It's got to be hard to be laid up like that."

Grayson nodded. "It hasn't been pleasant..." His eyes once again landed on Brook's. "For the most part," he finished softly.

"Don't look at her," Ken growled. When Grayson jerked, Ken continued. "I think you've done enough, don't you?"

Grayson blanched, but nodded. He turned his head to the side and kept his eyes on the carpet. "I was having a hard time recuperating at home with the media hounding me day and night, so we came up with the idea of escaping somewhere quiet where the paparazzi wouldn't ever think to look for me."

Ken snorted and leaned back in his seat, his arms folded over his chest. "Looks like that worked out well."

Grayson shook his head. "Everything was fine at first. I kept to myself, but had access to the peacefulness of the beach and was able to do exercises in my own home. Plus, my doctor was only a couple of hours away." He deflated a little. "Until Brook came along."

Brook stiffened, but Benny just sped up his rubbing. A silent signal to stay still. Despite wanting a good long cry, Brook obeyed.

"Brook not only saved me from a difficult situation in town, she broke down all the barriers I'd set up and worked her way into my life...and my heart."

A choked sob broke through. She wanted to believe him. Oh, how she wanted to believe him. *HE LIED!* her inner voice screamed. How could she believe anything he said ever again?

"Step carefully," Ken growled.

Grayson scowled. "You asked for the story," he snapped. "I'm telling it."

Ken's jaw ticked, but he didn't speak again.

Grayson shoved a finger in Brook's direction. "It can't be told without talking about Brook because everything...*everything*...comes back to her."

Ken waited a moment before nodding curtly and Grayson continued.

"She started spending time with Jude and me. I was sure she was going to figure out who I was." Grayson's gaze softened as it came back to her.

It didn't matter how many times Brook looked away, she kept coming back to watch him. It was like watching a train wreck in slow motion. Every word and action made her sick to her stomach, but she couldn't stay away. She needed to see it all.

"But she's so trusting and sweet that I was able to keep hiding who I was."

The tears had been held at bay fairly well up until this point. Brook's vision grew blurry as they came faster than she could stop them. Benny squeezed her tighter when they began streaming down her cheeks unheeded.

Grayson's face fell and he looked like he was about to get up, but when Ken cleared his throat, Grayson fell backward again.

"Hang in there," Benny whispered in her ear. "He needs to see how this affected you."

Brook nodded and took in a shuddering breath. *Let them fall,* she told herself. *Let him see what he did. Maybe it'll teach him that playing with people's emotions isn't quite as fun as he thinks it is.*

GRAYSON WAS GOING TO die. Right now. Brook's face was covered in tear tracks, her breathing was ragged, and another man had his arm around her. Each tear brought another stabbing pain to his chest and Grayson knew that at any moment, it was going to be too much. The emotional pain he was feeling right now made his back and leg pain seem like a walk in the park.

He clenched his fists uselessly. Even if he got up, Bennett and Ken wouldn't let him get close to Brook without laying him out first. Although, now that he thought about it, a black eye might be worth it if he could get closer.

"Keep going," Ken demanded.

Grayson pinched his lips together. He could appreciate that the man was doing his job and protecting a friend, but Grayson was starting to have a hard time being treated like a criminal. He hadn't meant for this to happen. He had never wanted to hurt Brook and had only lied in order to keep himself and others safe. Today's episode was a clear argument in favor of people not knowing where he was.

"This morning Jude had to fly back to California for an emergency. I had a doctor's appointment in Portland and asked Brook to drive me up." He clenched and unclenched his fists. "I wanted to take Brook out for a special dinner, but that proved to be a mistake." He shook his head. "Another patron took my picture, although between my hat, glasses, and the darkness of the restaurant, I'm not sure how anyone could tell it was me."

Ken scoffed. "I've seen the picture and I can't even tell it's you. The whole thing is a grainy mess because of the lighting, but it was obviously enough to have the media hoping for a shot."

Grayson groaned. "They never stop." He buried his face in his hands. "This is the exact reason I hid who I was when I came." Dropping his hands, he looked up, begging Brook with his eyes to understand. "I was trying to protect everyone. Once these paparazzi get going, they attack until there's nothing left. There's nothing they wouldn't do for the next big hit. While I was gone, they've been pulling all sorts of stunts to get past the security I have at my home down in L.A. Disguises, climbing fences or trees, long distance lenses, they won't let up and have absolutely no respect for privacy or authority." *Please understand,* he thought, willing the words to Brook. Surely she could understand why he kept his identity a secret. She had to.

Benny snorted. "You were trying to protect yourself."

"Yes," Grayson said through gritted teeth. "I was. But just like you, I have a right to be left alone. I was hurt," he continued. "So much so, we have no idea if I'll ever be able to go back to my career. My whole world had been turned upside down, but the media was hounding at me so much that I couldn't take a breath without it being reported." Despite the pain, Grayson leaned forward earnestly, meeting Bennett's fierce gaze. "Do you have any idea what that's like?" Grayson ground out. "Have you ever had your security alarm go off a dozen times a night because someone is sneaking across your property? Have you ever not been able to eat without someone taking a picture and reporting exactly how you chewed? Have you ever been a complete mess emotionally and physically, and yet no one cares? When all they want is to make money off your misery and spend time gossiping and betting about whether or not you'll ever be worth working again?"

The room was silent after his little rant and Grayson knew he had probably gone too far, but he needed them to understand. His deceit had not been personal. It was self preservation, and despite how much he had grown to love Brook, he wouldn't change what he had done. For the first time ever, someone liked him for him, not because of his name. His warts and flaws had been on full display during their time together and yet she had stuck around. She had kissed him. She had built him up and made him feel like he was worth something even though to the world, right now he had never been worth less.

"I have," Grayson said hoarsely. "So you're right. I was protecting myself. But by protecting myself, I was also protecting this entire town. No one would have been safe. While a few people would have enjoyed their two minutes of fame, most of you would not. The paparazzi aren't just annoying, they're a disease, like cancer, and they leave a place desolate in their wake."

A whimper came from Brook and Grayson's entire body reacted. She turned her head into Bennett's chest and began to cry in earnest. Grayson could stand it no longer. He shoved himself to his feet and nearly fell flat on his face. Curses rang through his head as he stumbled to his knees and grabbed for his cane. His leg was burning from his movements and was refusing to hold his weight, but he didn't care.

Using the cane, Grayson climbed to his feet. With every shuffling step, fire shot down his body, but Brook's despair was more important. He didn't deserve her, but she also didn't deserve to hurt so much. He hadn't wanted to hurt her. He loved her. If nothing else, he needed to help her know that he took the blame for everything. This was all on his shoulders.

He finally arrived at the couch, somehow free of any thrown punches, and allowed himself to fall to his knees again. Only this time, he did it at Brook's feet.

He dropped his cane and put his hands on her knees. "Brook," he breathed, ignoring the fact that she was in the arms of another man. "Brook, sweetheart, please give me a chance to explain."

"I think you've already done that."

The deep voice came from behind Grayson and he knew Captain Wamsley had stepped away from his desk, but Grayson ignored the jab. "I never meant to hurt you." His face fell when she still didn't look at him. "I..." He needed to tell her his feelings. He needed to share everything inside of him, but right now they had an audience. She deserved a better setting than a police station to hear that he'd fallen for her. Clearing his throat, Grayson dared to look back at the captain. "Can we have a few minutes? Please?" The last word was hard to say. In fact, if Brook hadn't worked her magic on him during these last couple months, he probably wouldn't have done so, but she'd helped bring his ego back down to earth and he would be forever grateful for it.

"I don't think that's a good idea." Ken's voice had softened and the empathy in his eyes said he understood, but he was standing his ground.

"I need to speak to her," Grayson snapped.

"And she needs support," Ken argued.

"She needs to hear the truth."

Ken's eyes narrowed. "What else haven't you told me?"

Grayson shook his head. "What I have left to say is for Brook's ears alone."

The darkening of Ken's face said he didn't like that answer. "You still haven't explained what happened when you got back to Seaside Bay."

Grayson pinched his lips together. Slowly, he looked back at Brook, gave her knee a reassuring squeeze, then climbed to his feet, only stumbling slightly as he steadied himself. "They were waiting in the dark at the house. I managed to pull Brook inside and we escaped around the back before they figured it out. The house had beach access and we got a head start before they spotted us." His hand was shaking as he pushed it through his hair. "I, obviously, am completely useless right now when it comes to running away, so Brook found me a hiding spot, then led the media away until she got to you. You know what happened after that." He looked back at her. Her tears had stopped, but her face was splotchy and her eyes were filled with pain. Even now, he found himself attracted to her. She was everything he never knew he wanted.

They stared at each other for a moment and the usual pull tugged at him. He sent a rare prayer heavenward that she could feel it too. Their natural chemistry was probably the only thing he had going for him at the moment.

"I'll talk to him."

Grayson blinked in surprise, but it was Ken who answered.

"What?" he roared.

Brook sat upright from Bennett's shoulder and put her chin in the air. "I'll talk to him," she said again. Her eyes never left his and he could see her slowly pulling herself away. She wanted closure. Her plan was to cut the ties between them.

His own resolve began to form. She might think they would be happy without each other, but Grayson had been through too many relationships. He knew better. This was it. The one thing people always spoke of with awe and dreaming in their voices.

True love.

And he had no intention of letting her throw it away because he was an idiot. His physical capabilities were limited right now, but he still had resources. Lots of them. And he would use every single one at his disposal to convince her he was worth keeping around.

CHAPTER 21

Ken and Benny weren't very happy with Brook's decision, but she knew, for herself, she needed the chance to set everything straight. There was no way she'd be able to move on otherwise.

"We'll be right outside," Benny whispered in her ear.

She stood as he got up from the couch, not wanting to be at a disadvantage when she was speaking to Grayson. Brook nodded and gave Benny a small smile, hoping he knew without her saying anything how much she appreciated his help. For someone who had grown up without any siblings, it was amazing to feel like she had the protective brothers her friends had always bragged about.

It took a few moments for the men to leave, and the silence left behind was deafening.

Brook tore her eyes from the door and turned back to C-Grayson. She closed her eyes and shook her head for a second. It was going to take a bit to get her mind wrapped around his real identity.

"I'm sorry."

Her eyes snapped open.

Grayson looked like a defeated man, and that was the last thing Brook needed—for her heart to completely leave her own possession and jump to his. Too bad he would never know it. "I'm sorry I lied to you."

Brook gave him a jerky nod. "Thank you for the apology. It's fine," she said automatically, shifting to move around the room a little. It was feeling slightly claustrophobic.

"No," Grayson said sharply. "It's not."

Brook backed up a step. "Excuse me?"

"It's not okay," he said, stepping toward her. "It'll never be *okay*. While I'm hoping with everything in me that you'll eventually forgive me, it'll never be okay that I lied."

Those dang tears were back. Brook blinked rapidly, trying to push her overwrought emotions into submission, but it was hard. She felt as if she'd been through a roller coaster tonight. One moment she'd been thinking they could make this work long term and the next, she'd found out the man she was in love with wasn't that man at all. "How much of it was a lie?" She snapped her mouth shut. She hadn't meant to ask that. It only brought out her gullibility. And besides, it didn't really matter how much of it was a lie. It wasnt like Grayson Cordova was going to stick around Seaside Bay. The odds of him sticking around were even less than they'd been when she'd thought he was a spy.

A completely inappropriate laugh slipped from between her lips. She pressed her fingers against her mouth. "Sorry," she said, another giggle coming out. She was out of control. She had snapped and now Brook couldn't hold back the tide. "Want to know something funny?" she asked, still laughing between words. She didn't give Grayson a chance to answer. "I thought you were some kind of spy."

The shocked look on his face caused her laughter to slowly drain into more tears. "You were so vague about who you were. I wasn't dumb..." She trailed off, realizing she had been more than dumb. "I realized that you weren't telling me everything," she corrected. "You wouldn't tell me where you were from or what you did for a living. You told me you wore contacts and you were always hiding your identity." Brook snorted and shook her head, turning away and walking a few steps. Her body was growing restless and she needed to move or she was going to do something drastic, and wasn't completely sure she would regret it. "Not to mention your little speech about not being able to have a long-term relationship." She swallowed hard, her mouth suddenly dry. How she could have pushed aside so many red flags, she didn't know. No, that was a lie. She'd used the excuse of love to push it aside. Love had blinded her to everything.

"The only reason I could think of for your behavior was that you were like in the CIA or FBI and went undercover for them." Her smile probably looked as terrible as it felt. "Can you imagine?" She shook her head. "How stupid is that?"

Grayson's jaw was set as he stepped closer to her. "You're not stupid," he ground out.

Brook hurried away from him. She couldn't think straight when he was so close. "Oh, no?" she asked sarcastically. "I went and fell head over heels in love with a man that doesn't exist." The words had started light, but they turned into a sneer by the end. The more she thought about it, the angrier she became. It was a split as to who she was angry at the most, herself or Grayson or even Jude. Each of them had a hand in the black hole that now resided in her chest.

"He does exist," Grayson begged. He dared to step closer again and Brook ended up backing up against the wall. "I'm still that man."

She shook her head, hoping he would back off just as much as she hoped he would come closer. "You. Lied." The words were quiet, but full of venom.

"I did," Grayson confirmed, stepping close enough to cage her against the wall. "I told you why."

Brook dropped her chin to her chest. "And I get it," she whispered, her righteous anger deflating. "I do. But that doesn't make it hurt any less." She managed to look up. "I trusted you. I did everything I could to help you. And it was all a farce."

"No," he breathed. He put out his empty hand and it landed on the wall next to her head. "It wasn't a farce," he whispered, leaning in close until their noses were nearly touching. "It was real, Brook. *RE-AL.*" He sighed and rested his forehead against hers.

The touch was agonizing and wonderful. She pressed her palms against the wall to keep from resting them on his chest.

"You brought out the real me," he continued. "I've lived a lie my whole life. I've played to the media, put on smiles for the cameras, pretended to be happy at every premiere, but it was all wrong. No matter how many people clapped or how many awards I was given...I was empty. Something inside of me was missing."

A soft sob broke free from her throat and Brook felt her knees begin to shake. She didn't want to hear this. She didn't want to fall any further than she already had, but when she shook her head, his hand went from the wall to cupping the back of her neck, effectively keeping her in place.

"It wasn't until I met you," he said, his voice was husky and full of emotion. "You were so bright, so kind, so sweet and innocent." He slowly moved his head back and forth. "So different from all the other women I used to spend time with. And somehow, that empty space began to shift. Something was growing. Each time you stood up to me, each time you told me no, each time you refused to let me wallow in misery or made me apologize for being rude, that spot began to fill up." He moved his face so they were cheek to cheek and his lips were at her ear. "I now have a piece of you inside of me, Brook. And even though you might hate me right now, I refuse to give it back."

His hand tightened when she tried to pull back again.

"I won't give it back because everything you filled it with has created something else. Do you know what it is, Brook?" He paused, but continued when she didn't answer. "It's love. Love like nothing I've ever known. I didn't know it at the time, but I had forgotten what it was like to love or be loved. You planted it within me and it's beautiful." He stopped and breathed, his breath washing over her ear and down her neck.

Goosebumps followed in its wake and Brook had to squeeze her eyes shut. His words were perfect, but how could she believe him? It hurt. Everything hurt. She wasn't sure she'd ever be able to recover, and it had all started because she'd been too trusting.

"I love you," he said. "I love you so much that the thought of losing you hurts worse than my recovery has been. I know it's hard, Brook. I know I don't deserve it, but please...*please*...don't push me away. You can trust me."

SHE HAD STOPPED BREATHING after his last words. Grayson's heart was ready to pound right through his ribcage and it only grew faster when she didn't take in any air. "Brook," he said a little more sharply than he intended. She needed gentleness right now, not rough, but she also needed to breathe.

Not knowing what else to do, he moved his hand up to grip her head and brought his lips crashing down on hers. The move was meant to shock her and it worked when he felt her suck in a long gasp through her nose. But now that he had his lips on hers, Grayson found himself not wanting to pull away. She was trembling under his hold, but she melted against him as he continued to move his mouth over hers.

A sliver of hope began to build behind the pain in his chest. He hadn't thought she would ever be willing to forgive him. The look in her eyes and the way she had reacted when they were alone had him feeling like it was useless, but he had chosen to persevere, and right now he was beginning to think it would pay off.

She met his affection with an eagerness he had yet to experience with her. Her hands landed against his chest and Grayson's bad leg began to shake. Oh, how he hated his vulnerability. He wanted to pull her into his arms and never let her go. He needed to feel her against his chest and reassure himself that she was real. But he only had one good arm and he was afraid if she leaned on him at all, they would both go tumbling to the floor. It was maddening.

Gasping for air, she pulled back much earlier than Grayson was ready for her to. Her face was flushed, but he recognized her ever present blush overpowering the redness of anger from earlier. "Goodbye," she whispered, her lips so close they brushed his as she spoke.

It took a moment before the word penetrated and when it did, Grayson jerked backward. "What?"

Brook wouldn't look him in the eye. Her chin was low and her eyes closed while tears leaked from her lids. "I don't think I can ever trust you again, Grayson," she admitted softly.

"Brook, I..." Grayson stopped. What could he say? What would it take for her to be willing to overlook his deception? "It wasn't personal," he finally said. "I never meant to hurt you," he continued. "It was never about you."

When her eyes flashed, he knew immediately that was the wrong thing to say. Where was a screenwriter when he needed one?

"Not personal?" she asked, her voice low. "You want my heart," she said, her jaw tight. "You want *me,* but none of this is personal?" Jerking to the side, she tore out of his hold and began to storm toward the door.

"I love you!" he shouted after her. "Doesn't that count for something?"

Brook stopped just in front of the door, her hand on the knob. Slowly, she spun, the anger gone as quickly as it had come. "And as stupid as it is, I love you too," she said hoarsely. "But it won't work if I can't trust you."

"And why can't you trust me?" He knew the question sounded odd in the situation, but he wanted to know. What did she need from him? "I've apologized, I've recognized that I hurt you, and I've explained the reasons behind the situation. What would it take for you to believe me?"

She let out a long breath. "It just won't work, Grayson."

"Why? Not?"

She looked at him sadly, breaking what little was left of Grayson's heart. "You're an actor," she said. "You spent our whole time together lying and you lie for a living." She shook her head. "You're too good at it. I would never be able to know if what you told me was the truth or not." A harsh laugh came from her mouth. "And that has nothing to do with the fact that I'm me and you're...you." She waved a hand between them. "We're so far apart from each other, it's amazing we ever met."

"I don't care about all that," Grayson shouted, stepping forward. "Can't you see?"

Brook put up a hand and shook her head. "Stop."

The word was soft, but it was enough. He stopped moving, but he didn't stop talking. "I will do anything it takes, Brook," he said. "I know full well that I'll never find someone like you ever again, and I didn't get where I am in life by being lazy. Somehow, someway, I will find a way to convince you I'm sincere."

Her sad look didn't change. "We'll see," she said, then opened the door and was gone.

Grayson hadn't had time to grieve yet when Jude slipped inside. "Man, you really stepped in it this time," he said.

"Don't start," Grayson commanded. "I've heard it all from the one person I didn't want to hear it from."

Jude looked over his shoulder to the open door. "She won't forgive you?"

Grayson shrugged. "Not yet. But I'm not ready to give up."

"Are you sure you want to go through that?" Jude pressed. "You've already got a media mess on your hands."

Grayson nodded decisively. "I don't care about the mess or fallout. I just want her."

"It doesn't seem like she wants you." Ken's words were said casually, but his large body standing in the doorframe was anything but easy-going.

"She loves me," Grayson argued. "But I hurt her."

"Shocker," Bennett said sarcastically as he stepped around his friend. "I'm pretty sure anyone would be hurt if the person they fell for wasn't that person at all."

"I had a good reason," Grayson argued.

"Maybe so," Ken said, stepping inside and closing the door behind him. "But Brook ended up as collateral damage, and so I hope she stays as far away from you as possible."

"It was never meant to go this far," Grayson murmured.

"But it did." Ken sat down and slapped his hands on his desk. "The question is, what are you going to do now?"

"In regards to myself or Brook?"

Ken groaned and scrubbed his face with his hands. "Truthfully, I want to hear that you're going back to L.A. and never coming back. But we could hear everything you said out in the hall and I hate to admit that I not only believe how you feel about Brook, but that she loves you and is simply afraid to try again."

Heat filled Grayson's neck, but he forced himself to stand taller. He had nothing to be ashamed of. Well...he did...for the lying. But not in regards to what he said about Brook. He'd meant every word. She was the missing piece, and ultimately, the most important piece. He'd give up everything, his fame, fortune, and career if it meant she'd take him back.

Bennett chuckled and rubbed his hands together. "Does this mean we get to plan some big elaborate scheme to get them back together?"

Ken gave his friend a look, but Bennett simply shrugged. Ken's eyes went back to Grayson. "So, I'll ask again. What do you plan to do next?"

Jude stepped closer. "I hate to say it, but first we need to calm the media storm. I realize Brook is more important, but convincing her of your sincerity will be much harder if you can't shake the vultures."

Grayson didn't like it, but his friend was right. "It looks like I need to go back to L.A.," he said regretfully. "As soon as I can, though, I'll be back."

Ken's eyes seemed to see straight through Grayson and he stood still for the exam. He had nothing to hide, not anymore. Finally, the police captain nodded. "I'll hold you to that."

Grayson nodded in return. "You have my word."

CHAPTER 22

Brook waited in Benny's car by herself while the men finished up inside the police station. She was grateful it was nighttime so that Jude and Grayson couldn't see her when they all came out.

She turned away, not wanting to see or know where they were going. She needed to make a clean break. Her heart would never be hers again, but Brook knew it would be far too easy to pine for Grayson from afar. She was pretty much an expert at it, after all.

She scoffed and shook her head, though no one was in the car with her. "And to think," she whispered into the dark, "I finally met my celebrity crush, and then I walked away." She sucked in a ragged breath. "Who knew he would end up being the love of my life?"

The driver's side door opened and Benny slipped inside. He sighed long and loud, then turned to her. "You doing okay?"

Brook shrugged. "As well as I can be, I suppose."

"That was quite the discussion you two had..." He left the sentence open-ended as if hoping she would say something.

Brook bit her tongue. She wasn't in the mood for interference. All she wanted was to go home, bawl her eyes out, and eat her weight in ice cream. Was that too much to ask?

"It sounded like he truly loves you."

Brook slowly turned and stared at Benny. The station was lit up enough that she had no trouble seeing him and it was a rare sight to see such stoicism on his usual happy-go-lucky face. "He lied to me, Benny."

"He explained why."

Brook shook her head. "Can you not understand how that makes me feel?" she asked, her voice soft but fierce. "He *LIED*! He lied about his name, about his career, about his family. And he was good at it. I mean, he's an actor for heaven's sake, so like a gullible idiot, I fell for every word. How can you believe anything that comes out of that man's mouth after that?"

Benny turned away and picked at his steering wheel. "I can see why it would be hard, but Brook...what would be the point of continuing to lie?" He turned back to her, his blue eyes full of sympathy. "He'd been caught. The gig was up and what did he do? He tried to protect you and insisted that he loved you." Benny cocked his head. "Why would he bother to do those things if you really meant nothing to him?"

Brook was too angry and hurt to let Benny's logic penetrate. "Please take me home," she said, turning to look out the window.

Benny didn't move right away and each second made Brook feel closer and closer to screaming, but she swallowed the urge. It wasn't Benny's fault that everything had blown up in her face.

"I'm always happy to take a beautiful woman home," Benny said lightly. It was much more his normal behavior and eased some of the tension between them.

The ride only took a few minutes, but they never got to her apartment.

"What is this?" Brook breathed, noting the dozen extra cars blocking the parking lot.

"Well...let's hope all this media is good for your store, huh?" Benny shot her a grin, but even in the dark, Brook could see it was strained.

"I can't go in there," she whispered, sinking back into her seat.

"I wouldn't ask you to," Benny said. He put the car into reverse and quickly backed out before anyone could get a good look at who was in the passenger seat.

Brook glanced over her shoulder multiple times, hoping no one would chase them down. When the street stayed dark, she blew out a breath and faced the front. "Where am I gonna go?"

"I hate to say it," Benny said casually, "but it probably wouldn't be a good idea to bring you home with me."

Brook gave him a small smile. "Probably not, but thanks anyways." She mentally went through all her friends, but most of them were still newly married and Brook definitely didn't want to stay with them. Things were awkward enough as it was.

Benny pulled to a stop and put the car in park.

Brook blinked a few times, coming out of her thoughts. "Where are we?" She peered into the dark and saw the closed sign on The Hidden Daffodil. "Perfect."

Benny buffed his nails on his shirt. "That's what I thought."

Brook looked at him. "Thanks, Benny. I appreciate it." She grabbed her door handle, but Benny stopped her by grabbing her forearm.

"I know you're hurt and upset, Brook," he said carefully. "But when you get the chance, think about what I said."

Brook leaned back for a second. "You really believe him? Even after all he did?"

Benny nodded. "I do. I don't think for a moment that his feelings were fake. And I believe that when you calm down enough to think about it, you'll come to the same conclusion."

Brook pinched her lips together, not wanting to argue, but she wasn't as convinced. Nodding, she opened the door and slipped out. The flower shop was dark, but Brook knew if she walked around back, she'd be able to knock on Rose's private apartment. She'd have to be careful not to wake Lilly, but Brook knew that Rose would welcome her with open arms.

Keeping an eye on her surroundings just in case the media was waiting here as well, Brook worked her way to the back of the building. Nothing moved in the shadows, so Brook continued to the stairs and slowly climbed to the upstairs apartment. She knocked, softly at first, then gradually louder until the door unlocked.

A small crack opened and Brook heard a gasp. "Brook?" The door opened the rest of the way and Rose stood there in pajamas with her hair in a messy bun. "What's going on? Why are you here so late?" Rose's eyes widened. "Are you hurt?"

Brook shook her head, then paused. "I'm not...physically hurt," she said. "Do you mind if I stay the night here?"

Rose's eyebrows shot up, then she nodded. "Of course not. Come on in." As Brook passed her, Rose leaned out the door and looked around before shutting and locking it.

Brook plopped on the couch and hid a huge yawn behind her hand. "I know I need to do a lot of explaining, but do you mind if we save it until morning?" She rubbed her eyes, knowing her mascara had been cried off hours ago. "I'm about to pass out."

"Of course." Rose rushed from the room and came back with an armful of blankets and a pillow. "Let's get you settled and in the morning we'll get it all figured out, okay?"

Brook stood and wrapped her arms awkwardly around Rose, though she was still holding her supplies. "You're wonderful, Rosalinda. Thank you."

Rose's cheeks turned pink. "It's the least I can do," she whispered. It only took five minutes to have the couch ready to go. "I'll do my best to keep Lilly from pouncing on you in the morning."

Brook laughed softly. "Don't worry about it. As tired as I am, I somehow doubt sleep is going to be an easy companion tonight."

The curiosity in Rose's eyes flared, but she didn't ask a single question. "Do the best you can. Things always look better after a good rest." With a final smile, Rose disappeared down the hall, leaving Brook by herself.

It turned out that her own company was not very pleasant since as soon as she closed her eyes, all she could see was Grayson's face. She could hear him saying he loved her and that he wasn't giving up. She could see the pain he was holding back and the way he could barely walk on his leg. Those vivid images were followed by hot bursts of shame at her gullibility and how stupid she had been throughout the relationship.

Regulating her breathing as best she could, Brook forced her body to relax and shoved aside all thoughts of Grayson Cordova. Even in her mind, she needed as much distance from him as possible. And that had to start now.

GRAYSON SHIELDED HIS eyes from the flood of sunlight that came through his bedroom window. By how high the sun was, he had probably slept through most of the morning.

After leaving the police station, he and Jude had gone straight to Portland and caught the next plane to L.A. Grayson would have preferred a private charter, but finding one in the middle of the night was nearly impossible, even with his clout.

Instead, he had bought out the first class section and then given strict instructions about keeping his traveling a secret. He knew it would eventually get out—it always did—but hopefully he could get home before it got any crazier than it already was.

"Up and at 'em," Carson called from his doorway.

Grayson groaned and scrubbed at his face. The beard rubbed roughly against his hands and he wondered, not for the first time, how Brook felt about kissing him with it there. It had been necessary when he'd gone up to Oregon, but now it probably didn't matter. It had served its purpose...a little too well. Maybe it was time to get rid of it.

"Gray," Carson called. "Come on, man."

"I'm coming," Grayson growled. Slowly and carefully, he sat up and maneuvered himself off the bed. His cane was resting against his nightstand and he grabbed it, then propelled himself to his feet.

Carson was leaning against the doorframe with his shoulder and his arms folded over his chest. "You look terrible."

Grayson laughed darkly. "You have no idea."

Carson's normally playful expression turned to sympathy. "I'm sorry it all fell to crap."

Grayson nodded. "Me too. Thanks for playing decoy, by the way."

Carson shrugged. "Being forced to stay in a mansion with a movie theatre and indoor pool was absolutely horrible, but I managed."

Grayson chuckled. "I hope you enjoyed it."

"More than I'm willing to admit."

"Tell Ameila I'll be down in a few," Grayson said, shuffling to his en-suite. "I need to clean up so I don't frighten Kaylee."

"Or the rest of us. I almost ran when that face crawled from between the sheets."

"Shut up!" Grayson shouted through the closed door. He huffed and smiled when Carson yelled something unintelligible in return. It was good to be back, but it would be better if Brook was with him.

At the thought of her, his chest began to ache again. He needed to get all this settled and turn his attention back to how to win her over. Despite her sweet and soft demeanor, Grayson knew full well how stubborn she was. She would never have become his friend if she wasn't.

Sighing in disgust with himself, he turned to the shower and got himself cleaned up. The hot water and specialty shower heads went a long way to helping ease his tension, but none of it touched the black hole in his heart.

Wiping the steamy mirror, Grayson turned his face one way, then the other, trying to see himself the way Brook had. She'd said she'd fallen in love with him. Not Grayson Cordova, but Cord. A grumpy know-it-all, who could barely walk.

His beard looked like he was wearing a dead animal on his face and he shook his head. It had to be love if she could look past all this. Grabbing a pair of scissors, he propped himself against the counter and began to snip away the coarse hair until it was only about an inch long. Now came the difficult part. He grabbed his vintage shaving kit and worked his face into a lather. The kit had been a gift from one of his girlfriends over the years. It seemed weird to be using it and thinking only of impressing Brook, instead of the gift giver.

The odds of him seeing Brook today were slim, but Grayson knew the kit did an amazing job of creating a smooth shave and he was going to do his best to start primping himself now that he was home. She might have fallen in love with him when he looked homeless, but he wasn't above using his famous good looks to recapture her heart if necessary.

By the time he shuffled downstairs, he felt like a new man. The only thing he was missing was a haircut. His locks were out of control and Grayson had had no idea there was so much curl in his hair. The longer it got, the more wild it became. If he wasn't on a mission, he might see what happened by the time it got to his shoulders.

Amelia catcalled when he finally arrived in the sitting room.

Grayson grinned at his sister. "Like what you see?"

"I like seeing your face," she shot back. She bounced her daughter in her arms. "How someone recognized you with that bush is any-one's guess."

Grayson grunted and worked his way to the couch. "I haven't seen the picture, but I heard it was grainy and dark." He laid down and shook his head. "I really don't know how it all fell apart."

Amelia tsked her tongue. "People are crazy. That's just all there is to it."

"Actually..." Richard waltzed into the room in one of his thousand-dollar suits. "I think I can shed some light on things."

Grayson raised his head. "What? No lecture? No 'I told you so'?"

Richard raised an eyebrow. "Would it matter if I did?"

Grayson gave his agent a sarcastic smile. "Not a bit."

Richard snorted. "Then I'll save my breath." He sat down opposite Amelia and Carson with Grayson off to the side. "Your father has been up to his old tricks."

"What?" Carson jumped to his feet. "You can't be serious."

All the tension that the shower had gotten rid of came rushing back. "Are you telling me that Dad is the leak?"

Richard nodded slowly. "I am."

Grayson turned his head so he was staring at the ceiling. "Why?" he asked hoarsely. "How?"

Richard sighed and looked around the room. "When are you going to get a bar in this place?"

"When I actually drink alcohol," Grayson snapped back. He'd seen too many drunken arguments among his parents to ever be attracted to the stuff.

Richard grumbled but moved on. "As you know, Dear Old Dad is still bitter about losing his meal ticket, so he thought he'd go about getting paid another way."

"Let me guess," Carson sneered. "By selling an insider story from the viewpoint of a star's father?"

Richard nodded in acknowledgement. "Close enough. He negotiated himself a healthy paycheck if he could get proof of your injury and give the paparazzi a way to get close to you. He found out about your doctor's appointment and had someone planted at the hospital to follow you. That's how they knew it was you at the restaurant."

"I hate that man," Amelia said tightly. She hugged Kaylee a little closer. "He'll never give up."

Grayson had to agree, but he also knew it wasn't all his dad's fault. Grayson had built his own trap when he'd continued his lie to Brook.

"What are we going to do?" Carson asked. "Can we sue?"

"No," Grayson said quickly.

"What? Why not?" Carson argued.

Grayson shook his head. "Let him go." He pinned his brother with a look. "We have more important things to worry about."

Carson's scowl slowly merged into a smile. "It's her, isn't it? It's that woman you were telling us about."

Grayson nodded.

"Oh, Gray!" Ameila cried. "I'm so excited for you!"

Grayson held up his hand. "Don't start throwing confetti yet. At the moment, she hates me."

Richard scoffed. "No woman hates you."

"This one does."

"Why would she hate you?" Amelia asked.

Grayson sighed and turned back to the ceiling. "Because she fell in love with the real me."

CHAPTER 23

"Are you going to tell me what's going on?" Rose had her back to Brook as she cooked breakfast.

Brook was still exhausted. There had been sleep last night, but it had been short spurts that were filled with nightmares. So rather than rising with energy and hope, she was dragging and grumpy.

Lilly bounced in her seat across from Brook. She was smiling brightly, not having heard her mother. The little girl's hearing aids hadn't been put in yet that morning, so if she couldn't read lips or sign language, Lilly remained blissfully unaware of what was going on.

"Maybe we should wait until Lilly goes to school," Brook said softly.

Rose glanced over her shoulder. "I have to open the store."

"Crud," Brook said, grabbing her phone. She hadn't thought about the store. If the media had tracked her to her apartment, odds were they were also at the store. "Ainsley?" Brook asked when the line was answered. "Thank goodness," Brook said softly. "Hey, look, Ains, I'm really sorry, but I'm not going to be in today." She listened for a minute. "Yeah, I'm fine, but there's a...situation and I can't come in." Brook pinched her lips together. "Actually, I'm a little worried things are going to be difficult today. Why don't we just shut down altogether?"

Brook listened politely to Ainsley's concerns and questions, but she didn't want to say anything more. "I'm sorry to do this so last minute, but I think it's best, at least for today." She nodded. "Mm-hm...yeah... If you would call Flo, that'd be great. Thank you." Brook smiled softly. "Thanks, Ains. I owe you a raise. You're so amazing."

She laughed at her friend's response. "I won't forget. Okay...thanks...
Bye."

Rose was seated, having set plates of scrambled eggs in front of
everyone. Lilly was happily chomping away, but Brook's stomach was
still in turmoil. "Thanks," she whispered, poking at the food.

Brook could feel Rose's eyes on her, but she kept her head down.
She didn't want to talk over Lilly's head. It was better to wait until
they were alone.

An hour later, they were just that. Lilly was in school and Brook
had followed Rose to the flower shop.

Rose came back from turning on the open sign. "I'm done waiting," she said firmly. "What's going on?"

Brook plopped onto a bench, careful not to sit on any of the dec-
orative flowers. "Cord isn't really Cord."

Rose froze. "What do you mean?"

"I mean he lied to me about who he was."

"Brook," Rose breathed. "Are you in trouble?"

Brook frowned and looked up to see her friend nearly in a panic.
Rose was usually very even-keeled. She was a single mother of a special needs child and nothing seemed to fluster her, so seeing her eyes
look wild took Brook off guard and made her realize how little she
knew about Rose's background.

No one knew.

Rose never spoke about her life before Seaside Bay, but she had
proven to be a friend that anyone could count on. She was a few years
older than the other women in their friend group and always seemed
so mature. Not to mention she was the most stunning woman Brook
had ever seen. Red hair and blue eyes and her daughter had inherited
both. Lilly was a living doll and you couldn't help but love her.

"Not exactly," Brook said carefully. "But it would appear that the
paparazzi are trying to find me. That's why I couldn't go home last
night and why I closed the shop for the day."

"The paparazzi?" Rose made a face. "What in the world is going on?" she cried, throwing her arms in the air.

Brook groaned and put her face in her hands. It was so hard to admit how stupid she'd been. "Cord is really Grayson Cordova." She waited for Rose to say something, but her friend was silent. Pushing her fingers to the side, Brook peeked through the crack. Rose was standing in shock with her jaw hanging open.

"Grayson Cordova? Are you sure?"

Brook nodded and dropped her hands. "It's a long story," she said softly.

The bell over the door rang and both women whipped their heads towards the sound.

"Oh, good," Rose said pleasantly. "Mary, I have some work to do in the back. Can you run the register today?" she asked her employee.

Mary nodded. "Let me grab my apron and I'll get on it." She stumbled to a stop. "Oh, hi, Brooklyn. I didn't know you were here today."

"Just visiting Rose," Brook said weakly.

They both waited until Mary was behind the counter and then Rose and Brook went to the back. Once the door was shut, Rose rounded on Brook. "We've got lots of time. Might as well share it all."

Brook wrung her hands together and took a deep breath, then spilled it all. It took longer than she expected, but by the end, the burden felt a little lighter, even if she still felt foolish for falling for everything.

"It's all so dumb," she muttered, looking at her hands. "I can't believe that I, of all people, fell for it. I've followed Grayson Cordova since I was a teenager. You'd think that if anyone was going to recognize him, it would be me." When she looked up, her vision was blurry. "But instead, I fell for every line. Every whispered word. Every lie," she grumbled bitterly. "I've always thought of myself as reasonably intelligent, but this…" She shook her head. "This just proves otherwise, I suppose."

"Don't you dare," Rose said sharply. She walked over, dropping her working gloves on the floor, and sat next to Brook before wrapping her arms around her. "You are not responsible for someone else's behavior. What he did, no matter the reason, was wrong and you are not responsible for that. If it wasn't you, it would have been someone else."

Brook tried not to wince, but the words hurt. The thought that he had only dated her because she was the most easily accessible female was worse than his lying.

"Where is he now?" Rose asked.

Brook leaned back and shrugged. "I don't know. I told him goodbye last night."

Rose tilted her head down until she could look Brook in the eye. "And?"

Brook looked up. "And what?"

"And how do you feel about that?"

Brook opened her mouth, then stopped. How did she feel? She'd been feeling like an idiot, she'd been hurting because her heart was broken, she was angry because she fell for a scam, and she was sad because she would never see him again. "I don't know," she answered honestly.

Rose patted her knee. "Maybe you need to figure that out before you do anything." She gave a soft laugh. "I can offer advice until I'm blue in the face, but none of it matters unless you want it to." She smiled sadly. "I'll be happy to listen while you work it all out, but until you know your own feelings, we won't get anywhere."

Brook nodded. Rose was right. She might have had the strength to turn Grayson away last night, but there was still a part of her that hoped he would come back. That wanted to believe him when he said he wasn't letting her go. And unless she could silence the voice or let go of her bitterness, no one would win.

GRAYSON GROWLED OUT one last push-up, then collapsed on the floor, his sweaty chest sticking to the hardwood.

"Your leg might be struggling," Carson quipped, "but your upper body strength seems to be flourishing."

"Shut up," Grayson mumbled, wiping at an annoying drip of sweat trickling into his eye. He'd been through therapy and then an upper body workout that morning and he was done. It had been almost a week since he'd seen Brook and each hour without her was eating at him until he thought he would go mad. His workouts had become more intense and his therapy sessions happened as often as Jude would allow. Anything to help take his mind off the fact that he still didn't know what he was going to do to get her back.

"Have you called her?" Carson asked.

Grayson didn't bother with a clarifying question. He knew Carson was talking about the same woman Grayson was thinking about. "Yes."

"And?"

"And it went to voicemail."

"How many times?"

Grayson pushed himself over onto his back. "I don't know. Five or six times every day?"

Carson whistled low. "That's one stubborn woman."

Grayson grinned fondly. "Yeah, but it's part of what makes her so wonderful."

Carson walked over and stood over Grayson's body. "Any woman who can say no to the great Grayson Cordova has my automatic approval."

Grayson reached out and hit the back of his brother's knee, causing it to buckle. "You're not funny."

"Neither are you," Carson called over his shoulder as he walked away. There was a blessed silence for a moment before Grayson's brother continued. "So, what are you going to do?"

Grayson frowned. "I'm not sure. I can't do anything big because if the media gets wind of it, they'll end up scaring her into hiding."

"I think she's already there."

Grayson sighed. "I know. She's obviously in hiding, or someone would have gotten a picture of her at this point." He'd been watching social media to see if her picture showed up and was ready to send security down if he had to, but nothing had popped up. A picture of their kiss and an article with all the generic information someone found online had splashed around, but no one seemed to have seen her in person since the night everything blew up. He knew she had some good friends and this only proved it. For Brook to have evaded everyone as long as she had, she obviously had help.

"Maybe that's why she's not answering her phone?"

"Maybe." But Grayson didn't think so. He still had the sinking feeling that she was avoiding him because she wanted a clean break. And each time that thought went through his head, his own stubbornness kicked in. She would be his. He just had to figure out how. The attraction, the desire, even the love was already there. It was just overshadowed by his lies and fame.

"Do you need help getting up?" Jude walked in with a bottle of water in his hands.

Grayson shook his head. "Nah. My cane is..." He looked over and realized he'd rolled the wrong way. "Kick that over, would ya?"

Jude picked up the instrument and brought it over. "Come on, let's get you on your feet and upstairs to your shower. You stink."

"Women love sweaty men," Carson called out from his place on a bench.

"I don't want women," Grayson said. "Just Brook."

"I'm sure she'll be thrilled to hear she's not a woman."

Grayson glared at his brother, who grinned in return.

"She'd have to be talking to him first," Jude quipped. He shrugged when Grayson turned his glare his way. "What? It's not every day you strike out. Do you really expect us not to enjoy it?"

Grayson pushed a hand through his sweaty hair. "I'm sorry. I just...this time it's different."

Jude's smile fell. "I know. Brook was something special. I'm sorry."

Grayson nodded.

"Ah, come on," Carson whined. "You're acting like you've already lost."

Grayson frowned. "No, I haven't."

Carson gave him a wry look. "Moaning and groaning about her being different? Yeah. You have."

"I never said I was done trying," Grayson argued.

"Well, then, what are you going to do?" his brother challenged.

"I don't know!" Grayson shouted. "That's the whole point!"

Carson pinched his lips together. "She's not answering your calls. What about texts?" He raised his eyebrows.

Grayson shook his head. "Nope."

"Can you sneak back into Seaside Bay?"

Grayson made a face. "Not easily."

"What if you appealed to her friends? Do you think they could get her to talk to you?"

Grayson paused. The thought had merit, but he wasn't sure if it would work. "Maybe...but somehow I think Captain Wamsley would rather punch my face in than help me win her back." He scratched his chin. "Although he did say he wanted her happy."

Carson nodded eagerly. "That's a start. We get her friends involved. Do you know any of their phone numbers?"

"The numbers won't be hard to get," Jude mused. "But I don't think a phone call is the best way to handle this."

Grayson looked expectantly at his friend and therapist.

"I think you'd do better if you could see her in person."

"If she saw me, I'm pretty sure she'd turn around and walk right back out of the room," Grayson grumbled. "Short of kidnapping her so she had no choice but to hear me out, what can I do?" He looked between the other men, but both of them were smiling. Grayson had seen that smile on his brother's face before and it never ended well. Grayson thought back over his words then slapped his forehead. "Guys, we can't kidnap her."

"No..." Jude said. "But you can work out a situation where she's taken somewhere you just happen to be."

"Don't you own like five homes?" Carson pointed out. "Can't you help her 'win' a vacation or something? She'll have no idea the place is yours, the media will have no idea where you're going, and BAM! You *just happen* to be in the same place at the same time."

Grayson pursed his lips. "That...might work..." Ideas were tumbling through his head. He had access to a lot of resources. Money was no object and setting up the situation would be a breeze. The only variable was Brook actually accepting the gift. But if he had her friends' cooperation and she didn't know he was involved, maybe, just maybe, he'd have a chance to speak to her again.

CHAPTER 24

Brook wasn't listening to any of the chatter going on around her as she stuffed flowers into her vase. Usually flower-arranging night was one of her favorite things, but right now she just wasn't in the mood.

The stupid media was still lurking around and Brook found herself having to sneak into work and stay in the back. Only Ainsley knew she was there and the store manager did her best to keep the piranhas at bay, but it was beyond annoying at this point.

Why the heck won't they just give up? Brook thought bitterly. It had been over a week and they still wouldn't leave. Who had that kind of tenacity? *The exact people that Grayson described while we were all at the police station.*

The thought of Grayson brought a deeper frown to her face. Even the mention of his name made her chest hurt. Why did he have to be so attractive and so kind once you got past the exterior grump? Remembering all their sweet moments together was making it more and more difficult to keep dodging his calls. She had finally given her phone to Rose and asked her not to give it back.

Yet there were days when Brook was alone in Rose's apartment and she had to fight herself to keep from searching the house for it. She wanted to hear that deep, smooth voice. She wanted to hear him say he still loved her. She wanted him to say he would give up his life of fame if only to be at her side.

He did.

Brook huffed. He hadn't *exactly* said that, but he had said he would be back for her. That he loved her and wanted to be with her.

And you sent him away.

"Be quiet," she muttered.

"What was that?" Genni asked, looking up from her vase.

"Nothing," Brook hurried to reply. "Sorry, I was just talking to myself."

Genni grinned. "I do that all the time. No worries." She went back to her work and Brook sighed in relief.

She probably shouldn't have risked coming tonight. If her stalkers got wind of it, they'd haunt the flower shop forever. She wasn't even sure what they wanted with her. They had one dark picture of her kissing Grayson and had decided she was a person of interest. It was ridiculous.

Her old high school photo and life stats had been plastered all over the media and suddenly Brook was getting hate-filled social media messages from every woman in the world who thought herself in love with Grayson Cordova.

Rose had had to cut her off from the internet, other than accessing work. She had been the perfect friend and Brook knew she could never repay Rose for her kindness and support. She had gone above and beyond, and yet Brook was still hanging on like a leech.

"Brook!" Caro shouted.

Brook jerked back and shook her head. "What?"

Caro pursed her lips and raised an eyebrow, then gave a pointed look around the room. Brook followed and gasped when she noticed the place was almost empty. "Oh, shoot. Is class over?"

Caro, Rose, Charli, Genni, and Hadlee were all standing together with varying looks of concern and amusement.

Brook shrunk back slightly, feeling suddenly intimidated.

"Come on to the back," Rose said softly. She led the way to a gathering room where the friends often met after class. Copious amounts of chocolate and gossip were usually involved.

Brook sat tentatively in one of the seats, unsure why everyone was so serious. When the rest of the women looked at her again, she knew she was in trouble. It appeared that tonight, she was the topic of conversation. "I'm sorry," Brook blurted out before anyone else could speak. She didn't like being the one who brought trouble into town and she had done a bang-up job of shaking Seaside Bay's foundation.

Caro frowned. "For what?"

Brook dropped her gaze to her hands, picking at her nails. "For causing so much trouble. I'm sure most of you have been hounded by the media as they look for me, and I'm sorry." She felt the sting of tears and she blinked rapidly, fighting the inevitable wave of emotion that hit her every time she paused long enough for her emotions to rise to the surface.

Charli snorted. "Like we blame you for those idiots," she muttered. "They can rot in—"

"Charli," Rose warned. She shook her head. "We're here to help Brook, not get our mouths washed out with soap."

Charli huffed and folded her arms over her chest. "All I'm saying is that if they don't give up soon, I might force Hadlee to make Felix use the cement shoes he keeps on his boat."

Hadlee palmed her forehead. "Charli..."

Charli shrugged unrepentantly.

"Anyway..." Caro said, making a face at Charli. She turned back to Brook. "Honey, Rose has filled us all in and we decided something needs to be done." She narrowed her gaze and studied Brook, who squirmed under her perusal. "Can you answer one question for me?"

Brook glanced up from under her lashes, then nodded. "Sure."

"Do you still love him? Even knowing he lied? Would you ever consider forgiving him?"

Brook made a face. "That was way more than one question."

Caro wasn't impressed.

Sighing, Brook leaned back in her seat and folded her arms over her chest. She debated how much to share. She didn't want to hedge the truth, but she still struggled with the truth herself. She wasn't comfortable with the actual answer because it felt wrong.

Genni rubbed her small stomach and nodded. "You do, don't you?"

Brook's lips were starting to tremble, but she did her best to press them into submission. "Yes," she croaked.

"Tell us why," Hadlee pressed.

"Why does that—" Charli began, then stopped at a look from Rose. "Fine. Brook, you know we love you. And we want to support you in any choice you make." Charli's eyes were intense when Brook managed to meet her gaze. "So feel free to share with us your feelings... All of them."

Brook laughed sarcastically and wiped at her eyes. "All of them? We'd be here all night."

"That's nothing," Caro said, getting comfortable. "Jack can fend for himself." She grinned. "Plus...I brought chocolate." She opened her purse and began handing out bags of truffles to each person.

Brook played with the ribbon, but didn't open the treat. She loved Caro's truffles, but right now her stomach was roiling. "I do love him," she admitted. "But I also hate him. I hate that he lied. I hate that I fell for it. I hate that the media won't leave him or me alone. I hate that he's so hurt and might never get his job back. I hate that I feel like a fool and even the fact that I still want him." She took in a shuddering breath. "When I met him, I just wanted some kind of purpose. Something to work towards. You all have families and significant others and I felt...left out. I was lonely and restless. When he was Cord, I found that. I helped a man who was hurting and brought out his smile." Brook smiled at the group. "It was amazing. Once I got past his grumpiness, he was sweet, kind, and fun." She snorted. "And a great kisser."

Laughter went around the group.

"And when those good feelings come rushing back, the hate begins all over again because I shouldn't still love him. I shouldn't still have good memories. There's no hope for a future for us, so why hold onto them?"

The room was quiet for several heavy heartbeats. Caro finally came over and leaned over to give Brook a hug. "I don't have all the answers, but you seem like you could use a little love. So here's mine."

Brook was pulled to her feet and soon the whole group was surrounding her. Brook sighed and relaxed into their hold. Caro was right. They didn't have all the answers right now, but maybe it would still be okay. They could keep taking things one day at a time and eventually, life would get better. No matter how her love life went, Brook would always have her friends, and they were amazing.

"DO YOU REALLY THINK it will work?" Amelia asked with a frown. "You don't think it will scare her?"

Grayson rubbed his chin. "I don't think so. I think at first she'll be more angry than scared."

"Hmm…" Amelia made a noncommittal sound. She had Kaylee on her shoulder and was patting her back. A loud burp came from the tiny bundle.

Grayson grinned while Carson snorted with laughter.

Amelia brought her baby down and Kaylee grinned at her audience.

"Pass her over," Grayson said, holding out his arms. He was in the recliner so he wasn't fully upright and it was too much trouble to get up to hold her himself.

"She needs a diaper change," Amelia warned.

Grayson made a face. "Is it bad?"

Amelia shook her head. "No. Just soggy."

Grayson sighed, but still held out his arms. "We'll be fine for a few minutes." His smile grew as his niece came closer. "Hi, sweetie," he cooed.

Carson laughed again. "Never thought I'd see the day when Grayson Cordova would talk baby talk."

"Watch it," Grayson growled. "It's not like I haven't heard you doing the exact same thing."

"I fully admit to acting like a fool," Carson said easily. "But I also don't have a public reputation for being stoic and well-mannered."

"Guess I'm a really good actor, huh?" Grayson said the words to Kaylee, who was smiling back and waving her arms. He bounced her on his lap, her chunky legs bending as she sprang off her toes.

"I'm still worried about your plan," Amelia said as she packed up the gear from the feeding.

"You worry too much," Carson said. He slid sideways on the couch and laid down, putting his arm over his eyes. "It'll be fine."

"Every stupid thing every man has ever done started with those words," Amelia scolded, pointing a finger at Carson.

"I hate to say it," Carson said from behind his arm. "But she's probably right."

Grayson made a face. "I'm not sure how else to get her to speak to me," he admitted. "She won't take my call or answer my texts. Going to Seaside when the media is still swarming would only cause a ruckus and she would *not* be happy with the attention." He shrugged as best as he could. "The only thing I can think of is to corner her somehow, and it's going to have to be away from her home."

"And her friends agreed to this?"

Grayson smirked. "It took a little persuasion, but I think everyone is on board."

Jude walked in, his hands in the air. "It's done!"

Relief flooded Grayson's system, followed by anticipation. He'd recruited Jude to help finish up the details so that Grayson stayed as far away from everything as possible. If anyone caught wind of his plans, it would completely ruin everything. "Thank you," he said sincerely.

A loud cry brought Grayson's attention back to the bundle in his arms. Kaylee's face was scrunched up and she was wailing loud enough to wake the dead. Grayson winced and looked at his sister. "What did I do?"

Amelia walked over and grabbed her daughter. "You quit paying attention to her," she teased. Amelia shook her head. "Just kidding. She probably wants out of that diaper."

"Can't say I blame her," Carson said. "Who wants to sit around in a puddle?"

"I don't recall it bothering you when we were kids," Amelia shot back as she left the room with her diaper bag in tow.

"Stinkin' sisters," Carson muttered darkly.

"I don't want to know," Jude said, holding up his hand. He disappeared into the kitchen for a second, returning with a cold sports drink. "So...what do we do now?"

Grayson groaned. "Now we wait."

"How long?" Carson pressed.

"Richard has to plant some seeds as a decoy and then if all goes well, I'll meet Brook in Kona in two days."

"Oooh, Kona," Carson teased. "Pulling out the big guns."

Grayson rolled his eyes. "It was closer than some of the other houses."

"Poor baby," Carson continued. "I feel so bad for you."

"Shut up," Grayson said, but there was no bite in his tone. How could he be upset right now? He was that much closer to seeing Brook. He physically still hurt from their separation and the pain wasn't going anywhere. It was a mess since he was still hurting everywhere else as well.

He frowned. His non-healing leg and back had been a source of worry for him. Jude and the doctors kept telling him to be patient, but he had expected to be seeing progress by now. He had felt better when he was around Brook, but now that they were separated, he knew it wasn't that his leg was better, but that she had lifted him mentally and emotionally. She made him smile and look forward to what was coming next, and that had helped his body feel better as well.

Now it had all slipped right back to where it had been and Grayson was struggling, though he refused to let anyone know that. It was the only thing he was nervous about when it came to seeing Brook again. He was hoping to present himself as someone to be in her life for a long time, even forever, if she would consider it. But he hated the thought of doing it when he wasn't whole. He was still weak and had no idea if he would ever work again. How could he ask Brook to take that on permanently? No woman would want to go into a serious relationship starting out like that.

"Knock it off," Amelia said as she passed back by, a dry and happier Kaylee in her arms.

Grayson jerked back. "Knock what off?"

"Whatever it is you're thinking," she said without even looking at him.

"How do you know what I was thinking?" he growled.

Amelia finally looked his way, raising her eyebrows. "Every time you get that look on your face, you're thinking something bad. It's been that way since we were little. It's your 'worst case scenario' face."

"I don't have a face like that," Grayson argued.

"Yes, you do," Carson said sleepily. He shifted, obviously in the process of falling asleep.

Grayson shook his head.

"What is it?" Amelia asked more gently. She laid Kaylee on her stomach with a few toys in reach, then scooted over so she could keep their conversation more private.

Grayson glanced at Jude, but the physical therapist was too caught up in his phone to pay attention. He looked back to Amelia. "I'm afraid she won't want me."

Amelia's jaw dropped. "Are you kidding me? Who wouldn't want you?"

Grayson made a face. "I'm serious, Amelia."

Amelia shook her head in disgust. "You. Are. The. Grayson Cordova. Most of the women in the world want you. And the others don't have television."

Grayson smiled. "Thanks, but she doesn't care about all that. My fame scares her." He blew out a breath. "But that's not what I'm most worried about."

"Then what?"

He pinched his lips together. "I'm worried she won't want me because of my injury."

Amelia grew very serious. "Tell me you're joking."

Grayson dropped her gaze and shrugged. "I'm broken, Amelia. What woman wants that?"

She reached out and patted his arm. "Do you love her?"

His head snapped up. "Of course."

"Does she love you?"

He scrunched his nose. "She loved Cord. So, yeah, I think she still does."

"The woman who loves *you*, not the actor, but *you*, won't care that you're hurt." Her eyes were heavy with sympathy. "And if she doesn't, then she wasn't worth it anyway."

Grayson grabbed her hand and gave it a squeeze. "I sure hope you're right," he said.

Amelia rolled her eyes. "I'm *always* right."

CHAPTER 25

"You won what?" Brook's jaw dropped open as she stared at Caro.

"A trip to Hawaii," Caro squealed, dancing a little jig. She sobered quickly. "But I can't take it."

"Why not?" Brook shouted. She winced when she realized how loud she was. "Sorry."

Caro laughed and fluffed her hair. "No biggie. I'd be just as excited if I was the one going."

Brook rubbed her forehead. "Tell me again why you can't go? It seems so crazy to turn down a trip like this."

Caro leaned in and dropped her voice, as if keeping their conversation private. They were currently meeting in the kitchen of her shop, so it wasn't like there were other people around, but drama was Caro's middle name. "Jack and I are working on some things for the store and the trip interferes with that."

"Yeah, but...Hawaii!" Brook said. "Can't the store wait?"

Caro rolled her eyes. "If only."

"When is it supposed to be?"

"Tomorrow."

"Wait...what?" Brook's eyes were wide. "You just heard about it today and you're supposed to go tomorrow?" She shook her head. "What in the world kind of notice is that?"

Caro shrugged. "I don't know. Maybe if we had a month to prepare, we could work it out, but we just can't leave so quickly." She grinned and the look was slightly devious. "So...I had a thought."

"Oh, no."

Caro waved away Brook's concern. "*You* can take the trip."

"Sure," Brook drawled sarcastically. "As if these giveaways are ever transferable."

"This one is."

Brook stilled. "You can't be serious."

"As a heart attack."

"How?" Brook leaned back, still shaking her head. "I've never heard of a giveaway that lets you transfer the grand prize."

Caro shrugged and studied her perfectly manicured nails. "I don't know, but I'm not about to look a gift horse in the mouth." She smirked. "I figured out of all of us, you could use the trip the most. Maybe by the time you get back, those man-eating fish will have jumped into the river."

"One can only hope," Brook murmured, her mind in a whirl. Could she take off for Hawaii with less than a twenty-four-hour notice? It was insane, yet it was intriguing. She felt like an empty shell, wandering around with nothing to do and everywhere to hide. A shadow of her former self, and until those dang paparazzi left, Brook knew she'd never have a prayer of getting back to normal life.

Not that life will ever be normal anyway.

How could life ever be normal when her heart was a shredded and bruised mess?

"Brook!" Caro snapped her fingers in front of her friend's face.

"Sorry," Brook said quickly, backing away from those red nails. "I was daydreaming."

"As long as it wasn't pictures of Grayson Cordova in a bathing suit, then we're fine," Caro said slyly.

Oh, great. Now that was exactly what was going through Brook's mind and the angry pulse in her chest began its hourly reminder that it was as empty as a homeless man's wallet.

"Now, what clothes are you going to take?" Caro tapped her chin.

"Hey! I haven't said I'm going yet," Brook argued.

"Oh, you're going," Caro said firmly. "There's no way I'm letting this thing go to waste. If I can't take it, then you better believe you will."

"What if I can't get away?"

Caro pursed her lips, looking unimpressed. "And just what, pray tell, is keeping you here? All those reporters who want to interview you?"

Brook deflated. "No."

"Then why not do something spontaneous for once?" Caro pressed, leaning forward in her seat. "Right now life is miserable. Hawaiian beaches will make it less miserable."

If only... Brook wasn't so sure she'd be less miserable in Hawaii. She'd be just as miserable, but tan and warm to boot. "Okay," she said softly. Really, what could it hurt? A change of scenery might be just what she needed to kickstart her life back up. The thought was a complete lie, but Brook latched onto it anyway. Being in Seaside Bay at the moment wasn't a good place for her.

"Yes!" Caro squealed. She jumped up and ran to grab her purse.

"Where are you going?" Brook asked, scrambling to her feet.

"I'm going to help you pack."

Brook put her hands on her hips and narrowed her eyes. "Wait a minute. I thought you were super busy with stuff for the shop, and that's why you couldn't take the trip."

"I can't take the trip," Caro said easily. "But that doesn't mean I can't let Jack run it for a while so we can get your bags together."

"Something smells fishy," Brook muttered, following her friend out the back door to her pink Volkswagen Beetle, Talula.

"It's the marina," Caro offered without even looking up. She turned the ignition and they buzzed out of the parking lot. "Think we can get inside your apartment?"

Brook groaned. "I haven't tried in a few days." She leaned her head back and closed her eyes. "If we can't, I'm in trouble. I don't have a swimsuit or anything with me."

"Eh, don't worry. If all else fails, I'll go in and pack for you."

"I do *not* like the sound of that," Brook said warily.

Caro's grin could only be described as devious. "That's because you know me so well."

"I would need actual clothes, Caro. Not just sexy dresses and bikinis." Brook scrunched her nose. "Actually, since I don't have either of those things, I think we're pretty safe."

"Liar," Caro sang out. "I've seen the clothes you hide in the back of your closet." She winked at Brook. "The ones you secretly want to wear but haven't had occasion for yet."

Brook folded her arms over her chest. "I still don't have any bikinis," she muttered. It was true though. Brook had taken things from her store more than once that she wished she had the opportunity to wear. They were the exact kind of thing she would wear if she were on Grayson Cordova's arm on the red carpet.

Seaside Bay might not be the place to use them, but in her daydreams, Brook had managed a lot of scenarios.

"Well, we'll just have to fix that," Caro said. She grumbled under her breath when they drove by Brook's apartment and there were people with cameras hanging out on the steps. "They just won't give up." Going past the building, Caro took a couple of turns to bring Brook back to her own house. "Out you go," she said, pushing Brook's shoulder.

"Caro..." Brook warned. "I'm really worried about this. You have to pack me regular clothes."

"Don't worry," Caro assured her. "I have everything under control."

"That's exactly what I'm worried about." Brook groaned.

GRAYSON COULDN'T STAND still. He shuffled back and forth over his hardwood floor until he was sure he was going to wear a hole in it. Brook should be here any minute. The car he'd sent for her had had plenty of time to get back from the airport and every minute that went by was making him more anxious than a man whose wife was in labor.

Headlights flashed through the front windows and Grayson hurried over as quickly as his cane would allow him to. A deep ache was pulsing in his thigh, but he shoved the pain aside. This was the moment he'd been waiting for. He peered through the blinds and saw Brook standing in front of the home with a look of awe on her face.

He supposed his beach home was pretty nice, but when he'd bought it, it had been for the tax benefits. He'd only been here a couple of times because he was always so busy. Now, however, he was hoping to make this house something special. It would be the place where Brook became his for real.

The chauffeur set her bags down and Brook gave him a tip, which made Grayson chuckle. The man had been paid well over his normal fees to do this without causing a fuss, but the tip was probably appreciated anyway.

Brook was still staring at the house as she walked up the sidewalk and onto the porch. As she got closer, he could see the lines of her face and the way her hair was rippling down her back. His fingers itched to run through the strands, and he found his knuckles turning white as he gripped his cane hard.

The sound of a code being punched into the electronic lock, followed by the front door opening, could be heard before her light footsteps sounded on the wood. "Whoa..." she breathed.

Grayson was encased in shadows and he closed his eyes, picturing her face and the pleasure that was on it. He was almost loath to reveal himself, knowing the look would surely disappear.

The door latched and she walked farther inside. He knew exactly where she would go next and he gave her a few moments to enjoy the sight. The house was built wide open and even from the front entryway, a person could see straight through the house and then the beach. The entire backside of the house was glass, giving uninterrupted views of white sand and crashing waves. While Brook would be very familiar with beaches, the lush, tropical green that accompanied a Hawaiian beach made a very different picture than the dry grass fields near the Oregon Coast.

He could hear her set down her suitcase and walk to the back of the house, sliding open the door and stepping onto the deck. Slowly, so as not to startle her, Grayson stepped out of the office he'd been waiting in and followed. She was standing at the railing, gripping the wood as if bracing herself for impact. The wind whipped her hair around her head, giving her a wild, mermaid look.

He stepped onto the deck and the wood groaned beneath his feet, giving him away. Instead of jumping and spinning like he expected her to, Brook sighed.

"I wondered when you'd come."

His heart sank. She didn't sound happy to see him at all. "How did you know it was me?"

A harsh chuckle met his ears. "It was all a little too convenient. Caro couldn't go on the trip? I had to leave now? She packed my bags and my friends all but shoved me onto the plane." Brook glanced over her shoulder, looking sinfully beautiful in the sunset. "Who did I know who would have access to a place as nice as this, on a deserted side of the island at a moment's notice?"

He gave her a sheepish smile and shuffled forward. "I had to speak to you."

"There are things called phones, you know."

"I tried that. You wouldn't answer."

Brook nodded sadly and looked down at the railing. "I know. I gave Rose my phone after the first day and when she gave it back, I scrolled around and saw how many times you'd called and texted." Her eyes were watery when she looked back up. "You were very persistent."

"So is every man who's in love," Grayson said, stepping up to her side. He wanted to touch her so badly. He wanted to take her in his arms and relieve the ache inside, but she wasn't ready for that. If he wasn't careful, she might never be ready for it.

Brook let out a soft but harsh laugh. "You don't love me, Grayson. I was just the most available female during your little mission."

"Now who's the liar?"

Brook's head whipped toward him. "Excuse me?"

He shook his head. "You have no right to tell me how I feel, Brooklyn Howell."

She opened her mouth, but snapped it shut again.

"I already told you, quite in detail, I might add, how I feel about you, but perhaps you need to hear it again." He stepped a little closer, just enough to make their situation feel more personal. "What I feel for you has nothing to do with you being my personal nurse, or the danger we were in when we were running from the paparazzi." He reached out and ran his knuckle against her jawline. "But it does have everything to do with you."

Her bottom lip trembled and he rubbed it with his thumb. "I don't know how to believe what you're telling me," she whispered.

Grayson nodded. Now they were getting to the crux of the matter. He had lied too many times and she was scared to trust him. It wasn't that she didn't hear or understand what he was saying, she was simply scared. Their separation had made him feel like half a man and he could only guess how much worse it had been for her, since she hadn't been holding out hope of a reunion. "Then let me prove myself," he said.

Her brows furrowed. "How would you do that?"

"Stay with me this week and I'll tell you everything."

Brook backed up. "Stay with you?" Her eyes darted back inside. "Like in the same house?"

Grayson nodded.

She shook her head. "I'm not... I don't..."

He put up his hand to stop her rambling. "Brook. Have I ever asked that kind of thing from you? Or ever made you feel like that was what I was aiming for?"

Her cheeks did that delightful flush and he smiled at the sight. It was just one more thing he loved and had missed. "No," she admitted.

"You'll have your own room, clear on the other side of the house if you want," he added. "But right now no one but your friends and my family know where we are. Let me show you the Grayson Cordova that the media never sees. The one that is reserved only for the people I love."

She hesitated. He could practically see the indecision in her eyes. She wanted to say yes. He honestly believed that. But would fear win?

"Would it help if I brought my brother here?" Grayson asked with a grin. "He can vouch for everything I tell you."

His joke worked and Brook laughed softly. She tucked a piece of hair behind her ear and smiled at him. "I'm not really sure what you're hoping to get out of this deal, but all right." She waved an arm toward the beach. "I'm already here, so I might as well stay a while."

"You want to know what I'm hoping to get out of this?" Grayson stepped closer, cursing the ache in his leg as he did so. It better not give him trouble this week while he worked to convince Brook he was sincere. He reached out and ran his fingers through her hair, then leaned forward to leave a chaste kiss on her forehead. "I'm hoping to get you."

CHAPTER 26

Brook was trembling with a mixture of nerves and anticipation as she dressed for dinner. Grayson had told her they would have a casual dinner on the deck, overlooking the water, but she still felt like she needed to dress up a little. He said dinner was being delivered, but the cook didn't know who they were delivering it to. He really had gone out of his way to make sure their little vacation was completely incognito.

The idea of no one knowing they were there only added to Brook's struggles. She wanted to believe Grayson, she really did, but it all seemed so fantastic. So impossible. She'd used the excuse that he, as a famous movie star, couldn't possibly love her, a nobody. That he had lied for too long for anything to be true, but standing down on the deck, knowing he'd gone out of his way to organize this... It caused her beliefs to waver.

Would he really have called forty-five times if he didn't care? Would he have left almost a hundred text messages? Very few people would perpetuate a lie that far. What was in it for Grayson if it was all fake? Nothing that she could see, other than the opportunity to humiliate her even further, but that didn't seem like his idea of a good time. Brook might have fallen for his gruff charm, and alias, but she was fairly sure he wasn't the type of person to take pleasure in another's misery.

Looking into the mirror, she ran a brush through her hair. The static in the air made her cringe. That was all she needed, her hair standing up like she'd been electrocuted. Nothing said "I'm spending the next week with Grayson Cordova" more than an out of control do.

It took another ten minutes to get her strands under control, but Brook was fairly pleased with the final product. She was wearing a flowy dress, courtesy of Caro, her hair was finally lying nicely down her back, and she had tried out the blush-colored lip gloss Caro had put in her makeup bag.

"I'll have to say thank you," Brook muttered to her reflection. Although, from the looks of the rest of her suitcase, Brook had a feeling she would be cursing her friend soon as well. Nothing she'd seen looked the least bit practical for a hike or even comfort. Everything had been to impress.

With a heavy sigh, Brook headed out to the front room. She paused to admire the view once more. It really was a magnificent house. She could get all too used to watching the water with a warm wind caressing her face. So different from the icy bite of the Oregon breeze.

"You look beautiful."

Brook forced herself to turn slowly. She wanted to savor the admiration in his voice before she looked into his eyes to see if he was sincere. She snorted in her head. *Like his eyes will tell me anything. He's been fooling me with his eyes for months.* "Thank you," she murmured, her eyes drinking in his own visage like a dying woman in the desert. He was wearing shorts with a casual T-shirt that showed off every hard line of his chest and arms. If he'd been dressing to impress, Brook had to admit he'd done well.

"The food should have been left on the doorstep by now," Grayson said, turning toward the door. "Let me grab it and then we can set up dinner."

"Oh, no," Brook hurried after him. "I can get it."

Grayson stiffened when she grabbed his arm and she quickly released her hold. "Brook," he said softly, turning to look her in the eye. "I know you love to help us invalids, but I'm trying to prove a point."

He gave her a sad smile, one she could actually see now that his beard was gone.

She had to admit his fresh-faced look had caught her off guard when she'd looked at him for the first time since arriving. The smooth skin was perfect, but Brook found herself missing the hair a little. Maybe he could just let a little bit grow?

"Brook?"

She blinked and stopped staring at his cheeks and chin. "Sorry," she rasped.

He chuckled and touched her chin with his knuckle. "I was saying that I want you to know I mean what I say, and part of that includes me taking care of you." His eyes crinkled slightly at the side when he smiled. "You've been taking care of me for the past while. Let me show my own feelings and sincerity by taking care of you."

She opened her mouth to argue. She wasn't hurt, she didn't need him to take care of her, but she snapped her mouth shut. "Okay," she said, trying to give him a smile in return. It felt rusty. "Thank you."

"I might not be as elegant as you," he quipped, "but hopefully that only makes it mean more." Turning, he walked away from her and retrieved the food from the step. Brook walked with him to the back deck, fisting her hands to keep from taking the containers from him. She could understand his point of view. Here was a strong, independent man who had suddenly become handicapped. She couldn't imagine how difficult that was for him. If she lost the use of her leg, she would probably break down and cry all day. But here he was, putting her needs ahead of his own.

Her heart slowly melted. *This isn't a joke.* There was no way he was playing some kind of joke on her or just stringing her along. Any man who would put his own needs and physical limits aside in order to take care of another was a definite keeper.

For the first time since the paparazzi had invaded her life, Brook felt some of the weight she was carrying lift. She felt a little less afraid of the situation and that allowed room for her anticipation to begin to build.

Grayson did his best to pull out a chair for her and Brook found herself smiling easier than she had only a few minutes ago. "Thank you," she said softly, taking her seat.

Instead of sitting across from her, Grayson pulled a chair over and sat down just to her left. "I always thought it was ridiculous for people to sit across from each other," he said, giving her his signature grin. The one Brook had seen splashed over every TV screen she'd ever owned. "If you like someone, don't you want to be close to them? Not clear across a table?"

There went a little bit more of that fear. If she wasn't careful, Brook knew she'd be caught, hook, line, and sinker before the evening was even out, let alone by the time she went home.

"I like that," Brook said. "But I have to admit I hadn't thought about it before."

Grayson shrugged. "I've had too long to think about these things, I guess."

Brook snorted a laugh and tried to cover it with her hand. "Like you're so old?"

Grayson chuckled. "Older than you."

She rolled her eyes. "Only by like four years."

"Four years of experience and hardship," he said with a completely straight face.

After a split second, both of them broke down into laughter. The uneasy tension Brook had been holding onto was gone. His name might have changed, but the teasing, smiling man sitting next to her was the same man she had fallen in love with. The question was quickly changing from whether or not he loved her to whether or not she would be willing to be a part of his life. Did they love each other enough to weather the media fallout? Could she handle being hounded everywhere she went? Losing all sense of privacy and being open to the criticism of the mass public?

Grayson began opening the containers and the wonderful sweet and savory smell of Hawaiian roast pork infiltrated the air. "Oh my gosh, that smells amazing," Brook said, taking in a deep breath.

"It tastes even better," he said as he helped dish up her plate. "I know the chef and he's at the top of his game."

"I thought you said no one knew we were here?" Brook froze with her fork in the air. With things softening between them, Brook wanted Grayson all to herself. She would need the time to figure out if this thing between them could really last.

"They don't," Grayson assured her. "Normally I go say hi, but not this time." He winked. "I'll see my friends another time."

Brook relaxed. "Thank you," she said.

Grayson raised his eyebrows.

"For going to all this trouble." She dropped his intense gaze and fiddled with her napkin. "It means a lot to me."

"Brook, I will do anything for you." He lifted her face back up gently so they were looking at each other again. "Anything."

HE COULD SEE IT IN her eyes and demeanor. Brook was definitely open to his suit. The longing he'd seen earlier had already started to fade. Her eyes sparkled tonight with enjoyment rather than trepidation and the green of her dress brought out his favorite color in her eyes. He was starting to have hope that this would be an easier week than he'd expected.

"So..." Brook finished chewing and swallowed her bite of rice. "You're going to be a complete open book this week?"

Grayson nodded. "Completely open."

"I can ask you anything I want?"

He felt like she was hedging toward something, but he'd promised, and he wasn't going back on it. "Anything."

Brook pursed her lips, not meeting his gaze for a moment before setting down her fork and looking him dead in the eye. "Will you tell me your story? Your *real* story? I got the feeling from the bits and pieces you did share that your childhood wasn't exactly idyllic." She made a face. "Which seems odd to me. I mean, you were famous so quickly."

Grayson poked at his food, his appetite gone. "That was actually part of the problem," he said darkly.

"You didn't appear to be one of those kid stars who struggled when they got older. Your transition seemed so seamless."

Grayson dropped his fork and leaned back in his seat. "That's the story we fed the media, for sure."

Brook's shoulders fell. "What really happened?"

He reached out to tuck a piece of hair behind her ear. It kept flying around and catching his attention, plus the move just gave him an excuse to touch her. He always felt better after that and right now was no exception. "I don't want to complain too much about my childhood," he said softly. "I mean, who wants to be the 'poor rich kid,' right?"

Brook rested her hand on his forearm. "I promise not to view you that way."

Grayson covered her hand with his other one. "Okay. But you asked for it." He took a deep breath, adjusting himself in his seat. He wasn't going to be able to sit up like this much longer. "I was the middle of three kids, but somehow I got the genetic lottery."

"Your eyes?" Brook guessed.

Grayson nodded. "Yeah. They were bluer when I was young and against my darker coloring, my parents finally decided they wanted to utilize my looks to their own advantage." He shifted their hands so their fingers were intertwined, taking strength from her touch. "I had never had the slightest desire to be an actor, but they both convinced me to audition for that teenage sitcom."

Brook smiled smugly. "I have to admit they were right. I fell for you when I was a pimple-faced tween in braces."

Grayson laughed. "I would have loved to see that."

"Not a chance!" Brook pulled her hand back and waved them both in the air. "I burned all the photos!"

He gave her a look and Brook shrugged. "Okay, maybe not, but still, I refuse to share anything about that stage of my life. It was more awkward than most. And you didn't look awkward at all."

His smile grew bigger. "The magic of makeup," he said with a chuckle. "Anyway, you know that I had some success from that show and it ended up launching my career."

Brook scoffed. "That's putting it mildly."

He winked. "When the show was over, I was actually ready to step away from the screen, but I was in a rough situation." He paused and turned to stare out at the water. This was where his life got weird.

"Please tell me," she whispered.

Grayson nodded. "Of course. My parents by this point were on the brink of divorce. They each wanted the money I made and still wanted to have complete control over my paychecks because they were acting as my agents and guardians."

"I remember seeing something about that..." she mused.

"Yeah. I ended up taking them to court," he said. That dark mood he struggled with was settling over him again. "I broke free and that's what made the news."

Brook was silent, so he plowed on.

"My parents were bound to split at any time, since all they did was fight, and now that their meal ticket had been taken from them, I figured it would only get worse." He sighed. "So I was this fresh-faced eighteen-year-old, free but still caught in the fact that I didn't know how to do anything but act."

"And you wanted to save your siblings."

His head whipped toward hers. "How did you know that?"

She smiled sadly. "Because I think I'm beginning to know you. You told me stories of your siblings, but never your parents. Not to mention, even the media talks about how close you are to Carson and Amelia."

He shook his head. This woman never ceased to amaze him. "You are a die-hard fan," he teased. "You even knew their names."

Brook winced slightly. "I probably shouldn't admit to that."

"No..." Grayson grabbed her hand again. "It's fine. I'm just glad you're willing to hear the story behind the reports." He raised his eyebrows to ask permission to go on and she nodded, tightening their grip. "I ended up back in court to try and get guardianship over my brother, but the courts wanted me to have a job. My sister was already a legal adult, but struggling through college. My money had been fine for my parents, but they hadn't given her much to go on when she moved out."

"So you went back to acting."

Grayson nodded. "Yeah. I had already been offered a chance to audition for a new action film and ended up jumping on it. When I got the role and was able to show the judge the entire situation, he awarded me custody."

"That seems crazy. Usually the courts want to leave kids with their parents."

"Right." Grayson's laugh was anything but humorous. "That just goes to show you how messed up my parents were by then. They actually had a huge fight in the courtroom and I think that was part of why the judge ruled in my favor."

"Wow. I can't even imagine," Brook said thickly. "I'm so sorry."

Grayson shrugged. "It's fine. We made it out, I made enough money to take care of them all and now they're all grown up and living their own lives."

"Thanks to you."

Grayson shook his head. "Thanks to themselves. None of what I did would have mattered if they hadn't chosen to break free as well."

Brook's smile was brilliant and made Grayson want to puff up his chest. "You're amazing," she said softly.

Grayson smiled. "Amazing enough that you'll stick around for a while?"

Brook laughed and looked out at the ocean, then back. "For a while."

Grayson brought her hand to his lips. "That's enough for now."

"Can I ask another question?"

Grayson nodded.

"Will you tell me about your injury?"

She was hitting all the deep stuff tonight. Although it wasn't like he could exactly blame her. He'd held back so much and she was probably itching to put all the pieces together. "If you want."

"It doesn't have to be tonight," she hurried to say.

Grayson glanced at his watch. "You're probably exhausted from traveling," he said. "What if I promise a full report over breakfast and a good night's sleep?"

"I'd like that."

Grayson kissed her hand again. "Then that's what we'll plan on." He wanted her to know it all just like he'd promised, but they had time. His whole team was working on keeping this trip a secret and even his dad wasn't going to ruin this for him.

And then, if she wasn't disgusted or as eager about being together as he was by the end of the week, he would let her go. It would be painful, and he didn't want to do it, but she was the one in charge here. Whatever she wanted would go.

CHAPTER 27

Dawn the next morning was unlike anything Brook had ever seen. Being raised in California and living in Oregon had made her privy to some fairly spectacular sunrises, but nothing could have prepared her for one on the lush island of Hawaii.

Ideally she would have still been sleeping, but the time difference had yet to settle into her system. Instead of being cozied up in Grayson's amazing guest bedroom, Brook was on the deck, nursing a cup of herbal tea and listening to the sounds of the island. She couldn't help but think about how she would have access to all kinds of luxuries if she and Grayson made a go of it, but the thought left a bitter taste in her mouth.

Brook had spent almost her entire life in love with the illusion that Grayson put on screen. She'd worshipped him like every other adoring female, dreaming and wishing that one day he would "happen" to see her through the crowd. Unlike those other women, Brook's dream had come true. Only she hadn't known it and it had come crashing down into an ugly reality.

She had Grayson's attention, but now she had to figure out if she wanted it. With each touch of his hand and each caress of his gaze, Brook grew more and more sure that he was telling the truth about his feelings. But his lifestyle still scared her. Her small experience with the media was enough to have her running for her life, if it didn't mean leaving Grayson behind.

She took a sip of her steaming brew, sighing as the taste of mint and lemon coated her tongue. Relaxing her back, she lay in a sunbathing lounge chair, her knees curled up to her chin as she sorted through her morning meditations. Why did it all seem so complicated? She loved him. The real him. And he loved her. So why couldn't they just be like every other person in the world and be together?

Fame was not nearly as attractive in person as it was from a distance.

"You're up early."

Grayson's deep voice wasn't as unwelcome as it would have been only two days ago. Brook peered over her shoulder and smiled. "So are you."

Grayson shuffled over and eased himself in the lounge chair beside her. "I wanted to be up to greet you."

Brook smiled. "And you thought I'd be up this early?"

He shook his head. "No. I seem to recall you like to sleep in." He shifted. "But my back was bothering me, so I needed to move."

Brook sat up and put the tea on a side table. "What can I get you? Have you taken any pain meds lately?"

Grayson chuckled and reached over for her hand. "No, thank you. Remember this week I'm taking care of you, not the other way around."

"Gray..." she said softly, not even noticing she had shortened his name, "I appreciate you wanting to prove yourself, but not at the expense of you hurting."

"Don't you worry," he said, leaning back and closing his eyes. "I've got access to everything I need to get better." He opened one eye a slit. "The last thing I needed was your company."

Brook felt her cheeks heat and she shook her head, though she was smiling. "You have way too many scripts to pull from in order to charm a woman."

Grayson's laughter grew. "Like any of my films would have those kinds of lines."

"I've seen you kiss a lot of women, mister."

He made a face. "No. You've seen my screen persona kiss a lot of women. I'm not one to play around and I'm definitely not one to sweet talk women for fun."

"Are you trying to tell me that you're writing your own script for this one?" Brook laid back again, enjoying the laid-back feel of the morning.

"I am," he said. His head turned her way. "I believe I promised you a story though."

Brook sobered. She knew this would be hard to hear. She didn't like it when people were hurting, and to hear how the man she loved had been injured would tug at her heartstrings. "Please," she whispered.

Grayson's brows furrowed. "It's not really that long of a story, but I can honestly say it's had a pretty big impact on my life."

Brook waited patiently, knowing he would get it out when he could.

"We were filming a movie." He glanced at her and she nodded, acknowledging that she had heard about it. "And we were all set to do an action sequence." His face went back to the ocean. "It was all a freak thing. I was supposed to be running along the top of some buildings and had to do a jump. It was set up for me to land on an inflatable mattress, while a body double jumped into action climbing up a wall. In the movie, it would look like I jumped onto the side of the building and began to climb."

Brook slowly shook her head. "You guys are crazy," she muttered.

Grayson grinned and turned back to her. "I'll admit the adrenaline rush is pretty sweet."

Her frown turned to laughter. "Of course it is."

Grayson settled back again and continued. "Everything went fine until I jumped." He pushed a hand through his hair.

Although his beard was gone, his hair was still longer than normal, leaving Brook with the desire to play with it. It was just right for running her fingers through.

"Marty, that's my stunt guy, was busy scurrying up the wall, when some of the scaffolding broke." His throat bobbed with a hard swallow. "One minute I was lying on the mattress, having just flipped over onto my stomach, when something hit me in the back."

"Oh, Gray..." He shrugged as if it were no big deal, but Brook could see how upset he was in every line of his face. His lips were tight and his hands clenched. Her fingers were struggling for blood flow, but she couldn't bring herself to say anything. This was truly hard for him. It would be for anybody.

"I've already told you all about the actual injury," he said bitterly. "But it was after the surgery where things got worse."

Brook clenched her hands into fists. She could barely stand hearing about how hurt he'd been. It made her own body ache with empathy.

"The media just wouldn't leave me alone," he said tightly. "I was in the hospital for a bit, and the security there was helpful, but I ended up having to hire a full security team when I went home. We had tried to keep the details of my injury under wraps because my producer was unsure what they were going to do about the movie and my agent was concerned that any bad press would affect future roles."

Brook pinched her lips together. She wanted to smack some sense into those people. How could they put their businesses ahead of Grayson's wellbeing? It was something she would never understand.

He pushed his hand through his hair. "So, in an effort to not only keep my injury a secret, but allow me a chance to recover without being bombarded from all sides, we picked a tiny town where there wouldn't be any paparazzi. The goal was a quiet recovery."

Brook huffed a laugh. "And then you met me."

His eyes were intense but warm. "And then I met you."

GRAYSON COULDN'T HELP but chuckle softly. It had probably sounded like he said he was upset they had met, when that was the complete opposite of the truth. "You turned my world upside down," he said, pulling her hand closer and toying with her fingers. They were small and thin and were a direct contrast to his thicker build. He thought they were a perfect fit.

Brook shook her head, but she was smiling. "I was kinda pushy, wasn't I?"

Grayson shook his head. "You were exactly how I needed you to be." He smirked. "You know, I thought you were so beautiful the first time I saw you on that bench, but not only was I undercover, I knew someone like you wouldn't want anything to do with a guy who could barely walk." He snorted. "It made me so mad that you were trying to help me." His humor disappeared. "I've never needed help before."

Brook squeezed his hand. "You *were* pretty grumpy," she admitted. "And I'll admit that I was first drawn to you because I wanted to help." Her eyes darted away before she looked back. "But I stayed because I fell in love."

Grayson tugged on her hand and pulled Brook out of her seat. Scooting over, he made room in his lounge chair just like they had done back in Oregon. The sun was fully up now and already he could feel the wet warmth filling the air. It was going to be a beautiful day.

Grayson could hear the contentment in her sigh as Brook settled onto her side and rested her head in the crook of his shoulder.

"Do you think you could ever forgive me?" he whispered into her hair.

"I think I already have," she said softly. Her hand rested against his chest and the spot was warmed by her touch. "I already felt that way before I came to Hawaii."

"Are you telling me you just came for the free trip?"

She shook a little as she laughed. "Maybe."

He grinned and kissed her temple.

"Kidding, but I already told you I was pretty sure you would be here." She pushed up onto her elbow. "And I needed to settle this once and for all." Her face turned serious. "I needed to convince myself for sure that you didn't truly love me. That it was all some kind of farce and a good bit of acting."

"And what have you decided?"

She gave him a sad smile. "I don't think it was fake."

It was still probably premature, but how could any man resist the vision in front of him? Cupping the back of her head, Grayson brought their mouths together. His body reacted instantly and he could feel his burdens lighten and his heart settle back into his chest exactly where that hole had been since their separation.

Earlier than he wanted, she pulled back. "Wait."

Grayson let her go, but the word worried him. He could practically hear the "but" in her tone. "What is it?" he asked, his voice husky with emotion.

"I still don't know how you and I would make this work." A single tear rolled down her cheek and it nearly tore the newly healed heart in Grayson's chest. "I love my life and my shop in Oregon. I love the small town and the fact that I know almost everybody by name. You live a life the complete opposite of that. You're in the spotlight *all the time* and I don't know that I can handle that. I don't know if I *want* to handle that."

Grayson dropped his hand from her hair. "What are you saying?"

Brook groaned and leaned forward, resting her forehead against his sternum. "I don't know. I love you. I was miserable without you. But I don't know how to move forward like this either." She brought her head back up. "How do we bring together two lives that are on complete opposites of the spectrum?"

Grayson gave her a sad smile and cupped her cheek, wiping the stray tears trickling down her face. "One day at a time," he said softly. "I don't have all the answers. In fact, if I'm being completely honest, I'm terrified of the fact that I might never be able to walk normally again. How can I ask you to jump into a relationship with someone who might never be able to work?"

Brook shook her head and opened her mouth to respond, but he put his thumb over her lips.

"Hear me out," he said quickly. When she paused and nodded, he continued. "I know my life is complicated—even for me, it's complicated—but Brook... I can't stand the thought of taking on anything in the future without you by my side. I don't know how it'll all turn out, but I know I don't want to do it alone." He tilted his head and raised his eyebrows. "Would you please give us a chance? We won't know how to make it all work until we actually try."

She stared at him for a long time, her eyes still full of sorrow. "I want to," she whispered thickly. "But I'm scared."

"About?"

"About it not working out. About losing you."

He slowly shook his head. "You'll only lose me if you don't give us a try."

"How are you so confident?"

Grayson smiled and rubbed his thumb against her cheekbone. "Because I've never felt this way about anybody before. Because you brought sunshine into a dark existence. Because I'm a different man for loving you. Because I love you too much to *not* let us succeed."

"I love you," she whispered.

"And I love you." He smirked. "Now can I please have a kiss that isn't filled with tears?"

Brook laughed and wiped her face. "Just for that, I should say no."

"But you won't."

"So confident," she teased, leaning down to give him a quick peck. "But it's part of what I love about you."

"Thank heavens," he whispered before pulling her back to him. He had been honest. Grayson wasn't quite sure how this was all going to work out, but he knew he would do whatever it took to see that it did. He thought his life had been ruined, but it turned out it had only just begun.

CHAPTER 28

It had been two long miserable weeks since Brook had seen Grayson. They'd been dating for close to six months now, but life seemed to have a knack for separating them for long periods of time. Or, at least, longer than Brook was comfortable with.

Grayson still wasn't back on the movie set, but he, especially lately, had been leaving more often than not. His back and leg were slowly improving, but he still walked with his cane and it was difficult to imagine at this point that he would ever be back to how he was before the accident. Doctors assured them both that this was normal and that it could take all the way up to eighteen months to fully recover from such an injury.

His frustration, however, had become tangible, though Brook assured him over and over that she didn't care, that she loved him no matter his physical condition, she could see the situation bothered him immensely. He hated being beholden to anyone and anything, and his anger had started to worry her.

During the last month she had only seen him for a couple of days, and though she had kept silent, she secretly feared that her original worries were coming true. Grayson was wonderfully attentive and loving while he was in town...but what happened when he didn't want to be in town anymore?

She had tried asking what he was doing and how things were going back in California, but it had been eerily similar to when she'd first met him. He'd been tight-lipped and vague about the details.

Now she stood in front of the home he rented, different from the original, but still just as beautiful, and wondered if it was worth going inside. Her poor bruised heart banged painfully against her chest and her back was damp with sweat from her anxiety.

She missed Grayson horribly and a large part of her wanted to rush inside and smother him with kisses, but another part was terrified. She was worried that one of the times she came to visit would be her last. She'd be relegated to just another girl in his life and he'd move on, his fame and fortune helping him forget all about her and little Seaside Bay.

Brook, for her part, knew she would never move on. Grayson had infiltrated every part of her life and she was changed forever. His screen persona had kept her from any kind of serious relationship before they ever met and now, who he was in real life would do the same.

Nausea churned in her stomach and Brook put a hand over it as if that could stop the sensation. As per usual, Grayson had texted her when he'd arrived, asking her to come over. He'd said he had something he needed to talk to her about. Words every woman feared.

Their relationship had been hard and yet amazing these past few months. During her bliss-filled week in Hawaii, the paparazzi had finally given up and gone home, leaving Brook free to come back to her store upon her return. Though she had to admit work didn't hold the same appeal it had before she'd become Grayson Cordova's girlfriend. Focusing on anything but his handsome visage had been very difficult at first, and had taken more self discipline than she cared to admit.

Luckily, Grayson had felt the need to pull Brook away often enough to help fill the gaps left by his absence. They had visited every house he owned over the last few months just to be able to spend some time together.

Her friends had been wonderfully supportive, as usual, and did their best to head off any media personnel who showed up randomly looking for the inside scoop. Ken kept complaining he needed to hire another deputy just for that job alone.

But when he could, Grayson always came back to Seaside Bay. He never rented the same home twice, jumping around to make it harder to find him, and it had worked out fairly well. They still had photographers if they went out, but for the most part, their clandestine meetings went unrecorded.

Brook wiped her clammy hands on her slacks. She wasn't quite sure why she'd dressed up for the occasion. Maybe it was with the intent to show Grayson what he was throwing away if he let her go, or maybe it was just to build her own confidence, but with the way Brook's heart was racing, it wasn't working.

It's not as if he's actually broken up with you, she reminded herself. "Maybe it'll all be okay." She snorted and closed her eyes. "And maybe fairy tales really do come true."

"Are you going to come in?" a voice drawled from the doorway. "Or just stand outside like a fangirl?"

Brook opened her eyes to give Jude a wry look. "I don't know," she said slowly, tapping her bottom lip with her finger. "Would I be required to scream, fan myself, and then faint?"

Jude smirked. "Pretty much."

Brook laughed. "Then no, thanks. His ego is big enough as it is."

"I heard that!"

Brook's smile grew. Just the sound of his voice was enough to have her feel excited and she knew better than to worry about him hearing her little joke with Jude. Brook walked the rest of the way up to the door and stepped past Jude. "Thank you," she said softly.

"Anytime," Jude said with a wink. "And when you're in there with the grump, remember who it is that has the good manners."

"Lay off my girl, Jude," Grayson said in a tone that said he wasn't impressed. He limped their way, coming closer to the door, and held out his arm. "She's taken."

Brook didn't hesitate a moment before melting into his embrace. Oh, he felt so good, so right. She loved how strong his hold was and the steady beating of his heart against her ear. She loved how he was big enough to completely envelop her and help her feel like the outside world had disappeared. He was bigger than life in personality and body, and she loved it.

"Come with me," Grayson murmured into her hair. Stepping back, he took her hand and led her deeper into the house.

Brook wasn't familiar with this rental, so she didn't know exactly where they were going, but she could guess that Grayson wanted to give them some privacy. She bit her lip, hoping the pain would help her stay in control, but it was hard. *Hear him out,* she told herself. *Don't jump to conclusions.* The words were smart, but hard to follow. She just wanted everything out in the open. No more secrets.

"In here," Grayson said with a grin. "There's a sunroom in this house that overlooks the beach, and it's beautiful."

He ushered her inside and Brook had to admit he was right. The space was stunning. It appeared to double as a greenhouse, as the walls were filled with greenery of all sorts, while the back wall and partial ceiling were completely made of glass that had an unobstructed view of the water. She could spend a lot of time in this room and never get tired of it. "It's wonderful," she breathed.

"I'm glad you like it," Grayson said softly in her ear. He wrapped his arm around her waist from behind and kissed her ear lobe tenderly, then worked his way down her neck. "I missed you so much," he whispered huskily.

Brook sighed and let her head fall back against his chest. "Same. This time felt like forever." She bounced slightly as he chuckled.

"That's because it was," he agreed. He pressed her into turning around and she got a flash of his brilliant smile before his mouth came crashing down on hers. "I need a minute to make up for lost time," he said between kisses.

Brook knew it would be smart to slow things down, but she couldn't do it. Standing on tiptoe, she threw her arms around his neck and threw everything she had into their exchange. She had missed him and until he told her otherwise, she was going to give as good as she got. If his kiss was any indication, her fears just might have been unfounded.

SOMETHING WAS WRONG. Grayson wasn't sure what it was, but Brook was slightly stiff and it worried him. Especially with what his plans were for the day. He knew he'd been gone a lot lately, but he had a good reason and he was excited to share it with her.

He had no complaints about her kiss, however. Her enthusiasm this morning was enough to knock him off his feet, if he wasn't still being held up with the aid of a cane. It was one of the few sources of contention between him and Brook. The other being how they had to sneak around to get any time together.

And Grayson couldn't blame her. He didn't like it either, but it wasn't brand new to his life, like it was to hers. He was hoping, however, that his announcement would help with at least one of his problems.

He pulled back, breathing heavily from their embrace. "I should be gone more often," he teased, "if that's how you're going to greet me." His favorite blush crawled up her neck and cheeks. Now that she was his girlfriend, he loved that he had every right to trace his fingers over the warmth and enjoy her soft skin.

"Sorry," she said, ducking her head and resting her forehead against his sternum. "I guess I got carried away." She was shaking slightly in his arms and he hoped it was from the intensity of their exchange, not whatever was making her nervous.

"Don't be." Grayson kissed the top of her head. "If I have my way, we'll make that a permanent part of our lives."

Brook looked up, frowning. "Permanent?"

A slow grin crept across his face. He knew it was bordering a smirk and he probably looked arrogant, but he'd worked hard to set everything into place and now, it would hopefully all come together. The only missing piece was Brook.

"Yes…permanent." He brought her hand to his lips. "I have some exciting news to share with you." With the way she was leaning against him, Grayson felt every muscle tighten in her body. He hurried on, hoping it would ease her anxiety. "I've been offered a job."

"What?" Brook breathed. She backed away, their connection broken. "You're going back to making movies?"

Grayson shrugged, some of his eagerness dying out at her horrified reaction. "Somewhat, but not in the same capacity." When she didn't say anything else, he continued. "I'm going to be a director."

Brook blinked a couple of times, as if waiting for the words to sink in. "A director? Like the guy who shouts 'cut' from a seat behind the cameras?"

He chuckled. "Yeah, something like that. It's a little more complicated, but still, the right idea."

Brook nodded slowly and began backing up some more. "I see," she murmured. Her beautiful gaze dropped to the floor and Grayson could see the tears were reforming. "So you're going back to California for good?"

Grayson ticked his head back and forth. "Not exactly."

Brook scrunched up her face and her hands turned into fists. "Just say it!" she cried.

Grayson leaned back. "Say what?"

"Whether or not you're breaking up with me," she said. Her tone was more calm after the initial outburst, but still thick with emotion. "Does this mean that you're going to be gone for good? That a long-distance relationship won't work?" She threw her hands in the air. "Just say it, *please!*"

Grayson's mouth dropped open. "You thought...I..." He had never been at such a loss for words. Hadn't he just hugged and kissed her a moment ago? Didn't she respond in kind? He could have sworn hers were the actions of a woman who was still in love with him. He thought they were growing closer, but maybe he'd been wrong? "Are you saying you don't love me anymore?" he asked, his voice cracking embarrassingly at the end. He'd just spent weeks working out a deal so he and Brook could end this traveling once and for all only to learn she wanted out?

"What? No!" she cried fiercely. "Of course not!"

"Then what in the world are you talking about?" Grayson was beyond confused. What the heck was going on?

"You've been gone for weeks," Brook said hoarsely. "You won't tell me what you're doing, you won't answer my questions, you're spending more and more time in California." She sniffled. "What am I supposed to think but that you've changed *your* mind? We're right back to the beginning where you lied to me about who you are, only for me to find out the hard way."

Grayson hung his head. She was right. He'd gone about this all wrong. Here he thought he'd been creating a surprise for their future, but when she was already still on edge from how their relationship started, he could see how that would frighten her. "Brook, sweetheart, I'm sorry." He took a couple of steps in her direction, holding out his hand. "I don't want to break up with you. I want to marry you."

Her eyes widened to the size of dinner plates. "Marry me?" she mouthed.

Grayson nodded. "I haven't been running around behind your back. I've been working out the details so we can get married and never have to say goodbye again."

Her chest began heaving and her shallow breathing was audible. "Where will we live?"

Grayson made a face. "Well...that part gets a little tricky." He continued holding out his hand. "Will you come with me and I'll explain it all?"

Brook nodded, eagerly taking his hand and wiping her face with her free one. "I'm sorry," she said as they settled themselves on the couch. "I didn't mean to get so dramatic."

Grayson shook his head. "No. I shouldn't have been so secretive. That wasn't smart on my part, not after everything we've been through." He laid back into the corner of the couch, and Brook snuggled into his side. It had become their favorite way to cuddle, especially since it got chilly on the back deck sometimes. "I have enough money for us to live on for the rest of our lives," he said softly, running his fingers through her hair. "But I don't think I'd be happy doing nothing."

Her hand patted his chest. "I agree. We all need a purpose. It helps us feel worthwhile."

Grayson nodded. "Agreed. Anyway, even if my body actually heals, I'm not sure I want to go back to action films." He shrugged when she looked up at him. "I did fine at it, but I don't think it's where my heart lies. Plus acting would pull me away from you constantly."

"And directing is better?"

"It's a start," Grayson said. "It's something new, something to try." He gave her a sad smile. "And it's something I can do now."

Brook nodded.

"If I stick with it, it'll mean some traveling, but right now, the movie I've been offered is being shot here in Oregon."

"You're kidding." Brook gasped.

Grayson shook his head. "Nope. In fact, I went ahead and bought this house."

"You bought..." Brook's mouth gaped open. "I'm not sure I'm ever going to get used to how free you are with your money."

Grayson grinned and leaned forward to kiss her on the tip of her nose. "I'm hoping you'll more than get used to it. I'm hoping you'll learn to help me spend some of it."

"Grayson," she said adoringly. "I want to marry you, so bad. But what about my store? My life here?"

Grayson frowned. This was going to be the hardest part. "I'll admit that I'm asking a lot, but I'm hoping you'll meet me in the middle. If I keep directing, we'll probably end up house-jumping in order to be wherever the movies are being shot." He tilted his chin down, looking her directly in the eyes. "It would mean either hiring someone to run the shop in your stead, or closing it." He tilted his head back and forth. "Or moving the whole thing online. And in return, I'll make sure you're always with me, no matter what part of the world I go to. I'll make sure to take projects where we can be together with whatever family we have. We never have to be apart again and the paparazzi should settle down some since I won't be the star."

Brook snorted. "Like they don't follow directors?"

"Not as much," Grayson said sheepishly. He knew that one was a stretch, but still true enough. "What do you say?"

"Is that your proposal?" Brook asked, her lips twitching.

Grayson answered with his best smile. "Brooklyn Ann Howell, I can't get down on one knee, but I love you. I love everything about you. Your kindness, your light, your persistence, and stubbornness." He paused while Brook laughed. "Your ability to see past my rough edges and pull out the real me, the one I rarely showed anyone. You pulled me from my own pit of despair and I will never not be grateful." He pulled her hand from his chest to kiss her palm. "I can't guarantee I'll ever walk normally again. I can't guarantee we won't have to run from the paparazzi at times. I can't guarantee moving around will be easy. But I can guarantee that I will always love you. I can guarantee that any house we're in will be filled with laughter and goodness.

I can guarantee that I'll bring you back to Oregon to see your friends every single year, no matter what."

"Really? No matter what?"

Grayson nodded sagely. "No matter what."

She pulled loose of his hand and cupped his cheek. "Then Grayson Damien Cordova, I wish you to know that I love you as well and am totally willing to meet you in the middle. Thank you for opening my eyes to more than the surface of a person. I would love to be your wife and will hold you to your promise to come back every year." She blinked teary eyes. "You're my most important family, but the rest of them are here."

Grayson cupped the back of her head and pulled her in. "Baby, we're going to start a family of our own," he said huskily before kissing her. "And then they'll be wherever we are."

Their kisses might have been a little saltier than usual, but they were no less intense or sincere. It would be a change for them both, and Grayson knew it would be bumpy, but if Brook could help him heal from a life-altering injury, he knew that together, they could tackle anything that came along.

It was funny how his Brook had started out just wanting to help an injured man, and instead had caught herself a star. The strange result had ended up being the best thing that had ever happened to either one of them.

EPILOGUE

Bennett rolled his eyes when he saw how big the stack of packages was for Brook and Grayson. They'd been married a month now and were still getting mail from every corner of the world. *Half of it's probably hate mail that Brook took Gray off the market.* Benny snorted at his thoughts.

It seemed like a pandemic these last couple of years as each of his friends slowly began starting new lives with their significant others. With each wedding, Benny grew more and more restless. And bored. And depressed. But mostly bored.

Rose and Ken were the only other singles in the group now and they only had eyes for each other, even if Rose resisted it. Which left Benny by himself. He couldn't just drop in on his friends unannounced anymore. He actually had to cook all his own meals, leaving his mooching skills severely lacking lately.

And apparently, getting married did something to a person's sense of humor because nobody seemed to want to join in his jokes anymore. Not that they had been incredibly eager before, but they had laughed and given him attention. Now all they did was glare until he stopped.

He didn't want to admit it, but Benny was also lonely. His sister, Melody, was positive that if he would simply find his own significant other, he would feel better, but he had no desire to become the besotted, grumpy man he saw his friends turning into.

He might be a little past thirty, but he still enjoyed his freedom. He didn't want to answer to anyone or anything. He liked to laugh and play, and marriage had a way of draining that from a man, no matter how happy his friends claimed to be. There was no way catering to their wives' every whim was exciting. It just wasn't.

Maybe I'm too much like my mother.

The words hit home. His mother was living her best, off the grid, carefree boho life down in California, having shirked every responsibility she had once taken on. Or, at least, he thought she was. They hadn't heard from her in so long that Benny actually wasn't sure where she was or what she was doing.

"I'm not nearly as bad as her," he muttered to himself. He held down a good, solid job as the mail carrier of Seaside Bay. He met up with friends and helped when they needed it. He dabbled in art at home as a fun creative outlet, though few knew about it, and he enjoyed surfing on occasion. Life wasn't terrible, just slow.

Whistling a tune to try and cheer himself up, Benny stopped at the next house and made a face. Allison Mayer had graduated school a year behind him and yet everybody knew who she was. She'd moved into Seaside Bay in middle school and had shown up looking like the perfect porcelain doll. Even at the young age of thirteen, she wore enough makeup to star in a movie.

Perfect makeup.

Perfect hair.

Perfect clothes.

Perfect grades.

Those were the qualifications of Allison Mayer, and her attitude reflected the fact that nobody else lived up to that ideal. She had been as snobby and jerky as any teenage queen bee had ever been.

Benny had taken great enjoyment in ruffling her feathers any time he got the chance. It had been the ultimate challenge. Nothing ever seemed to break through her stoic face. She showed absolutely no emotion and only once had he ever seen her lose it. The moment was one for the record books when Allison sent the star quarterback running for his life for daring to ask for a kiss.

Now Allison was the local piano teacher and still lived with her mother, who was the town cougar. Benny doubted if Allison would ever be the type of woman to let a man into her life. Heaven forbid he might burp after dinner. She'd probably kick him out without looking back.

Muttering under his breath, knowing that Allison would either open the door with a glare or her mother would flirt inappropriately, Benny braced himself. He knocked, holding the box in front of him like a shield.

There was some shouting behind the door and Benny held back a groan. The door was still closed and he could already tell this was going to be rough.

"Open the door!" The screeched words became louder as Allison wrenched the door hard enough to nearly pull it off its hinges.

Benny froze. This wasn't an Allison he was familiar with. Not a speck of makeup was on her face. One side of her face was clean and fresh and still beautiful, the other half was covered in a port wine birthmark. He had no idea that it had existed under all that powder she wore.

She must have realized the situation, because as Benny continued to stare, Allison's mouth began to flap like a bass out of water. Her brown eyes were wide and Benny could have sworn a flash of fear went through her gaze before it disappeared behind the icy look he'd seen since they were young.

The door slammed shut just as quickly as it opened and Benny found himself staring at brown painted wood. It kind of reminded him of Allison's eyes, actually.

As he worked to process everything that had just happened, a slow smile spread across his face. His boring, uninspired life had just taken a turn. Benny knew something he hadn't known before.

The door swung back open and Mrs. Mayer stood with her hands on her hip. "Hello," she purred.

Benny held back a shiver. This woman was way too old to speak to him that way. "I need Allison to sign for this," he said, indicating the box.

Mrs. Mayer raised an eyebrow. "I'm her mother. Can't I do it?"

Benny shook his head. "No. It's addressed to her."

Mrs. Mayer started to roll her eyes, then stopped as if realizing she had an audience. "Just a moment," she said breathlessly, then disappeared into the house.

Benny shifted his weight when he heard yelling start again. It was clear only Mrs. Mayer was doing the talking and Benny found a trickle of sympathy forming toward Allison. He shook himself and shoved it aside. That was the last thing he needed right now. The mystery of her birthmark intrigued him, but he wasn't about to feel sorry for her. She'd been horrible since they were kids, and it wasn't going to change now.

"Allison is...indisposed," Mrs. Mayer said when she returned. "Can I take it in and have her sign it? Then bring it back?"

Benny figured that was as good as he was going to get, so he shrugged and handed her the tablet.

Mrs. Mayer disappeared again, then brought it back with a smirk. "Will that do it for you?"

"Thanks," Benny muttered, handing her all the mail. He tried to glance one more time into the house, but all he saw was the twitch of a curtain. The door closed behind him as he walked away, but the entire situation sat on Benny's mind for the rest of the day.

Allison had a birthmark. Her mother treated her badly. Allison still lived at home and rarely spoke or showed emotion.

It felt like there was a mystery behind the situation and for a bored, restless bachelor, nothing had ever looked so exciting.

Don't Miss Reading Benny's story in

"Her Unexpected Delivery"

www.ingramcontent.com/pod-product-compliance
Lightning Source LLC
Chambersburg PA
CBHW061232210726
48293CB00003B/739